plexigirl media

Pam Alster

Robin's Blue

Pam Alster studied fiction at UCLA and authored the critically acclaimed plays *Shop Bloomingdales, Find Mother and Millennium's Eve.*

Robin's Blue

a novel

Pam Alster

Plexigirl Books
A Division of Plexigirl Media
Los Angeles

For J.J.

Robin's Blue

Prologue

I don't remember Mommy dying, only the finned taillights of my father's car pulling away from Nana's curb, the smell of skinless paprika chicken baking in the kitchen, the chime of a grandfather clock. Fragments: Up, Up and Away by the 5th Dimension, Chanel No. 5, a guitar. Mommy's death marked the passing of my happiness but since I learned early that people didn't respond well to gloom, I achieved an astounding ruse of lightheartedness.

Saying my mother died of complications due to infectious pneumonia became like saying my name was Robin Elizabeth Daniels. It was my moniker, like being born in Philadelphia, October 25th 1962, like being the skinny, funny one of the two Daniels girls, like having a stepmother who didn't attend PTA meetings. It wasn't the grief that fell like a curtain over the face of the recipient of this information, it wasn't my daily incubus of suffering to bare, it wasn't my mother, the floating apparition, who haunted my waking hours, because her image faded with each day that passed. Pictures. I have them. Flat perfect squares of color —a diaper clad toddler at the beach, a woman kissing her, holding her with one hand, a bucket in the other, my sister Melanie in the background splashing knee-high in the breakers.

Daddy didn't talk about my mother; he didn't not talk about her either. She was the pervasive sidestepped presence. Melanie and I only spoke about her in private. For me it was because I didn't want to bring our desolation out for inspection, but for my sister, I think it was because she kept her grief like a polished trophy for herself and never trusted Daddy to share in it. She involved me in remembrances as a sounding board, not as a confidante, I'm certain. But it wasn't like Daddy ever referred to Mommy in any of the ways I'd seen in movies or on TV when a mother has died, like "You remind me of her," or "She lit up every room she entered," or "She loved the rain." Instead, she was a constant vaporous tableau, mentioned randomly, thoughtlessly and regrettably at once in the same breath.

And I assumed that because Daddy lived instead of Mommy, he loved me unconditionally despite his absence, his anger, and my striking resemblance to the woman who'd forsaken him.

July 1979

Chapter 1

I waited in the designer living room for my boss to surface from the recesses of his house. He told me to come by after work and pick up inventory. Though I was technically the hotel lifeguard, my duties included manning the suntan oil sales cabana. I got the job two weeks after coming to Myrtle Beach, despite Melanie's insistence that I'd make more money at my first job slinging disco cocktails with her. But I wanted my nights to go out and the gig allowed me to be paid for being in the sun all day.

"There's vodka in the fridge," Joe called from the down the hall.

For some reason, I called him Joe McClure instead of just Joe like everyone else. The whole name fit him, and it was our private joke. I'd say, hey Joe McClure! whenever he came by my pool. He was well-liked and popular, the big daddy of the beach and I felt at ease with him, more of a friend than an employee.

I wiped a smudge off the framed picture of him and his wife holding clubs in front of a golf cart and put it back on the end table. She was attractive for an older woman. She looked confident, deserving and rich. Prettier than my stepmother, but she reminded me of her just the same, how she possessed the Kodak moment the way her leather-gloved hand held the irons. I shuddered at the thought that I might become that.

I found the vodka in the well-stocked bar and smiled at the mirror behind the sparkling bottles. My hair was in a greasy ponytail and I was still in my shorts from work but I felt sophisticated retrieving the sturdy highball glasses, even stood a little taller when I walked to the kitchen, as if cocktail hour was as natural an occurrence for me as breakfast cereal.

The refrigerator was full and there were Tupperware containers with celery and carrot sticks. I thought I'd eat healthy too if I had a nice house. I found the tonic and poured it over ice.

I was squeezing a lime when Joe emerged, showered and changed, renewed, like he'd molted. His golf shirt had drip spots from wet hair, and it was tucked, as usual, into belted Bermuda shorts.

"Hey there, Joe McClure," I said, smiling.

He took the drink from me, stirred it with his finger and drank half of it. "Ah," he said, grabbed cigarettes, then sat at the kitchen table.

I took a sip from my glass and the lump of ice splashed the cocktail on my face. I thought how silly I must have looked but laughed as I grabbed a napkin. I knew more than to be embarrassed by my klutziness, it worked better to let stuff slide, anything else seemed childish.

"You don't have to be nervous, I'm not going to attack you," Joe said, his chuckle neither harmless nor threatening. He smiled, patted the chair next to him, lit a smoke, offered me one. "You're eighteen, aren't you, Robin?" he said.

I'd worked for Beach Buff for a month and the issue of my age had never come up. I was suddenly nervous and thought about lying, but then decided that it didn't matter. I was selling suntan oil, not booze. "You know I'm sixteen," I said. "How old are you?"

"Thirty-six," he said.

That explained the golf. It's what grown ups did. It was their religion. My father not only played, he *designed* courses. It's how we first found Myrtle Beach. For years, he traveled weekly back and forth from Pennsylvania to South Carolina overseeing whatever project.

Joe was only a couple of years younger than Daddy, but a hell of a lot more fun. Every week he held a barbeque for all his employees at the Pool Boy house, a kind of dorm for the beach and pool lifeguards. There was always a keg and live music. Joe partied and danced with everyone.

Here, he seemed fidgety and preoccupied, exhaling smoke over his shoulder, tapping ashes in the crystal.

Maybe his wife was on the way home. I'd heard she was an interior decorator. "Where's the Missus?" I said, retying the string of my bikini top which was digging uncomfortably into my neck from under my t-shirt.

"Clients in Charleston. She'll be there for a few days," he said, impatient.

I was worried I'd done something wrong, when he pulled an amber bottle from his pocket. "You do coke?" he said.

"Sure," I said, hoping he didn't see the lie on my face. I was flattered he trusted me.

He spilled the vial of white powder onto the table and used a credit card to divide the pile into thin lines. Then he dug in his pocket, produced a short straw and handed it to me. "Ladies first," he said.

"You go ahead, I'm going to have a little more of my drink." I wasn't afraid, I'd done plenty of other stuff. Various pills, pot. But I didn't have the slightest clue what to do and hoped to stall long enough to fake it.

He held one nostril closed and inhaled the powder through the straw up the other, then he snorted hard. His eyes watered and he shook his head like a dog. "Good stuff," he said. He stuck his finger in the residue, rubbed it on his gums and licked his lips.

Low orange sunlight reflected off the toaster, making me squint. I took the straw, pretending I'd done it a million times before, it was how I got by hanging out with college kids all summer. The coke burned a little but I didn't feel anything except awake. I was relieved that I wasn't instantly addicted and I didn't feel like jumping out of a building. I copied what Joe did with the gums. It tasted bitter and my mouth got numb.

Joe's expression changed, he was a greedy cat and I was the bowl of canned food. My face got hot with embarrassment. In spite of his thin frame, his pot-belly hung over his pants while he straddled the chair. "You're very pretty," he said.

It wasn't a revelation but I'd never heard it from him and I vainly liked that he thought so. I drank the rest of my drink and a relaxed dizzy haze settled in with the liquor. The curtains ballooned from the open window and I held my up hair for the faint breeze to dry the day's stickiness from my neck.

He tilted his chair toward me, then reached over and brushed the inside of my thigh. I wasn't shaken, but we'd never touched beyond a friendly squeeze. "I see how the

12

guys fawn over you. You're getting around this summer."
He said this quietly like a secret he knew about me.

I hadn't realized my recklessness was so obvious. I let go
of my hair, fanned myself with my hand, tried not to look
at him.

"You're a horny little girl, aren't you?" he said, tossing his
allegation at me like a basketball from the free-throw line.
His usually bland marble eyes turned feral.

I blushed at his directness. No one ever talked to me this
way before. Despite the privacy of the house, I looked over
my shoulder. I didn't feel safe, uncertain where it would
lead. "Maybe," I said, unable to think of anything clever to
deflect his confusing scrutiny.

I tasted the coke settling in the back of my throat and
went for the cigarettes but before I got to them, Joe reached
over and pinched my nipple through the shirt.

"Nice tits," he said.

I batted his hand away. His vulgarity shocked me. But it
was my own fault for assuming he wouldn't put the moves
on me. That he should've been looking out for me was
immaterial.

I got up, filled my glass with ice, tried to act casual.
Would it be unbearable? It's true, I wasn't hot for his body
but maybe since he was experienced he'd know how to
make me come. Up to now, I'd been with boys my own age
and they didn't know any more than I did. Sex had hardly
been the explosion I'd expected.

Joe put out his cigarette, finished his drink, stretched.

"What about your wife?" I said.

His arrogant smirk suggested I had already consented. "We have an open relationship," he said, shrugging, as if I should know what he meant.

I hoped it implied secrecy. There were sure to be some advantages to it. A better deck assignment, drugs. He was clearly a liar and a letch, but not dangerous. Otherwise, why would all my co-workers have stuck around? The thing that scared me the most was the seediness of it all, but maybe he'd let me drive his Mercedes. I poured more vodka than I needed and took a gulp.

Classical music from a passing car floated in and then disappeared down the street.

Joe came from behind me where I stood, stuck his hand down the front of my pants, moved my swimsuit bottom to the side and shoved a finger in me. I tried wriggling free but he was persistent, and I realized I'd finally got myself into a mess I wasn't getting out of. Whatever was going to happen, I'd deserve it. I should have run right then. He was disgusting. But what if he wouldn't like me anymore, or worse, fired me? I'd have no way of explaining it. Melanie would love that. And, shamefully, it felt good.

I resisted, turned my head so he couldn't kiss me but I let him pull me to the floor and open my legs on the kitchen tile. The crickets chirped beyond the screen door in the waning daylight.

He was presumptive, pushy, lacking self-consciousness. He pushed his face in my crotch. "You're so clean," he said.

I thought: wasn't everyone? I hadn't even showered.

The year before I was sent to boarding school, my best friend Donna and I hitched to Center City. We walked into a head shop and I danced in my brown corduroy Levi's and a pink angora sweater to Play That Funky Music for the stoned Indian owner while Donna lifted a pipe and some incense from the front of the store. The guy didn't touch me but I saw then how easy it was.

I hovered like my ghost, eyes squeezed shut, while Joe dined on the remains of my innocence. And though I thought how a nice girl wouldn't dare give herself to a married man with twenty years on her, or use her body for personal gain, I also knew nice was boring and I never wanted boring. I felt brave for permitting this and surviving it. It was like ripping off a bandage to minimize the pain of what I knew the adult world held for me. Men whose cruelty could only be managed if weakened at the altar of my sex.

Chapter 2

At the end of the summer, a week before we were to return to our respective campuses, Melanie and I drove back to Philly together, me with a hangover and her full of reproach.

We passed South of the Border. I silently counted down the one hundred miles of billboards meant to build one's anticipation for the state line crossing that I long ago learned was merely a glitzy truck stop. We hadn't stopped there in years, not since we'd begged Daddy as little girls, expecting an amusement park but finding only cheap Mexican-themed trinkets and blue plate specials with watered down mashed potatoes.

We drove the distance through North Carolina and were now in Virginia, close enough to Pratt that Melanie could have dropped me there on the way. I would have preferred it to forcibly sharing the ten hour ride with her, but my school wasn't scheduled to open for another week and it would be empty except for the staff. So instead of the loneliness of a dark dorm, I'd spend the time like a hostage in Bala Cynwyd.

Laine would be packing for Princeton. I'd been too distracted to return her last two letters. She probably hated me but would forget about it once school started.

Fitting in wouldn't be a problem for the daughter of a New Jersey Senator.

I felt pain in my stomach at the thought that I'd hurt her. I hugged my arms around myself and kept quiet; she wasn't someone I'd ever discuss with Melanie.

I looked at my sister. Even watching the road, her silence was pregnant with her sacrifice of having to carry me home, while she suffered through the labor of driving.

That morning, I'd been remanded to one of the stripped beds of our furnished apartment while I listened to my sister offer a long distance compendium of my crimes to Daddy: not paying the rent on time; not saving a dime of my money *—God knows what the hell she did with it, she never bought groceries*; partying every night with one of our roommates who was a total slut; and finally, being a total slut myself.

Slut. A stupid word. I didn't for a minute believe it defined the sexually progressive girl that I was. But I had no defense for Melanie's indictments. I'd tried to get a year's worth of boys packed into two months, though I wasn't interested in chastising myself for it.

"I did you a favor and look how you act," she'd said repeatedly. Her constant reminder that I would have been back at camp if she hadn't convinced Daddy to let me tag along.

In fact, it was Daddy who sent me to live as one of Melanie's roommates in Myrtle Beach —a concession, I felt, for having sent me to boarding school —and Melanie agreed to it. But hers was hardly the selfless gesture she called attention to daily. She was desperate for an extra body so she could afford the outrageously expensive rental she wanted one block from the beach. Any suffering she'd claimed as a result of my presence was part of her persistent act to extract sympathy in the form of weekly dollars from Daddy. Her unflinching use of my presumed flaws for her personal gain never failed to surprise me.

We pulled out from the last of the four tolls on I-95 through the Richmond stretch. Another two hundred and fifty miles and we'd be home. Melanie pushed the Celica into fifth gear; we hadn't spoken since we stopped for gas outside Petersburg. "You're lucky I have Daddy's Exxon card or I'd have left you back in South Carolina," was the last thing she said to me.

But our silence lacked the anger that initiated it. We were spent, done with our summer long fight, done with each other, and biding the hours until we'd go our separate ways.

I'd changed so much since I left Carpenter Lane. Being away helped me realize that I'd never been at home there. Living a year at school and the summer without parental restraints proved to me that I could never go back.

Though, what did it matter? I'd suffocate in Melanie's car before we even entered Pennsylvania.

I thought about the guy I'd been seeing for the last two weeks. I could still smell the Prell in his sun-blond hair. He was a bartender at a college bar in North Myrtle Beach where my roommate Karen and I had been going for the end-of-summer parties. He was on his way back to Clemson for his junior year. Karen was lucky, she was twenty-one, she didn't have to go back to school. She'd stay on, get a winter job.

Melanie switched the radio station from *Born to Run*; it figured she didn't get it and I knew better than to say anything.

She started disliking Karen shortly after she'd moved in with us. We'd met her at the disco where we had our first job, needing to take on a fourth girl because Melanie's Yale roommate backed out at the last minute.

Karen was pretty, in a blonde Pepsodent sort of way, a straight-white smile and swish in her stride that said I'm foxy. She said things to me like, "That cutie pie over there's checking you out, you ought to nab some of that." I liked that she was older than me and thought I was cool enough to tag along, so I'd take her up on the challenge. Because she was a local girl, she knew everyone and we got into all the clubs for free. And she had a car, so I never had to ask Melanie for a ride. Before long, Karen and I were staying out all night and sleeping all day.

"The only thing you're getting from her is a bad rep," Melanie had said.

The car had gotten hot and the smell of the vinyl interior began to nauseate me. The air vent was little help but I knew better than to adjust the fan —Melanie's car, her rules —I kept my focus instead on the power lines, hoping it would subside. Then mercifully, as if she read my mind, my sister turned up the a.c.

Though Melanie griped daily about all she'd sacrificed for me, her dominance and guilt trips had been no match for my impetuous nature. I liked the drinking, the boys, the lack of curfew. At first, I felt accountable and apologetic, then I got sick of her dogma. She wasn't in charge of me. All I had to do was pay my rent and stay as far away from her as possible. Being around her was like being doused daily with a bucketful of castigation and contempt. Part of me knew she was right but I resisted her and deflected her words with the armor I'd grown to shield myself from her derision. As if the only way to distinguish myself was to reject all that she was.

I closed my eyes and meditated on a picture of me, alone, driving away from her.

A chill ran through me in the hot afternoon when Melanie and I arrived. Gnats swarmed in the late sun beneath the basketball hoop in our driveway as we emptied the trunk. When we dragged ourselves in, Daddy and Cheryl barely spoke to me.

I didn't deserve to be ostracized. I'd given them what they wanted: I walked the straight line at Pratt. They didn't know about Laine, and I was never once caught doing anything against policy. I reinvented myself as a high-quality young lady, with a B+ average and clean reputation. I proved I could take orders, that I was a gracious, first-rate daughter. If I'd kissed Melanie's ass all summer, would that make them love me?

As long as they didn't have to hear about it.

I carried my suitcases down the hall to my room, closed the door. My head hurt. The air was stale but I was too lazy to open the window and flopped on my bed. I wasn't sure if I'd have felt any better had my father hugged me hello; he still intended to send me away at the end of the week.

And I was infuriated that I wasn't entitled to a defense. There was some legitimacy to Melanie's view but I wasn't convinced I didn't warrant compassion; a glimpse of acknowledgement from the members of my family, even a shoulder to cry on. Hadn't I been harassed daily, abused by Melanie's authority? Wasn't Daddy the recipient of her weekly complaints about me and didn't he regularly threaten me with disinheritance and banishment? Hadn't I already been expelled from the family the previous year, and wasn't returning home for a trunk full of clothes merely a formality before being shipped off again?

My bedroom felt small. A blue and white flowered bedspread, a poster of a couple holding hands in a sunlit field decreed *If you love something, set it free.* A picture of John Travolta sandwiched between Ringling Brothers ticket stubs and a dried corsage, all thumbtacked to a bulletin board. My Wilson cheerleading uniform hung in the closet. Distance had changed me. And events couldn't be taken back. Work, Quaaludes, sex with my boss. Laine was gone and returning to Pratt would be torture. I couldn't pretend the world hadn't happened to me.

My red phone was on the bedside table. Daddy had put a separate line in for me and Melanie. It wasn't to spoil us, but because my stepmother didn't want us using hers. I wiped the dust under the receiver and around the push-buttons. I was saddened remembering the hours I'd spent on it, despondent. It was the lifeline to my friends.

Now, the only person I felt like calling was Karen. The number where she was staying was on a folded piece of paper in my pocket. Daddy would be livid about the long-distance charge but I called anyway. I was relieved when she picked up, like hearing her voice was the only evidence that she still existed, that anyone cared.

"You don't need to go back to that prison," she said, "You can stay with me."

I felt liberation at being given the option. That it was a friend who'd given it to me was not unexpected. Karen wasn't the first person I'd felt loved me more than my own family, she was only the most recent and the one who presently knew me best.

I stared at my unpacked luggage in the faded daylight. Still not a word from my father. I cracked the door, heard voices from the far end of the house. Daddy, my sister's shrill pitch. Was Cheryl with them? No. Hidden, as usual, behind her locked bedroom door.

Hopeless, I packed an extra suitcase with winter clothes, a picture of my mother, big round plastic curlers. I tiptoed to Melanie's room and pilfered fourteen dollars from her wallet, then wrote a note: *Dear Daddy, I'm leaving. I just can't do this anymore. I'm sorry. Please don't try to find me. I'll be OK. Know that I love you always.* A tear fell from the tip of my chin onto the paper. I wiped it, smudging the R in my signature.

My heart was loud while I crept down the hall, slipped out the back and jumped the fence between ours and the Jameson's corner house. The streetlights had come on and honeysuckle permeated the humid evening. The cab I called was waiting, its exhaust a grimy cloud against the curb. "I'm running away and I only have enough for the bus ticket," I said to the driver. "Please take me to the Greyhound station."

At first he shook his head, then he got out and opened the trunk. Said he'd make up the fare on the return.

I closed the taxi's door without looking behind me, afraid of being caught, unwilling to glance back at the neighborhood where my only memories were unhappy ones. In that instant when decisions are made that change irrevocably the course of one's life, I ran. Away from Carpenter Lane, from Daddy and Cheryl, from my relentless sister, from my senior year at Pratt and the Class of 1980.

The bus driver was unsuspicious of my pile of suitcases. "Back to school, huh?" he said, his hat propped from his forehead so it wouldn't fall off when he tagged my bags. I nodded and climbed the stairs. The inside was a cool contrast to the muggy night. The people onboard were as tatty as the bus. A black guy with short gray hair and horn-rims read by the dim light, a man in workpants and a nametag shirt drank a Pepsi, two nuns in matching flowered dresses and traditional navy head garb talked without noticing me.

I sat midway at the window on a seat that wasn't obviously stained. It'd be a challenge coping with the odor of ammonia, stale cigarettes and hidden mold but I didn't have a choice. I was relieved at having made it, but also remorseful.

It was well into dinnertime. I'd be found missing, though surely not missed. Would Daddy call the police?

Scour the neighborhood? Better the cops find me than my father. He was thoroughly intolerant of being disobeyed or inconvenienced and I was infinitely more frightened by him than any unknown ahead. I'd been gone from home for over a year and it'd been at least that long since he'd lost it with me. Being out of the way was my best defense but this could be the act to flip him back into the violent monster I'd suffered too many times before. If he came after me, then what; one never knew.

I took a deep breath to slow my pulse. Things would be fine when I got to Karen's. She said the house was huge, I'd have my own room. Getting a job would be easy. My stomach growled. I'd been too amped to realize I hadn't eaten. I opened the Peanut Chews from the vending machine, ate one. They'd have to last, I only had two dollars for food.

A guy smoking on a bench was orange in the parking lot light, the counter inside looked stark and fluorescent where a final passenger paid. My departure was made distinctive only by its lack of hoopla. The hiss of the accordion door closing, the squeak of the wheels as we pulled away from this dreary place I hoped to never see again.

Chapter 3

Less than seventy-two hours after leaving home, the night of the day I returned to Myrtle Beach, I was arrested. The reason, underage at an unsupervised party, wasn't an actual offense. In fact, the cop who took me in said I wasn't being charged, I was only being held until I could be spoken for by an adult.

Karen planned the soiree at her boyfriend-of-the-week's house while I was en route. The guy was rich, old, and, as Karen insisted, in love with her. Though he was out of town, he purportedly knew we were staying at his place.

When the party was raided, we hid in the burgundy-tiled powder room and Karen smoked while I peed, staring at the pretty white unused guest soaps. The buzz from the grain alcohol punch kept my panic at bay.

Karen confessed, "He doesn't really know we're here."

"You told me we had a week," I said, elbows on knees, head dangling, waiting for the relentless stream to end so I could bolt.

"I was just supposed to water the plants while he was gone. I figured what he didn't know wouldn't hurt him," she said.

I felt surprisingly betrayed. Thankfully, I'd left everything but a small suitcase in the car. I grabbed it and my purse, my zero options running through my mind as I headed for the door.

Karen's stilettos clacked on the floor behind me. "If anyone asks, act stupid," she said.

Where was I going to sleep that night was all I was thinking, would that be stupid enough? I thought of a guy we'd worked with who still lived in town, he always liked me, maybe he'd let us crash for awhile.

The police stopped us in the driveway. Karen reapplied her lip gloss and dropped names while one of the cops checked our i.d.'s. They didn't ask if we knew the owner of the house but when my Pennsylvania license revealed my age, I was thrown into the back of a squad car.

Karen held a lit cigarette to my lips through the car window. "My cousin's a State Trooper," she said. "He'll get you out."

I didn't have the option to think otherwise.

They kept me in a cage in the hall of the Sheriff's Department. I was a spectacle dressed in purple disco Danskins and three-inch heels, pacing like a lion in a circus wagon. I tucked my cold hands under my armpits and I prayed that Karen was getting things handled on her end. I didn't know how long I'd be able to take the freezing air conditioner, but more than anything, I was anxious about a missing child report with my name on it.

I curled into the bench and pictured Daddy bursting into the station. My father was never one to hold back an embarrassing tirade. Or hitting me —he'd done that in front of people before, too.

And this wasn't the first time I'd been arrested. I was fourteen when Donna and I were busted for shoplifting clip-on earrings and Great Lash Maybelline from McCrory's Five and Dime. We barely took it seriously when the security guard snapped our Polaroid mug shots. Me, the impudent suburban girl giggling when fingerprinted and cuffed to a desk at the Lower Merion Police Department. My stepmother, smug, with the smell of winter trailing her mink coat, barely able to conceal her pleasure. "Too bad your father's not here to see this," she'd said.

But Daddy had been surprisingly cool, he said he'd been caught shoplifting a pocketknife from Sears when he was fifteen. Kids did that. He said I'd been through enough for one day.

His response would hardly be the same, now that I'd stuck my finger in the face of whatever Daddy had done to try to be a good father. Maybe he'd simply deny my existence and not come at all, because his real power over me was that I believed his love was never a given.

One of the deputies leaned on my cage. "Cigarette," he said, and slipped one of his Kool's through the bars. The corner of his eyes drooped in a sad way. Thirty, I guessed, probably married because he wasn't flirting.

I took the light, though I didn't even want it.

I fell into wakeful sleep. Dreams of running, my eyes filled with cobwebs. A red light beyond netting that I pulled and pulled, endless moist threads, and I cried out help but no sound came.

I woke to my arresting officer knocking on the gate. He took his time sorting through his keys on the big round ring. The lock turned over with a clunk.

"Why didn't you tell us you're kin to Clay Causey?" he said, shaking his head. His hair, parted on the side, looked freshly combed but his wire-rimmed aviator glasses were greasy and his nose hairs needed trimming.

I followed him down the linoleum hall, past a doorway with a hanging sign that read: Warrants, and refrained from collapsing into Karen's arms at the booking desk. Her Highway Patrolman cousin beside her in his uniform, shoulders slumped and hands shoved in his pockets like he'd spent a lifetime denying his height. He fit right into the small town law enforcement diorama.

He was exactly what I needed.

Chapter 4

I awoke on the frayed Herculon sofa to the loud bark of Clay's Husky. When he started to howl, I shaded my eyes from the high noon sun and unchained him from the tree. I gave him half my dry toast and brought him into the dilapidated two-bedroom Clay had been sharing with his brother since his wife ran off.

"Clay best not catch Nanook in the house," Karen said, still damp from a shower, her long hair twisted in a perfect towel turban.

I blushed at the scolding, and scratched at my legs which were itchy from the knee-high weeds in the yard. I thought the dusty secondhand furniture and soiled wall-to-wall carpet hardly needed protection from the suffering mutt. "I can't in good conscience leave the poor thing out there in the heat," I said.

A blinding reflection cut through the curtains as a patrol cruiser pulled onto the dirt lawn. I wanted to pull some jeans on over my underwear, but Clay got to the door and caught me in my long sleeping tee before I had a chance.

Nanook greeted him, tail wagging. "What're you doing inside, boy?" he said, looking at Karen. He draped his gun holster on the back of armchair. I'd never seen a real gun and appreciated its distance.

"Don't blame me," Karen said, throwing an annoyed glance my way. "You know I'm no dog lover." She marched into the kitchen, fished a Tab from the fridge.

Her hostility puzzled me, since I was the one who should've been mad at her for having me come all the way down from Philly only to end up in this dump. But I kept it to myself, sat Indian-style on the couch and lit a cigarette.

"It's OK, I guess," Clay said, trying not to stare at my legs. He took the seat next to me and patted the dog on the head. Then he pulled a metal cake pan from under the coffee table, cleaned the seeds from the pot and rolled one.

We smoked and watched *I Love Lucy*. I was cool to just veg-out and laugh with Clay, who didn't have much to say.

When we heard a car, he peered out the flimsy curtain. "It's Jeff," he said, as if he'd been expecting him.

An imposing dark-haired guy in jeans stepped out of a shiny black Lincoln Continental; his motorcycle boots stirred the dirt.

"Is he your dealer?" I said, thinking I'd better get some clothes on.

"He's Ed's boss," Clay said.

I was too stoned for introductions. I grabbed my suitcase and ran for the cramped bathroom. The drain was rust-stained and the sink a mess with toothpaste and soap scum. I wanted to cry.

I knew what I was doing when Karen convinced me to come back to the beach, excited to be free of my family and escaping the restrictions of school. But now it all seemed distressingly naïve. I wasn't an eight year old who'd run away with a jar of peanut butter and a loaf of bread, home in time for dinner. Once I stepped on that bus I knew couldn't turn around. And regrettably, I'd made out with that Marine on the leg to Spartanburg so I didn't panic in the loneliness. The act only made me feel it more.

How long would I have to stay in this dump? I shuddered at the thought that it might simply be a weigh station on route to another odious form of detention.

I showered and returned in shorts and a tank top, hair towel-dried, but still sticky from the steam.

Ed had come home and Karen and the guys were playing cards.

"You must be Robin," Ed said. He made an awkward gentlemanly gesture of standing and dusting off a place for me on the couch.

Clay and Karen shot each other an amused look.

"Hey," I said to the room, so as not to encourage Ed's corniness.

"Jeff, Robin, Karen's friend," Ed said, with respect toward his boss.

Jeff nodded. His serious eyes kept him at a distance, but his reserve didn't tame his room-filling presence and the sense that everyone seemed to be kissing his ass. I pretended not to notice when he gave me the once-over, and I sat on the far end of the couch. "What are we playing?" I said.

"Strip poker," Clay said and dealt me in.

Ed's Salem dangled from his lips while he checked out his cards. "You use that Atra razor in there?" he said to me.

I was thrown by his question. I wouldn't have dreamed

of borrowing a grooming implement from their filthy bathroom; as it was, I had to wash the soap before using it. "I had my own," I said.

"You can, anytime," he said, like he'd just offered me a ride in a brand new race car. "I'm telling you, they're worth the money. Leave that leg of yours smooth as a baby's behind."

I pitied his pathetic attempt to ingratiate himself and sorted my useless hand.

Jeff studied me from his end of the couch with a hint of superiority, then his attention shifted to the erratic path of a fly. He snatched the insect in mid-flight, got up, threw it out the front door, then resumed his place on the sofa. I was impressed.

The card game continued until I was down to my shirt and panties again. When I lost the next hand, I lifted my top and flashed the room.

"Put your clothes back on," Jeff said, his tone a rebuke. I blushed at the scolding, but what right did he have to judge me? I didn't work for him. He stood, grabbed his keys. "Wendy's anyone?" he asked, but directed the question at me.

I pulled on my shorts, feeling more naked than I was, embarrassed by the fool I'd made of myself. "If you're buying," I said. "I haven't eaten all day."

White leather interior. Everything automatic. Totally turned out. I was surprised by the car's lavishness. "What's with all this? It looks like a pimp's," I said.

He shook his pack of Winston Lights and popped one up for me, grabbed one for himself with his teeth and lit us with his Zippo. "Ed told me you're a runaway," he said.

The word was a crushing anvil. I took the cigarette, watched the road. Things couldn't have gone more wrong. My best thinking had me crashing in the equivalent of a trailer with white trash. As much as I tried to stretch reality, I wasn't freshly emancipated with options, I was a teenage runaway.

"How long have you known Karen?" he asked.

"She was my roommate this summer," I said, unable to look him in the eye. I kept my gaze on the expensive watch on his well-defined forearm. He wore it on his right wrist. The wrong wrist. Was he left-handed or trying to be cool?

"She's trouble," he said.

I didn't understand what he had against her. Maybe he had sex with her. I instantly regretted the image. For some reason, I expected him to be above a random fling.

At Wendy's he smoked through the open window as he ordered, his other hand rested on the shifter. I wondered if his skin was as smooth as it looked. Five frosties, he said. He was right about Karen. She lied to me about the house, got me thrown in jail. And even though she talked Clay into springing me, he wasn't really my guardian. After a night at Ed's house, God help me if he was.

"Where are you from?" Jeff asked.

"Philly by way of boarding school," I said. It sounded flippant, but I was beginning to feel less so.

He took a drag, rolled his eyes. "You don't belong with those idiots."

I lowered the visor, checked myself in the lighted mirror. Jeff smirked. I snapped it shut, looked at him.

"I'm not spending the rest of my life there. When Karen and I get jobs we'll get our own place," I said. Why was I defending myself to him? "At least they're not trying to get into my pants."

"You go right on thinking that," he said.

"Did you sleep with her?" I said, unable to stop myself.

He smiled, then said, "None of your business." Which meant he did. Well, it wasn't his business who I'd be sleeping with either.

I read the menu in the line for the pick-up window. They had the fat kind of fries. Not as good as McDonalds, Melanie always said, but she loved Wendy's. She got a single with cheese and a Mr. Pibb every time. I bristled at the thought of her gloating over my disappearance. "Clay checked last night, my parents aren't even looking for me," I said.

Jeff shook his head. "My father would have hunted me down and kicked my ass all the way home."

I had no home to be kicked to, that mythical place was yet to be found. And why *wasn't* Daddy calling the hospitals or police stations? Did he even care I was gone? "There's nothing there for me anymore," I said.

The greasy smell wafted over us as Jeff handed me the hot bags of food. I dug for fries. "I'm so hungry," I said. I offered one up to Jeff's mouth while he drove. He shook his head, then ate it. I continued feeding us while he drove. An ease had settled in the car.

"I never slept with Karen," he said without looking at me.

I wondered why he told me, but for some reason, I was relieved.

"You can stay in my guest room until you decide what to do," he said.

It didn't matter that I didn't know him, I was in need of rescuing. His place couldn't be worse than Ed's. "Until I get a job," I said.

"Yeah, yeah. Until you get a job," he said. "But you should think about calling your parents."

"One thing at a time," I said and turned up the radio.

Elvis sang *All Shook Up*. When we were little girls, Daddy'd put Elvis on, pick up a broom like a mic, sing along. Melanie and I would dance around him, we knew every word. A moment fleeting when he wasn't berating and punishing, a flash where I believed he loved me. I flipped the station. I couldn't bear it now.

Karen was pissed when I collected my things. "He's divorced," she said. "He won't want you hanging around for long." Her jealously made it easy to leave.

As Jeff and I cruised down Kings Highway, a pressure released from my body and for the first time in a week, I was able to breathe. The sun was setting and the lights switched on down the endless stretch of restaurants and mini-putts. We hadn't spoken since we left Clay's. I needed to fill the quiet. "How long were you married?" I asked.

"Five years," he said, unfazed. "We met in high school."

"Do you still see her?" I said for lack of something better while I tried to figure his age. He was a grown-up. Twenty-five, at least.

"She went back to Canada with my son," he said. He leaned to get his wallet and handed it to me. Inside was a picture of a boy with blond curls. "He just turned three."

Telling me about his child softened his edge. I had an urge to console him. I wondered about the ex. Was she pretty? "He must have gotten the hair from his mother," I said.

"Let's hope that's all he got," Jeff said.

We turned off the highway on the north end and parked outside a fourplex a block from the beach. Jeff helped me carry my stuff to a second floor apartment. His divorce condo was sparkling new, with bare walls and furnished with remnants from his previous life: brightly upholstered furniture and glass tables. A substantial bedroom suite. But the place was a mess.

He showed me to a guestroom with faux bamboo twin beds in white with yellow bedding. Feminine. More wife.

"I'm going to hit Piggly-Wiggly before it closes. Get some provisions," he said. "Make yourself at home."

I set my bags against the wall. There were boxes in the closet visible through the open sliding door. I pulled one out, looked. Books, Beatles albums. A belted leather coat with fur trim smashed underneath. A picture of Jeff much younger. Longer hair, sideburns, in a suit, and a redheaded girl in a long royal blue velvet dress, cutting a tiered wedding cake. Her teeth were big, her jaw long. I was suddenly ashamed, like I'd read Jeff's diary. I buried the picture under the coat, then I shoved the box back in the closet.

I checked out the kitchen, found mac and cheese in the cabinet and decided to make dinner. I washed a pot, put the rest of the dishes in the dishwasher and cleaned the stacks of paper off the kitchen table. It was the least I could do to show my gratitude.

The water boiled. I stirred in the dried noodles. I'd never made Kraft Macaroni and Cheese, but I learned how to follow a recipe in Home Ec where I'd made fried chicken and brownies. I liked measuring, mixing and seeing the end product.

Jeff returned with two bags stuffed with groceries. "I got cigarettes," he said, tossed me a pack of Winston Lights. He seemed pleased by the table I'd set. "And she cooks," he said.

I spooned the macaroni on the plates, proud of my achievement. "So, what else do you do besides rescue runaways?" I asked.

He poured two 7Up's over ice. It was easy, like we already knew each other. "I thought Ed told you. I own an arcade on the boulevard," he said.

"Which one?" I said. I knew the strip well. Daddy used to drop Melanie and me at the Strand across the street during spring break to hang out and ride the roller coasters.

"Across from the museums, beachside," he said.

"That huge one, you *own* that?" I said. The place was always packed. I figured he had to make a mint. I was impressed and intimidated at the same time.

"It's a family business. We have a couple in town and up and down the coast," he said.

"And Ed?" I said, curious as to what his possible value was.

"My brother hired him years ago. I inherited him. He does whatever. Gives change, empties the garbage," Jeff said. "We're open until Labor Day. You can come with me tomorrow."

We ate. "What will you do for the winter?" I said.

"I'll go home to Canada for awhile," he said.

I was disappointed that he'd be leaving soon, but mostly worried about how quickly I could pull it together.

After dinner, we smoked a jay, me curled on the loveseat, him laid out on the couch. We watched *Saturday Night Live* in the dark. Ricky Lee Jones was on. "She's good," I said. "I'll have to get the album."

"When you get a stereo," he said.

"Exactly," I said.

"And a place to put it."

We laughed, but I was embarrassed.

Jeff stretched. Stood up. "We open at ten tomorrow," he said.

I was stunned he didn't make a move on me. But I liked that he didn't; strangely, it made me want him to. Then I felt insecure –didn't he think I was pretty? I must have been looking shabby after all the moving around. The thought, *he's not over his ex*, didn't ease my rejection. Daddy told me once: The only man who doesn't want you is your father. Jeff didn't want me. He probably thought I was jailbait. "Thanks for everything," I said.

"No problem," he said and disappeared down the hall.

His door pulled shut and the TV became background noise. I was alone for the first time. Displaced like a refugee. Not that I hadn't been lucky so far. I didn't think it possible I'd land on the street, but I was in the third place in a week and I'd have to be careful. I needed work immediately. In the morning, I'd go to Castaways, a local bar that stayed open after Labor Day. I knew one of the waitresses, she was dating the owner. Maybe she'd get me a cocktail job. It was a plan. I finished my cigarette, then got ready for bed.

I gagged on the toothbrush. The mirror reflected an exhausted stranger. Keeping it together was the only control I had and it was making me ill. I wore sweats but I shivered, unsure whether it was the temperature or the loneliness. My stomach was raw nerves and the dark room sucked dry what was left of my courage. I balled up and tried to rock myself calm the way I always had since Mommy died. There'd be no sleep.

I went to Jeff's room. The door creaked loud enough to wake him but he didn't move when I crawled under the blanket. I touched his arm, he shifted, made room for me, as if it was expected. He smelled faintly of Safeguard and dried sweat when he pulled me to his chest, wrapping me in his heat. I cried there until I fell asleep.

Chapter 5

The Grand Strand Game Emporium was across from Ripley's Believe It or Not on the ocean side of the boulevard. Jeff opened the gates on both sides of the building so that the salty breeze cleared the stuffiness of metal and stale popcorn. He turned on the power and the place came alive with a buzz. Bells, neon, electronic music. I felt like a trespasser in its immensity and followed Jeff past the sign that read Employees Only.

Ed was already in the office. "Mornin'," he said unceremoniously and acknowledged me with a nod. He'd missed a button on his melon Panama shirt but I didn't mention it.

"Any calls?" Jeff said and walked past him to an interior room, dropped his keys on the desk, searched the mail before taking a seat.

"No calls. Payroll needs signing," Ed said, his drawl more evident in the confines of the office.

I felt conspicuous hovering between the two, then Jeff said, "Give Robin the tour." He smiled at me, reconnecting our thread of intimacy. "Ed probably knows more about this place than I do."

Ed and I traced our way back to the arcade. The morning haze had dissipated and leftover vacationers loitered on the boardwalk.

"Couple hun' thousand or more tourists come through in the summer," Ed said, with the same bland expression he carried on his face. I shuddered at Ed's resemblance to his brother and the memory of their shack. He slugged ahead of me, keys rattling on a pull chain.

"How long have you worked here?" I said. I couldn't care less, was only fishing about Jeff.

"Goin' on five years about now," he said.

"Must be a good job," I said.

"The Burkes are good people," he said.

I was encouraged by that.

"Flash Gordon. I know this one," I said, stopping to touch the buttons on one of the pinball machines.

Ed used a key to turn it on. A ball popped out. "Ladies first," he said.

I lost my turn immediately and moved aside for Ed to takeover the flippers. Looking at his lazy posture, I wondered how much work actually got done around the place. "Do you know Jeff's ex-wife?" I said.

He nodded, expertly shooting the ball into some groove that lit the thing up like a casino.

"Did you like her?" I said.

"Christine was OK. Her family's rich, but they seemed regular to me," Ed said. "Jeff says they're Mafia."

I flashed on Al Pacino, tommy guns, Diane Keaton in tears. Did that mean Jeff was in the Mafia, too? I didn't think divorce got you out. But what did I know about Italians. "Maybe they're still watching him," I said, chin in my palms, elbows resting on the glass while lights strobed and Ed's score ticked up.

"Naw, she's the one who left," he said.

I thought about the horse-faced girl from the wedding picture and felt sad for Jeff. I'd been dumped before – months of me listening to Linda Ronstadt, hugging the stereo speakers, barely touching food –I almost failed tenth grade that year. Daddy didn't know what to do with me, it was one of the reasons he sent me to Pratt.

When I got bored watching Ed show off, I went to the skeeball machines, checked out the plushy prizes. I'd mastered the trick of running the ball up the side rail and into the middle hole and won at it every time. I could get one of those stuffed bears fair and square. Jeff would be impressed.

Thinking of him made me impatient to get back to him.

"Let's see what Jeff's up to," I said, taking pleasure that Ed jumped when I commanded. He released the flippers and his bonus points chirped behind us.

The bar was small and lifeless in the daylight. I entered through the propped-open side entrance. Sun cut through stagnant dust-filled air, the bar was imbedded with liquor and smoke.

Jeff had let me borrow his car. I took the responsibility seriously, drove the speed limit, used the turn-signals and made sure to lock it when I parked outside Castaways.

"I'm losing a girl this week," the owner said. A thick gold chain peeked from beneath his close-cut gray beard. "Come by on Tuesday."

I couldn't wait to tell Jeff. I burned through the side streets, windows down, singing along with Rod Stewart *Do*

Ya Think I'm Sexy. Something changed in me after I'd seen his business. I felt like I wanted to be capable in his eyes.

"How do you plan to get to work?" he said when I told him about the job he said.

I hadn't thought about that.

By the end of the day, he bought me a 1972 pink Plymouth Duster for three hundred dollars from a used car lot on Highway 501. It was clean and had an AM/FM radio. I promised to pay him back.

"I have to do something really nice for you now," I said and gave him a hug.

He shrugged it off but I didn't want it to mean nothing. I climbed into the driver's seat, seized the steering wheel, and when Jeff looked in the open window, his mouth close enough to kiss, heat flooded my cheeks. I fumbled to turn over the ignition.

"I'll help you look for a place after Labor Day," he said, then tapped the roof and returned to his Lincoln.

I nodded but dread crept in. Labor Day was Monday. The job and car gave me independence but I'd planned on living with Karen. Now an apartment meant I'd be alone. I'd never been by myself, not one night, and the thought terrified me.

But for now, Jeff said I could hang with him. And I realized that's all I wanted to do. Stay with him, put it all on hold. Stop moving, stop running, stop thinking. Just be. With him.

I put the car in gear and followed him home.

That night, he took me to Bamboo Gardens. I wore a blue dress and took time to roll my hair and put on make-up. I wanted him to see I was beautiful, because it felt like a date, as close as we were going to get to one. My life had shut in on me and I was aware of my loss, sad for the future dates I was going to miss, because I'd already screwed my life up.

Jeff was greeted as a regular. He ordered Mu Shu pork and Peking Duck. We drank Mai Tais from laughing Buddhas with miniature umbrellas and fruit. We had wonton soup and ate fried things from a flaming Pu Pu platter that spun on a Lazy Susan, and opened fortune cookies. *Good luck come you always.* I prayed for it to be true and stuck the souvenir in my purse. I tried to act natural when the check came and Jeff slid the waiter his credit card, like going out to dinner with a man of means was a regular thing for me.

"Thank you. For everything," I said again, and it felt significant and my throat ached while I suppressed tears. He brushed it off, like the car, as if it meant nothing, and again, I wondered if he thought of me as anything more than his good deed.

The chill hinted at the coming autumn and I shivered while Jeff jiggled the front door key.

"You're cold," he said, rubbed my arms, pulled me close.

I let him kiss me, like I didn't want the choice, as if my circumstances had made the decision for me. His lips were soft and his mouth smokey and sweet from the cookies.

And it was effortless, as if I'd already given myself to him.

I felt him watching as he held the door open for me, turned the lights on.

"I'm going to change," I said, when the silence became awkward.

When I returned, Jeff was waiting on the sofa, partially lit by the kitchen and the room seemed too large for what we were considering. What I sensed he wanted from me. What I needed him to want of me.

"Let's go to bed," I said, as if by some invisible agreement we were now sharing one.

I let him lead me by the hand down the dark hall.

"Are you sure you want this," he said in the tussle of sheets.

I nodded, nestled into his neck. But he didn't let me hide, he lifted himself and searched my eyes, his face striped by moonlight cutting through the Levelors. And I pushed any doubts aside for the warmth that I needed to feel whole, and because my body was the only thing I had to give. And he erased my limited expectation for the act by the gentle force with which he moved inside me. And I let myself fall for him because I was defenseless.

Chapter 6

October 15, 1979

Dear Donna,

How's jail this year? I got the address from your mom. She told me you lit a cigarette on the headmaster's lawn. You're totally nuts.

So much has happened. I have a boyfriend named Jeff. Brown wavy hair and green eyes. He's twenty-five. I know. But it's cool. You're going to love him. We've been living together for like six weeks. Well, I'm living at his place. For now. I keep saying I'm going to get my own apartment but between you and me I hope I don't have to. The big deal is that I'm in love. I haven't told him yet. He loves me, too, I can tell. So, I'm going to wait for him to say it first cause I don't want to blow it. He owns the biggest arcade on the beach. I know, it's weird, but it's not.

I still haven't heard from my dad. It's kind of sad, man. I can't believe he didn't send the cops looking for me. He's probably happy to be rid of me. You're the only one I've contacted besides my grandmother. I called to let her know I wasn't dead. She sent me $100 to get by.

I know you're not going to Philly for Thanksgiving, so Jeff said you can come here. He even bought you the roundtrip from D.C. on Piedmont Airlines. (What did I tell you, you're going to love him.) I'll pick you up at the airport and we'll make the turkey ourselves. Don't lose the ticket, it's like cash. And don't forget to bring your guitar.

I heard Don't Let The Sun Go Down On Me on the radio today. Of course, I thought of you. Jeff's still so into the Beatles. I think it's a Canadian thing. Did I tell you he's Canadian?

My hair's still long, is yours? Dying to see you. Call me collect. -R

Chapter 7

When the temperature dropped to an annoying wet fifty degrees and the South Carolina winter chill became unrelenting, Jeff took me to the mall and bought me a jacket the Crayola color of Burnt Sienna. Though it was frivolous and expensive –suede and faux fur-lined with a hood –I cherished it, as if it held an unspoken intent.

We'd settled into a rhythm where Jeff took care of things like clothing, food and shelter. Took care of me. But I didn't know what it meant. It felt temporary. Despite what we'd thought we'd planned, what we'd said we were going to do, we were living together, and I worried daily that he'd ask me to leave. But he didn't. And though my circumstances said I was, I refused to act desperate.

As I'd hoped, Jeff asked me to go to Canada with him for Christmas, which meant family introductions, making me feel our progress as a couple and further delaying any life decisions.

He'd scheduled a plane change in Philly. "Call your dad," Jeff said, tossing the tickets on the kitchen table.

I was seized with adrenaline at the sight of the word Philadelphia on the flight coupons. But hadn't the worst already happened?

The dread of an eventual confrontation with my father was at a constant simmer, but as the weeks went by, I had less reason to believe that he was in a rage and looking for me. That he intended to drag me back to boarding school. Or that he even cared. My sense of loss increased with each day. I distracted myself with playing house and smoking weed. As I drifted, Daddy bled into the horizon.

But Jeff's tone was not gentle prodding, it was a demand, and my only choice was to make the call.

I waited until I was alone in the house. Circled the phone. Smoked. Ate Milano cookies over the sink, as if I'd find my bravery at the bottom of the foil bag.

I'd thought for months how to explain myself but remembered none of it as I dialled his office. I was startled when he picked up on the first ring. "I'm going to be at the airport in Philly. Can you meet me?" I said, and did not draw air until he answered.

"What time," he said. "I'll be there."

I traveled in my new jacket, a turtleneck and jeans, carefully chosen to look my best. I knew I'd changed, grown, but the little girl in me wasn't sure that I wanted my father to think so.

I followed the sea of people up the ramp and immediately spotted Daddy waiting at the gate. As usual, he looked underdressed for the frigid winter in a trenchcoat, without a hat or scarf. He'd always toughed out the weather, would scrape the icy windshield without gloves and me always wishing he would get into the car before his hands froze.

As I got closer, I was struck how his blond hair had

turned completely white, making him appear much older, and I felt responsible. We reached at each other like starved troops, white flags waving. I nearly fell apart in his arms, his lingering scent of Old Spice bathed me in momentary absolution. And though I expected anger and intimidation, when he shook Jeff's hand, there was only distracted exhaustion.

I cringed when Jeff addressed my father by his first name. The moment felt disrespectful, and I wanted him gone. Daddy and I were wounded animals who'd abandoned the struggle for dominance and Jeff hadn't earned the right to witness our intimate exchange.

"I'll see you at the gate," I said to him and watched self-consciously until he disappeared into the terminal.

Daddy and I sat under a poster of a Hawaiian girl with a lei, Honolulu scrawled across it in bright orange exclamation. I hadn't figured beyond the moment. I was the one who'd been brutal. Any justifications I'd had for leaving could be reduced to desertion or ingratitude and I deserved the torture of witnessing the pain I'd caused.

Cigarette butts spilled over a sand-filled ashtray.

I craved a smoke but didn't dare. Instead, I studied the laces of my snow boots for the glimmer of forgiveness I needed from my father. "Why didn't you come for me?" I said.

He looked away, thought about it. "I knew you'd be okay," he said.

But I knew I hadn't been, and wouldn't be, no matter what he needed to believe.

Daddy bought me a hot chocolate at the cafeteria. We watched, the bitter air almost seeping through the plate glass, as snow fell and stuck to the blacktop and uniformed men threw suitcases from loaded carts.

"What about school?" Daddy said.

"I'll finish at Myrtle Beach High next semester," I said. "I only need English to graduate on time." It was an embarrassing option but not as bad a being a drop-out.

When my Air Canada flight was called, we walked, avoiding further eye contact, beneath a piped-in jazzy instrumental of *California Girls*.

At the gate, I cried, my face buried in my father's sleeve. His overcoat repelled my tears, smeared what was left of my carefully applied make-up. There were no words. The beeping of a motorized cart interrupted our hold. He pushed some folded bills into my palm. "Finish school," he said, then kissed my forehead.

I gripped his hand until the last possible moment. Our connection, though physically severed, remained unbroken as I continued down the ramp, turning to look back with every other step. We didn't pretend with smiles.

I caught the last glimpse of him and waved before rounding the corner, and our goodbye felt permanent in a way that it hadn't when I left for Pratt, or even when I boarded the bus to Myrtle Beach. I was now on my own, my choices solidly irreversible, and I knew I'd be lonely for my father every day of my life from then on. The half of me left over after Mommy died was discarded on the faded carpet of the concourse, trampled by hundreds of passengers on their way to nameless destinations.

Chapter 8

It took less than a day to adjust to the cruel Niagara winter. The Burke family home was buried in snow, though the drive and walkways had been proficiently shoveled. The three-story Victorian had thick walls, steep staircases and delicious smells emanating from the kitchen. I marveled that four of Jeff's siblings still lived there, struck by their unspoken bond.

A pick-up hockey game at the nearby rink was my first and while surprised by the brutality of it, I dug that Jeff was a kick-ass goalie. He blocked a slapshot with his whole body and snatched the puck off the ice. His brothers high-fived the win.

"Wish you were always here, man," Mark said, punching Jeff's arm. The youngest brother was *Junior A* and the family's big hope for going pro. I was envious of their pride in him.

Jeff skated to the board, facemask cocked. "I'll meet you in front," he said to me.

Heat pumped in the truck, *Breakfast in America* played a cassette. It was good to finally be alone. Every private moment had been stolen since our plane landed. "Your hands are freezing," Jeff said. He rubbed my fingers between his palms, blew on them and I let him baby me.

We smoked hash oil rolled in tobacco and drove alongside the gorge that divided white Ontario from sepia New York. The neighborhood was new but familiar. It's international difference highlighted by cleanliness and speed limit signs posted in kilometers, an alternate place I'd gladly disappear to.

Jeff was starving so we stopped at the corner Italian bakery, the aroma inescapable. It was warm inside. I wanted to crawl for a nap among the safety of the lined-up loaves.

"Don't be dainty," Jeff said, sticking his hand in the middle of the steaming bread. He put the clump of white in my mouth. "Try some real food." He kissed my stuffed lips, my mouth filled. It was the bliss of that I took with me when we emerged from the trance of our exclusivity.

I had no expectations of the Falls. My only reference was Marilyn Monroe in an inappropriate dress, tormenting her husband in the movie *Niagara*. As we got closer, the river spewed frozen water on the windshield. Jeff parked illegally, took me to the brink of Horseshoe Falls. Snow blanketed the ground but the walk had been salted, the hash and my intoxication with Jeff made me impervious to the cold.

Sightseers gaped. Mist rose high in a funnel from the foot of the spillway, glazing everything in petrified droplets. I wasn't prepared for the knee-bending pull. "God," I said, awed by this violence of nature. I thought what a horrible suicide jumping would be, how you'd be ripped to pieces before you drowned.

"Will you take our picture?" Jeff said, handing the camera to a Japanese man who was burdened by his own professional photography equipment and unsuitably dressed in a flimsy raincoat.

The river roared behind us and Jeff stood, arms wrapped tight around me. The man smiled and snapped and bowed. I wanted to give him my scarf in thanks. I wanted him to share in our folly.

I stared at the perilous wall of water, but even that failed to distract me from the dizzying thoughts of us. It would have been romantic but for the wind chill. "Your mother said I should call her *mum*," I said.

"Yeah, no one's made a bed in that house for thirty years. I think she's in shock," Jeff said.

Before arriving, I'd resolved to be the model houseguest. Helping with the daily dinner preparations and keeping our room neat seemed to work. "It's not my classic beauty and utter perfection?" I said as a joke, but it's what I really wanted to hear.

"Everyone likes you," he said.

"And you?" I said.

The air burned my sinuses. I wasn't self-conscious when he wiped my dripping nose with his glove. "We're here, aren't we?" he said.

In the morning, Jeff's "mum" Alice told me we were going to make gravy, their word for spaghetti sauce. I was nervous about being left alone with the women while Jeff took off to catch up with his dad and brothers, but staying busy with kitchen duty held its comfort.

Since I'd been with Jeff, I considered it my job to make meals for us. It helped with making me feel like we were a real couple. I'd learned a lot from the shelves of Piggly-Wiggly and using things like Hamburger Helper and recipes from the back of soup cans.

I knew enough to hide my general ignorance and I picked up a knife and quietly copied whatever Jeff's sisters did beneath their gossip. As I chopped an onion, I watched humbled, when Alice pulled real garlic, like sectioned orange slices, from inside a dry-skinned bulb. I assisted her by mixing her ingredients in oil at the bottom of a giant kettle, opening cans of stewed tomatoes and browning the meat.

"And two heaps of sugar," she said, dumping them into the pot while Rhonda, Jeff's sister held open the lid. "That's the secret. Takes the bitterness off the herbs." She winked, blended it, then spooned some for me to taste. Already good. "Leave it, we'll stir it in an hour," she said, satisfied, drying her hands on the dish towel.

I'd never understood the care that could be put into making food. It'd taken me all of fifteen minutes to boil noodles and heat a jar of sauce. Dinnertime on Carpenter Lane had always been a reminder of the burden of my presence instead of something festive. Maybe this was how the rest of the world did things. The house filled with the aroma of the simmering pot. I was transported back to the smells from the halls of the apartment building near my elementary school. My third grade friend who lived there was from India and there had always been a tub of something curried on the stove. I thought then that only people from foreign countries made their own stews and that the exotic spices emanating were something from the wrong side of town. Meal preparation that took all morning was reserved for Thanksgiving or Christmas and I'd never stepped a foot in the way of my stepmother in her kitchen.

But I pretended that this perfectly natural for me, and I absorbed it all. Being asked to help, following a recipe known-by-heart, now handed to me and already committed to my memory. The cracking open of the cloves, smashing them with the side of the knife, the heating of it all until see-through to release the flavor, the touch of sweet to finish. And the squeeze from Jeff's mum to make me feel welcome, as if I'd already taken a seat at the table.

I could do it forever.

Christmas morning, I sat cross-legged on the family's living room floor wearing the paisley pullover Jeff's parents gave me, tags still attached to the wrist. "Open mine," I said, handing Jeff his gift.

He yanked the green curling ribbon until it snapped and then ripped open the present. The new Ricky Lee Jones album, a green scarf to match his eyes and musk oil which I knew he was running low on. He wrapped the scarf around his neck, removed the cigarette from his mouth and gave me a kiss on the lips. "We'll listen to it later," he said, checking out the album cover, "I wouldn't dare screw with *Jingle Bell Rock*."

The Burke's choice of Christmas music created an atmosphere of fun that I'd never experienced with my own family. Cheryl had always been so formal, wearing her Santa-red dressing gown with white trim. Bing Crosby on the stereo while she stood on the perfectly decorated staircase waiting for the flash of Daddy's Polaroid.

"This one's for Robin," Jeff's sister said. Suzanne was twelve, in reindeer long johns. She had been thoughtful and unselfish our entire visit and required only that I sit next to her during meals to listen attentively to excruciating detailed accounts of her current school crush.

"Jean Naté. I love it," I said, hugging her. The dusting powder came in the familiar springtime yellow box. I was touched that she got me something, and embarrassed that I piggybacked my name on Jeff's gifts for his family.

I thought of the previous year. How Melanie yelled at me for buying her the drugstore perfume —one she'd always liked but had become too adult to appreciate. She chided me for how much money I spent and ordered me to take it back, give her the cash equivalent. Her gift to me was a Yale t-shirt and plastic tortoiseshell vanity mirror that broke when I threw it at her. Daddy sent me to my room, and later, feeling bad, I gathered the pieces, glued them back together.

"Don't forget, you're doing my hair later," Suzanne said, touching mine with reverence, making me feel like I had something to offer.

Jeff handed me a big white box tied with an elaborate red bow. I'd waited to open his present last and was immediately disappointed by the size of it: it wasn't jewelry. The lavender robe resembled a choir gown with a zipper up the front and angel sleeves. Prudent, sexless. I was confused. I wanted to cry. I expected something more indicative of his love for me. If it was the thought that counted, I had difficulty translating what was behind the housecoat. And though I might have needed one, it was hardly the style I'd have chosen for myself. Like he didn't know me at all. "Thanks," I said, my tone less than enthusiastic.

"What. Not the right size?" he said.

Rhonda nearby, ponderous and guarded had spied on our exchange, so I was mindful to appear gracious. "No, it's perfect," I said.

We sat in Jeff's sister-in-law's trashed living room while Jeff's son played outside with the cousins. Joanne was twenty-eight with four kids. She was still in her nightgown after lunch but seemed too worn out to care. We watched through the window as they threw snowballs, tackled each other.

"Look at the fun they're having. You'd think she'd bring him round now and then," Joanne said, meaning Jeff's ex-wife, nudging me like we were buddies. "You're so much nicer than her."

It's what I'd hoped the family would think and they'd made it easy to be that way. I couldn't imagine anyone not being happy here. I sipped my coffee, settled into the threadbare recliner while Joanne folded laundry.

"Be careful with the Burkes, they'll suck you in," she said, matching up a basketful of holey tube socks. "You'll be spitting out kids before you know it and living round the corner wondering how your ass got fat."

The notion horrified me. I had no intention of having children. Not for awhile. Even if Jeff and I stayed together, I planned to have a career. My father had said, *I won't have any illegitimate grandchildren running around my house* when he found out I wasn't a virgin anymore, and I believed him.

The group came in from the snow, red-faced, noses running. Wet coats and boots in a puddle at the door. "Hot chocolate, Mum!" they said and flew up the stairs screaming, laughing.

"Boys," Joanne said. "There's no point in cleaning up."

Despite the chaos, she'd been welcoming and friendly, in contrast to the other brothers' girlfriends, whose suspicions were palpable. They'd been distracted in conversation, letting their gaze linger too long at my chest, and their men had been all too helpful, opening a door, pulling out a chair. Showing off. Ray the firefighter had been blatant, sending signals as if he were trolling for strange at the disco. It was troublesome, so I consciously paid the women more attention.

But Joanne seemed unthreatened, even glad I was there. "You'll come by tomorrow, then?" she said when I left and it felt like I'd made a friend.

Outside the window, the snow fell big as cotton balls in the gray morning light. I'd gotten up early to shower in the one bathroom before the rest of the house stirred. Cold seeped from under the damp mat despite the spitting radiator. I dried myself, wrapped the towel tight for the run to the bedroom and smacked into Ray when I opened the door.

"What's your hurry?" he said, his grip on me longer than needed.

"You know how it is once everyone's up," I said and stepped back, squeezed myself tight, shivered. "I'd never get in."

"Too bad I didn't catch you earlier," he said, his huge arm on the wall blocking my passage, his warm body radiating while he probed my eyes.

I laughed casually because indignation seemed an out of proportion response and ducked past him without looking back.

The night before we were to return to Myrtle Beach, Jeff and I played *Risk* with Ray and his girlfriend who would've been a natural beauty were it not for her self-conscious slouch and buck teeth.

I pretended to disregard any of Ray's previous advances and the night had been fun, though his lusty gaze had made me uncomfortable.

We kept at the game for what seemed like hours while Ray attempted footsie with me under the table. I ignored him, tucked my feet under my chair, relieved when I rolled a three and had to surrender Australia to Jeff, who now dominated the board.

"I'm going to get some more wine," I said.

The kitchen was cozy, lit by the stove. The pots I helped wash were draining on the counter. I filled my glass from the gallon of boxed Chablis in the fridge and walked into the living room. The tree and fireplace glowed. Opened gifts were scattered in piles. I took the poker and rearranged the logs. Orange sparks popped, then fizzled to floating ash.

The visit had been a success. Despite the emptiness of the meeting with my father, I took comfort in turning my attention to Jeff. Being his girl gave me a purpose and a reprieve from the usual tensions of the holiday. I envisioned our future home where we'd entertain, learn to play bridge, build our album collection. I'd cook, get my nails done. We'd have passionate sex and passionate fights. He'd say I was crazy, he'd say I was beautiful. I'd believe every word.

A meaty arm encircled my neck from behind, interrupting my daydream, and I jumped. "I lost," Ray said, "They're fighting it out in Kamchatka." He put his Labbatt's on the coffee table. "Too bad you're leaving tomorrow," he said.

"We'll be back," I said, acting impervious while I secured lopsided ornaments on the tree.

He put his hands on my shoulders, rooted his nose in my hair and kissed my neck roughly. "You can tell how much I want you," he said into my ear.

I pulled away but I was careful not to insult him. "I love your brother," I said; the words felt strange coming out. I hadn't even said them to Jeff. I moved toward the dining room but Ray grabbed my arm, spun me around and shoved me against the wall.

"We can't do this," I said, turning my head to avoid his beer breath while he pressed his hard crotch against my leg and pawed me.

"If not now, when?" he said and held my face, put his tongue in my mouth. I froze, frightened that if we got caught, no one would believe my version over his. The visiting tart could be easily disposed of and things would go back to normal.

His lips covered mine. I was small in his grasp and the thought —*no one's here, would it be so terrible?* —popped up like Door Number Two in a game show. I'd made out with plenty of boys I'd barely known before Jeff came along, it didn't have to mean a thing. Still, this was beyond the beyond, so cosmically wrong, yet I caved, kissed him back. Suddenly, electric with my submission, I needed him to pull me to the floor, thrust inside me, say nasty things. Maybe it was his brutishness, or the covert flirtation-turned-foreplay, but I'd never wanted it like this before.

Jeff materialized from nowhere. "Your girlfriend is looking for you," he said to his brother, then yanked my arm and pushed me upstairs to our room.

"It's not what you think," I said, devastated. Because I didn't want to lose him, because I didn't get to finish what was started with Ray.

Jeff shut the door. "When we get back tomorrow, I want you gone," he said, detached, as if he was ordering take-out. "I should have known better than to bring you here."

I was shocked that he immediately assumed the worst of me. The robe he gave me was folded neatly in my suitcase for the trip back. "But I love you," I said, too stunned for tears.

"That's irrelevant," he said. "You can't be trusted."

I was horrified by what everyone was going to think. Fucking Ray. He was probably a weeping victim in his girlfriend's arms. "He was drunk," I said.

"He's my brother, I have to forgive him," he said, then walked out the door.

Jeff had been gone for two hours and I didn't know if he'd found another place to sleep, if he'd talked to anyone, or if the entire house knew. Fetal position wasn't comfort enough and failed to keep me warm while I replayed the events.

I'd momentarily acquiesced to Ray. *I was turned on.* But I wouldn't have chanced such a breach in his parent's house if I wasn't forced. It didn't make it right. But it would have felt right, if I hadn't been busted. I was complicit. Guilty. It was all true. But, Jeff didn't know that.

I pulled the covers tight and schemed how I'd convince him of my unabashed love and my renewed faithfulness, regardless of the indiscretion.

The past months had taught me to be myself with someone else. Jeff rescued me, protected me, treated me like family, which made this situation more calamitous. I thought of how Jeff's mum had made a big deal at the dinner table of all I'd done to help. I'd been valued.

I got up and tiptoed to the bathroom, terrified I'd run into someone in the hall, but all was quiet. The toilet seat was ice.

I washed my hands in frigid water, annoyed by the separate old-timey hot and cold faucets. I could still taste the beer on Ray's breath and shuddered from the memory. Why couldn't I be good? Ray was another shameful digression like skipping classes or lifting weed from the couple I babysat for on Carpenter Lane. I hadn't played it out beyond the moment. My impulses never paused for consequences.

The bed was only warm in the spot I previously occupied. I positioned myself to get the most heat but my body stiffened as I contemplated what would become of me. Jeff's decision to scrap me was conceivably permanent. Surely he'd let me get an apartment first. Would it be enough time to prove I was worth another shot?

The door creaked opened. Light knifed through blackness. I waited like a statue. Jeff slipped into bed. We lay there face to face. My cold hands curled so as not to shock him. "Please try to forgive me," I said.

"It's too late," he said.

I wriggled closer. "We deserve a chance."

"It's too late for me," he said. "I already love you."

August 1981

Chapter 9

Jeff and I had lived together for two years when I caught sight of him coming out of Kroger's with the tall blonde girl from the pro shop. They were holding hands and nuzzling over a bag of groceries.

I tried to wring a confession, but my attempt at force only succeeded in making me contemptible to him. These were days I'd spent in shock, replaying our battles, obsessing over timelines, trying to figure when he had time to cheat. How could I be so pathetic, unable to picture a life without him, and how could he not want me?

I blamed myself. Was it because I threw a jar of Grey Poupon at him during one of our fights? He'd caught it mid-air. The expression on his face suspended my fury. I thought he'd kill me, instead, he made threats. If you ever do that again, he'd said. We wrestled over everything. His friends bumming weed, socks on the floor, Willie Nelson versus Elton John. I assumed all passionate couples fought endlessly.

Jeff was holding the girl's hand. He'd held mine, too. So what? Mommy died, Daddy sent me away, I broke Laine's heart. Had she felt the same when I stopped returning her calls?

The trees and power lines looked impressionistic as I drove into Center City. The real estate firm's address, which I'd written down on a scrap in a netherworld of rote action, lay on the passenger seat. Each effort, waking, dressing, putting the keys in the ignition, was dulled by an undercurrent of pain. The goal: act normal. It had been sixty-eight days since Jeff had asked me to leave and this step in the direction of serious employment was my attempt toward permanence.

I'd returned to the Main Line because Daddy was living alone, separated from Cheryl. His lapse in devotion to my stepmother condemned him to a bachelor house to reflect upon his crime. His other woman was in advertising and lived downtown. After she and my father had their honeymoon, reality hit like ice water in the face. The moment she complained about my father's excessive business travel and eighteen-hole days, and refused to have dinner waiting, it was sayonara and I suspected it was mutual. It all worked in my favor because Cheryl would never have allowed me home.

I got a waitress job near Daddy's to prove I wasn't a bum. Caruso's Italian Restaurant, fine dining with opera singers, and a sweet-faced bartender whose flirtation reminded me that I was still alive. But I wasn't interested in anything but sad.

The already hot day felt like a simmering pot; it was only ten in the morning and I had the a.c. pumping to protect my blow dry. I wore my red t-shirt dress for the downtown interview with a wide eggshell-colored belt and the new matching shoes that Aunt Liv had purchased for me at Wannamaker's. They were my first pair of designer shoes. Aunt Liv *wanted me to have them.* It was her pretense of care, but the gift felt judgmental. I wore them to denounce who I'd been before the shoes and wondered if they'd help me re-enter like Dorothy, to this place that was supposed to be home.

My stomach hurt. I hadn't been eating. Not that I wasn't trying. I foraged through Daddy's kitchen for snacks; I grazed at work. That morning I ate yogurt and drank vitamins with a glass of Welch's grape juice. It churned inside me. So skinny. I liked it though, being a size two made me feel ironically superior. I'd weighed myself the day before at Daddy's insistence. Ninety-two pounds, disguised by a C-cup. Even in my emaciated state, my boobs prevailed.

I was on time. I was good at on time, I could control that. The city was in view, but the curves of the Schuylkill made me nauseous. Maybe I was pregnant. My period hadn't come yet. Would that bring Jeff back?

I pulled alongside the river and puked out the open car door into the gravel. Partially digested blueberries swimming in violet with chunks of curdled milk. Scull teams forged by at a clip, rhythmic oars skimming the surface. I found a tissue and blotted and wiped and chewed some Bubble Yum, the piece fat and juicy, and I thought how I'd buy a pregnancy test on the way home. It gave me hope.

I heard myself thank the parking lot attendant for my ticket like I was campaigning for homecoming queen, then dipped below street level to visitor parking. Two hours free with validation. Would they validate me with a new job? Would they see through the eyeshadow?

Love had only weakened me with false security then shredded my paltry illusions of forever. I'd have died from grief, but I made myself a pact: when I get through this, I'll never hurt like this again; I'll never be unable to live without another human being.

I refreshed with powder around my lips, reapplied color. I was pretty, hadn't that been the consensus? Not enough for Jeff, he wanted the blonde —but for the job, yes. And wasn't it a career that was supposed to matter? I smoothed my clothes and willed myself across the oily concrete to the elevator.

The next day I was doing chemistry with my pee. An eye-dropper into a test tube positioned over an angled mirror. Wait two hours. I watched the Price is Right, then crawled into bed among the boxes of unpacked shit in Daddy's second bedroom and masturbated. It seemed to be the only activity that was remotely satisfying, though pathetically so. I wondered, should I be playing with myself if I was pregnant?

I thought about things I wouldn't be able to do if the test outcome was positive. Wear a bikini. Couldn't I get an abortion? Donna had one. Melanie had one, too, when she was dating that cardiac resident. The only reason to keep it would be to get Jeff back. And that would be ridiculous.

The phone rang. It was Mr. Slate from the realty job. I wondered if I was the only one who thought of the Flintstones when he said his name. He had salt and pepper curls and wide lapels. You can start immediately, he said. But they'd expect a year's commitment, he'd told me at the interview. I'd sat in his mauve wing-backed club chair next to the pedestal ashtray while he showed me brochures with glossy pages of towering properties and agents with stunning orthodonture. That could be me, I'd thought, sitting straight to appear as if I were listening.

The decision to marry Jeff came the next day when Daddy and I had lunch at the country club. My flowered halter dress and high-heeled sandals were a little flashy for the golf and tennis crowd.

"What are you *wearing*?" Daddy asked.

I had gotten used to that question. It was one he'd been asking me since I was a teenager. Hard to believe I was still one, sitting depressed in front of my father, explaining my clothes and justifying, once again, the reasons I couldn't keep food down.

Though technically we lived together, I rarely saw him. We'd run into each other after he spent several nights in a row with Cheryl in her new townhouse, trying to get back into her good graces. Seeing Daddy in this bewildered mid-life state, and having been betrayed less than three months before by my own boyfriend, only confirmed to me that no man was capable of being faithful.

During my internment, I updated Daddy on my job hunt or depression, whichever was winning.

"I have an offer to sell commercial space in Center City," I said. "I have to sign a contract, though, before they'll pay to get my license."

"How long?" he asked.

"One year." A lifetime to me. There was still the possibility of a call from Jeff begging for forgiveness.

"You're not still waiting for him." It was a statement. He'd been observing my lugubrious condition and knew, despite my declarations to the contrary, that I hadn't let go.

I chewed on the club's chicken that wouldn't go past my throat, watched the bees in the potted begonias.

Then my father said, "I'm moving back in with Cheryl."

"Whatever makes you happy, Daddy." I meant it because I saw my father's dilemma. He needed me to be OK. Even in the face of my own confusion, I wanted to take care of him. But it was selfish of me that healing his strife took precedent over healing my own. If he was unglued, then how could I focus?

"Stay in the house until you find a place in the city," he said.

I intended to, I could barely take my next sip of iced tea much less begin an apartment hunt. I was still disappointed from the negative pregnancy test and unresolved about the job.

That afternoon, after two and a half months, after my force-feed with Daddy, after my limp agreement to move to Center City and sign my life away, Jeff called. "I miss you," he said.

"What about the girl?" I asked, barely audible, breathless. I knew that absolution was out of the question and it had nothing to do with her.

He groveled. I can't live without you; you'll never find anyone who loves you like I do. He offered the kind of love I deserved. Tainted, conditional.

"I have to think," I said. I hadn't been able to recover. I went on some dates but couldn't get Jeff off my brain. Love only came once. Jeff was right, without him, I risked being alone forever.

My hand still held the receiver when Daddy walked in. "That was Jeff," I eked out. "He asked me to come back." If my father was disappointed, I couldn't read it. "What do I do, Daddy?" I asked.

I couldn't sort my thoughts. I needed my father to realign my options, I needed to know that my future was important to him. I needed him to tell me that he didn't want me gone just so he could go back to Cheryl. I needed him to be a different father.

"I can't make that decision for you," he said.

I thought, please Daddy, make it! I promise this once I'll listen. Tell me not to go back to the man who killed my hope —that you won't discard me. I watched my soul leap from my body and throw itself at my father's feet, wrap its arms around his legs, press itself to his knees, beg for him to tell me he loved me, that I was a good daughter, a worthy person.

What I did was stand there. What I heard was *go away*. What I said was, "Okay."

Chapter 10

If only I was fearless, if only had a sense of worth, if only my father hadn't said, I can't make that decision for you.

Jeff and I burned a joint on the way to the Montgomery County courthouse. It had been a long time since I'd smoked and I found myself more than a little paranoid despite the fact that we'd gotten high the previous night in our hotel room.

I wore jeans, Frye boots and a western shirt with a ribbon tie at the collar and hated that I didn't have the strength to argue with Jeff about what I'd wanted to wear –the white knee-length dress and shoes I'd already purchased. He'd smirked at my notion to honor the occasion with appropriate attire. "We've already lived together, for godsake," he said. "I doubt anyone will buy the virgin thing."

Everything felt wrong. I'd let Jeff talk me into sleeping with him instead of staying at Daddy's the night before the wedding. He'd flown up from Myrtle Beach to marry me and he intended to take ownership of my body upon landing. I wasn't given the time to reconnect, to feel what I was supposed to. I felt numb. I needed to transform my ambiguity into intention but there was an incurable rupture that kept me distant as the dream you can't remember.

I didn't look at Jeff for fear I would jump from the speeding car.

Weren't the two years I'd lived with him happy? They were. We shared our friends, our hobbies. He took me to New Orleans, we went to Disney World and Gatlinburg, twice to Canada. Sure we fought, but who didn't?

We moved into the three-bedroom home with the sunk-in living room and white wall-to-wall. Nana helped me pick out the furniture at Maxwell's, she'd embarrassed me when she haggled with the owner. We purchased floral sofas, hand-painted Chinese lamps and a white dining table with bright yellow chair cushions for the eat-in kitchen. I hung an emerald green shower curtain in the master bath, bought appliances at Sears and hooked up the cable. Jeff set up a professional sound system and the Betamax. Melanie even came for Christmas. Weren't we settled?

But what of the blonde I saw him with in parking lot? A punch to my stomach, I hadn't been able to shake the image. The idea of Jeff fucking her on our king-size bed sickened me, but at the same time, I took a meager satisfaction in knowing that my spirit prowled the house. She had surely seen the things I left behind. My winter clothes, the avocado Oster blender, the lead-crystal ashtrays. Jeff had probably stuffed the framed pictures in a drawer, along with our albums filled with snapshots from our travels, birthday cakes, kissing under the mistletoe. The blonde must have known I'd be back, that he wasn't entirely hers.

We parked among the sea of cars, the courthouse daunting in the gray day. I stubbed out my cigarette, pretended to be merely running an errand like buying tampons or gas; I hoped the game would keep me from fainting. I prayed I didn't look stoned.

I never asked Jeff why he didn't want the girlfriend anymore; I only needed to hear that he wanted me. I had won. But what? The time when all I required from Jeff was for him to marry me and forever make me safe from the world was a memory. Now he was only an apparition of someone I used to trust. He would be an acceptable guardian, but that was all, and I didn't know how to articulate it, and I was too afraid to reject it.

I was surprised to see Donna's mother, Mrs. Milpas behind the counter in the registrar's office when we paid the license. Apparently, she worked there. Seeing her here was incongruous, like seeing your civics teacher at Safeway tossing a Salisbury steak TV dinner in the cart. She looked different without her housecoat and curlers.

I was embarrassed because Donna didn't know I was marrying Jeff, no one knew, I hadn't even called Melanie, and Daddy wasn't spreading the word. The hastiness of the marriage might have implied it was forced at the barrel of a shotgun, but no one felt that passionate about it.

Mrs. Milpas walked with us to the Justice of the Peace. The marble under my feet felt solid and final and I might have been walking to my execution for the dread I felt. "We're all doing well," I heard myself say to her, "And yes, Melanie is at Yale. We couldn't be happier."

The room was a soap opera chapel with a few rows of pews and a pulpit. The brides held flowers, buoyant in sherbet-colored dresses. I shook from the air conditioner. Then I saw Daddy. He wore a pale-green summer suit, he had a bouquet for me. I'd never seen him formally dressed unless he was going to the rare party with Cheryl. How handsome he was, how his prepared smile failed to mask his defeat. But still he didn't stop me.

And I hated Jeff even more for not wearing a suit. He'd worn one in the picture I'd found of him and Christine at their wedding. Yes, he'd been through it all before, but I hadn't, and he needed to tarnish my experience because he was cynical and selfish. I only saw it clearly now, in the glare of the courtroom.

"What are you *wearing*?" Daddy said.

This time he was right. I was ashamed that I'd let Jeff talk me into the jeans. The anti-establishment look wasn't a genuine display of ideals, but a mistake, in accord with the monumental one I was about to make.

I deflected Daddy's comment by introducing him to Donna's mother. She'd offered to bear witness, be my matron-of-honor. I smelled the lilies, cried for all the loss they represented, and then corked the imminent flood. It would have been hard to mistake my sobs for joy.

I never so much as looked at Jeff; I'd abandoned him at the door like I abandoned myself. At that moment, I only wanted Daddy.

We conferred in a corner, pressed against polished mahogany molding. "If you're ever unhappy, Robin, get out immediately," he said. "Because eventually it will end, and you'll have wasted years." But still he didn't stop me, and I thought, OK, the remark was meant as a waiver for what was about to happen. Like I had silently agreed to a provisional life, a temporary fix, so that we, Daddy and I, could both escape the hole where we'd accidentally wound up. Daddy would never judge my decision to leave the marriage if ever I had to, and knew implicitly that it couldn't last. And then I thought, why couldn't *I* just stop it? Take my father's arm, walk straight out of the building, propel myself on an alternate trajectory. Why was nobody saying what they meant? Why was I not being rescued, why couldn't I rescue myself?

The whys swirled unanswered in a blur until I heard the "I dos." There was a solemn goodbye at the car, another in the line of too-many-for-my-short-life, and Jeff and I rode the ten hours back to Myrtle Beach in silence.

August 1982

Chapter 11

Ready the house for your father and stepmother. Dust each vase, each trinket, Windex every surface, so they will notice how clean and responsible you are. How well you maintain your home, even in a foreign country. Vacuum every square inch and thank the good Lord that the pipes burst a few months back and forced the landlord to replace the trodden wall-to-wall with an updated plush pile.

Wear the striped-belted shirtdress with the gold-plated buckle instead of the trendy mall corduroy knickers and ruffled blouse, to show the preppy wife you've become. Wait coiffed on the sofa that was transported over the border in a U-Haul from South Carolina. Stare at the tree, decorated with ornaments tastefully arranged with enough space between each one so that the tiny lights catch their unique quality just so. Refrain from nibbling at the cheddar block and Wheat Thins that are arranged perfectly on the crystal serving platter.

With horror, see the 4 x 6 foot portrait of yourself hanging on the living room wall. The one you were talked into by the local photography studio. Know it would be deemed too conceited, too garish for your parent's sensibilities. Fear the inevitable glance of repugnance thrown your father's way when your stepmother judges it, but realize it's too late to replace it with another picture or putty up and paint over the nail hole.

Answer the door with smiles and verve.

Easy trip, sailed through customs, Daddy says.

Hug him a little too desperately; shy from eye contact, so he doesn't see the desperation. Yearn for a compliment on your home, get none. Serve Cheryl ice water instead of the orange pekoe tea you'd set out with the cups Nana brought back from Japan. Pour some for yourself and let it sit until it's too cold to drink.

Split-level, Daddy says. Nice layout.

Explain the bidet in the powder room. It's French, everyone has one here, you say. Try not to imagine anyone using it.

Listen while Jeff talks with Daddy about Atari. New games, you hear. Innovation. Good money.

In the kitchen say, I'm unhappy, like an echo that reaches through your hand from some distance to the arm of your stepmother. Want for her embrace, for her absolution as the only mother you ever knew, to send you back to *Go*, to collect two hundred dollars. Need a woman's touch, but not the Canadian kind, not the kind that says it's OK to be twenty and married. To drift like seaweed in the wake of someone else's life.

Recoil from Cheryl's blank expression when she says: Why are you telling me this? Don't cry. Excuse yourself to the washroom. See the bidet, drop tears in sink. Fix yourself like a collectible doll before returning with cheer. Dinner anyone? Stuff the sadness into a silver box of Du Maurier Lights, tuck it in your purse. See your breath in the carport and appreciate the numbing sting of the night air. Know that unconditional love is a premise that only exists in childish hope.

August 1983

Chapter 12

I returned from visiting Melanie at Yale and drove myself home from the Myrtle Beach airport, hypnotized by the windshield wipers, and I knew I had nothing left in me for Jeff.

It was the eve of our second wedding anniversary and dumping rain by the time I pulled into the garage. The place was dark. No Jeff. I ran across the 16th green to the house next door.

My neighbor Rick saw me through the glass doors. Annoyed. Wet. He got up from the sofa, barely slid the panel open so as not to let in the storm. "Hey, Robin. They're not here," he said. "Maybe you and I can double date with them next week," he said jokingly, but we both knew there was nothing to laugh about.

Jeff and Susan had become best buddies. They took her toddler out for dinner, movies, to amusement parks when Rick was away on business and I was at work. They golfed, though I didn't think it was the only game they were playing. Was my husband missing children or sex? I didn't care anymore.

I tromped back through the flooded terrain.

I despised my situation in comparison to what I'd just seen of Melanie's. Her law school apartment, minutes away from campus on a beautiful tree-lined street, resembled a picture from a magazine complete with the sky-blue comforter and matching curtains she made from sheets bought "on sale." Smart shopping —Melanie's answer to everything. I'd enjoyed New Haven without the anchor of marriage. Maybe it was the flirtatious grad students living across the hall who made me feel I could aim for more.

I left my wet clothes in a pile. Dried my hair with a towel and climbed into the empty bed. Knowing that I'd eventually leave Jeff had clouded the sun from our marriage. I'd felt that way since the courthouse nuptials when I settled for scraps. Oh, to be rid of him, I thought in the dark. Never see his socks on the floor again. Never see him roll another joint for the back nine. Never sit through another game of bridge with Rick and Susan. Never play another round of golf with women who kicked their ball onto the green from the rough when they thought no one was looking —women who passed around Sidney Sheldon books and competed against each other with their pedigree dogs.

The visit with Melanie forced me to think of my future. Of course, she was no help, her opinions leapt from *Jeff's never going to be anymore than a small-scale business owner* to *You should be happy with what you have*. But New Haven was a traditionally elite world compared with my hollow nouveau golf course existence. And it opened my mind to the possibility of living elsewhere, learning something new. And though I didn't desire the things my sister did, I needed something for myself that didn't include Jeff. I didn't know who I was without him, I only knew that I should.

Staring at the ceiling, I vacillated from enjoying the fantasy to strangling fear at my traitorous thoughts. But the tempest beating against the roof cleared away the miasma and I saw plainly what needed to be done.

I awoke to Jeff's back.

I got dressed without showering, fixed my hair in a high ponytail. The aerobics class I taught at the local fitness club started at seven. I was good at the job and my classes were full. Before teaching, since I'd adopted Jeff's world, my own friends had been non-existent. I'd supplemented my loneliness with semi-annual visits to Melanie, which only left me wanting and sad. I hungered for girls my own age –like my sister who were educated, paid for their own cars and had roommates; who were interested in current events, music, their personal betterment. My new social life interfered with my marital purgatory. Jeff was not one for expanding his circle, and he didn't want to mingle with mine. But I'd become increasingly disinterested in Jeff's wants.

Daddy was down consulting on a nearby course the week before I visited Melanie in Connecticut. At the driving range, I told him, "I want a divorce."

He silently teed up another ball.

"I don't love him anymore," I'd said.

"You should've thought of that before you married him," he'd said, and swung the wood without looking at me.

What happened to "If you're ever unhappy?" I thought. If my mother were alive, wouldn't she have told me to pack my bags and come home? Futile. Orphans didn't have beds waiting for them. And I *was* an orphan: a person with a dead mother; a girl whose father didn't want her.

I focused on the half-empty basket of balls and swallowed any further urge I had to confide in my father. If anything were to happen, I knew I'd have to brave it alone.

The clock read six-thirty. I studied my reflection in the master bath mirror; cute in hip-high candy-striped leotard and Reeboks. Jeff was still sleeping. Not tee time yet. I watched him breathe. "Jeff, wake up," I said.

He was totally out of it.

"I'm leaving you," I said. My announcement was resolute, dispassionate.

He sat upright.

I'd rehearsed the line an incalculable number of times and had imagined his responses. Things like: *I'm keeping the Blondie album* and *Don't let the door hit you in the ass on the way out.* But I didn't predict he'd spring from the bed and fall to his knees. "Please don't leave, Robin," he said. "I'll change. I love you. Anything."

Chapter 13

I rolled down the window and the world smelled like honeysuckle. Dew covered the grass and sprinklers showered the fairways as I drove through the winding roads of the golf course Daddy designed. The water reflected a brightening sun and though the August humidity would make the afternoon unbearable, there'd be no rain. Perfect for moving.

I went home after class while Jeff was golfing and packed all I was taking. I threw suitcases and hang-up clothes in the front and back seats of my car. I didn't feel guilty. I cared more about how I'd fix up my new room.

I was shocked when my father came through the open door.

"Where are you going," he said, the rage I'd successfully avoided for the better part of the previous five years beneath his words.

As it stood, Daddy had co-signed on the mortgage as an incentive to get Jeff and I owning. The reason, I was certain, he'd been so negative about my leaving –he didn't want the inconvenience of divvying up the property between us and the legal expense it would entail. But I'd need his help to make it through the first couple months. As usual, it was something I should have secured *before* I jumped.

I spilled the details of the day in a rush while I

scanned the foyer for the last of what I was taking, before I chickened out, before he could protest.

He looked over the living room that was barely touched except for a couple of half-filled boxes I'd brought from the A&P. "The poor guy," he said, almost to himself.

Always me. I'd fucked my life up repeatedly and now I was continuing down the path of fuck-updom. Again. Daddy would forever see me as irrational, errant. And this time, I was taking down some *poor guy* with me. Robin the Impaler. How he thought of Jeff while my suffering should have been his priority, I'd never comprehend.

But then he'd never heard the smug let's-get-a-manicure-sometime invites from Susan. And her insincere *You have to work? Too bad's.* Or witnessed her and Jeff together yucking it up, drinking their poolside lemonades.

"He was cheating on me with the next door neighbor!" I said and grabbed my purse and keys, stood by the open door to let my father pass before closing it for good.

"Listen to me, Robin, you're going to get your ass back in that house and work it out," he said, grabbing my arm. "Forgive and forget. If you don't, you're never going to get another cent from me."

He was hurting me. "Is that all you think I want from you?" I said, struggling.

"I'll cut you off," he said, enraged.

"Then do it," I said and stalked off, leaving him in the threshold.

My head jerked back suddenly, his hand yanking a clump of my hair. He turned me around and smacked my face. Then a backhand, and I went down.

"That's it. Get out now," he said, then dragged me down to the sidewalk, my skirt up high on my hips. People strolled down the sidewalk in the bright day, a child rode a bike, the gardener witnessed him kick me toward the driveway, me clutching my keys and bag.

I got in the car, threw it in reverse while he chased me fists aiming for my head through my open roof as I pulled away, tires screeching.

I was numb to my bloody knees and bruises, but cried all the way to the month-to-month rental I found near the beach.

I'd taken one of the eight furnished bungalows for three hundred dollars including utilities. There was a parking space in front. The furnishings were sparse, the decor was monastic: a rustic wood floor, stained glass on the bedroom door and a working phone in the kitchen; but its simplicity appealed to me.

I unpacked, stared at cracks on the ceiling from my new bed. There was no turning back with my rabid father lurking. But doubt muddled my resolve.

"What the hell do you think you're going to do out there?" Jeff had said when he realized his pleas were useless. "You're used to the good life, Robin," he said.

He was probably right. I failed shamefully at financial independence before and was more than wary of another *I told you so.* There was the real estate license I'd never used, the life insurance sales classes. Six months earlier, I even became a Mary Kay distributor, talked into it by a close friend of Susan's, and by the possibility of a pink car and the promise of a black rabbit fur jacket as a welcome gift from the company.

When Jeff found out I'd signed for the personal loan to buy the initial inventory, he was incensed. It's a good thing the woman isn't an Air Force recruiter, he'd said.

I'd left most of the product at the house, but I could see the jacket hanging up in my new closet.

I drifted asleep, in a crust of dried tears atop bedding I'd commandeered from the house. When I woke, headlights blazed across the wall. I shut the drab flowered curtains, got a Diet Coke, sat at the kitchenette.

Money was going to be an issue. My paycheck at the club was barely enough to pay for the apartment and car. Jeff's business was all cash and it was already on the downhill side of the summer. He'd hide it, cry poor. Our credit cards were fairly maxed but I had a half-full one in my purse and had taken a couple hundred from the checking.

I was faint when I stood and steadied myself on the stovetop, squeezed the edge until my knuckles turned white. I sobbed. I didn't care if the new neighbors heard or if I drooled on the burners. I sank to the floor, pressed my face against the oven door and wept until I fell asleep on the linoleum.

Chapter 14

It was overcast and balmy; the air left a damp film on my skin, not an ideal day for a barbeque but it was a real date, *God, had I really ever been on one,* and I wasn't complaining. When Doug slipped his Mercedes into gear, I felt like I'd already shed my previous self. Days of doubt and trepidation were now fuzzy gray in the rearview.

I'd run into Doug, drinking margaritas at Rosa Linda's with the girls from work. I'd met him before; he was my ex-next-door-neighbor Rick's corporate marketing director, always pleasant, glossy black hair, poignant eyes and cheekbones. When he realized Jeff and I had split, he asked me out on the spot.

In the past, the drive to Litchfield Beach would have taken forty-five minutes, but with the new Highway 17 bypass, we got there in twenty. I felt a stab of sadness when we passed by Socastee, the exit to the old subdivision where Jeff and I once lived; we had driven the two-lane rural route to and from town then. That time, like the place, now a remote haze. I pushed regret aside; the road had changed and so had I.

"Corbin owns Strand magazine," Doug said about the guy whose house we were heading for. Then he talked about running ads in various publications for Rick's restaurants and clubs, providing promotional items for local radio, sponsoring contests. There was nothing captivating in what he said, nothing I hadn't heard before with Jeff, but I listened, near fascination, if only because Doug seemed genuinely interested in my response, and because I was blissful with possibility.

I'd let him kiss me at the end of the night, maybe even sleep with him. I needed to be pursued by a handsome man who had his shit together. Things would be different than when I was seventeen. I was aware that having been married granted me social freedoms. I was soon to be divorced and clearly no virgin and I didn't intend to be coy.

Doug forgot what he was saying when I smiled at him from the passenger seat. He looked at the road, then back to me. I knew how pretty he thought I was. I knew he wanted to impress me, to be respectful. If things were to go well, I'd have to make the first move.

But I wasn't deaf to hypocrisy, aware of the dangers of scandal. I'd been a victim of high school gossip and the double standard –boys could scratch their horny little itches, but if a girl did, it meant *slut*. If I did sleep with Doug, I wouldn't tell anyone at Fitness International, they were all such Ivory soap jocks. What did they know about the prison of marriage, about longing for change? We were all the same age but they'd spent their life on campus, or at home with mommy, protected by their fantasies of ideal love. Time for them had unfolded at such a pace that they still perceived themselves as naïve budding tulips.

The sleek beachfront home was on stilts planted among sand dunes and sea grass. The air, thick with moss and salt, permeated my every cell. I surrendered to the feel of my clammy hands, sticky clothes; moisture beaded on my upper lip and I felt beautiful and feral when we entered.

It was a crowded party, unlike any barbeques I'd been to, an immense improvement over the keggers the summer before I met Jeff. *Safety Dance* played, the beat moved the floor and envious eyes followed us, the gorgeous couple, as Doug pulled me into the nest of bodies.

We danced, got drinks. Doug was a gentleman at every turn, finding a place for me to sit, proudly introducing me to friends, feeding me chicken chunks from a skewer. I was lovely and sexy, tossing my hair, laughing at all the right moments.

After we ate, he led me upstairs by the hand. We found a sprawling bedroom which overlooked the dreary matte horizon. I watched the sand below pocked with the beginnings of a torrential thundershower and the wind blew rain through the open wall of windows; thick drops were cool on my arm.

Doug produced a vial of coke and I thought, could this get any better? It had been years since I'd had any— Jeff abhorred the hard stuff –and I reveled in the independence of saying yes to it. The first hit felt like I'd been let out of a cage –it was like a dense fog had lifted. Cocaine was expensive, and I was happy that the world hadn't changed much for a single girl; it was still easy to come by free drugs.

It was early when we left Litchfield. I wasn't ready for the night to end but I felt unsure about bringing a man to my bungalow, as if I was being watched. We decided to go to Doug's townhouse only after he promised to return me in time for my morning classes.

He kissed me up against the door. His mouth was saline, the residue of his cologne a whisper beneath a layer of perspiration. I wanted this.

Inside, it was housekeeper clean, with a burgundy sofa, overstuffed silk pillows and glass tables. High-end electronics filled an étagère.

"It's cold," I said, all goosebumps and nipples. He turned off the a.c., put Alan Parsons on the stereo, cut lines on the kitchen pass-through.

"I'll make screwdrivers," he said, running a hand through his perfect hair and suddenly I wanted to do the same.

"Later," I said and placed his hand between my legs. He dug inside me with his fingers while I unzipped him. Not as thick as Jeff, I thought, and then flashed on the perils of rug burn before I straddled him, half-dressed, on the floor, consuming the newness and feeling little guilt for the relief that flowed from me.

I awoke in his bright room, sheets in a wad at the foot of the king-sized brass bed. The sunlight was an accusation. The length of his body pressed against me, his kiss zealous through morning breath.

I closed my eyes, afloat in memory of the night before and I wanted to run and tell everyone what we had done. I wondered what Susan would say if she knew I'd slept with Rick's hunky marketing director. She'd be fuming with jealousy. But there was something to be said for discretion. It worked for Melanie, who had always been private about her affairs, though I'd hated her fraudulence –she'd been Miss Virginity in high school when I found Blake Carson hiding in her bedroom closet.

"I love your skin," Doug said, lifting himself slightly to look at me, the back of his hand brushing wisps of hair from my face.

I took him in, ignoring my self-consciousness, and I saw in his eyes that he already needed more from me than a passing romp. He'd want to introduce me to his friends, have exclusive Saturday nights, rides from the airport. But as I moved in perfect rhythm with him, I knew I had enough of being owned by a man. And as tempting as it was to fall for Doug's obvious charms –looks, money, his apparent adoration –I'd already learned that fairytales were a myth. No. He wasn't going to get any of that from me. I offered my lips instead and the moment disappearing into our lust.

Chapter 15

The autumn exodus from Myrtle Beach was a sore reminder of my consummate bad timing. I was lucky that my job was not tied to the tourist trade, but two aerobic classes a day barely paid for food and gas.

My qualifications as bookkeeper, secretary or office manager were enough for me to hit the big hotels for a year-round position. After filling out a couple of applications, I landed an executive secretary desk at the Hilton.

With the nine-to-five ticked off my list, I needed more permanent digs since my bungalow would be boarded up for the winter. There were vacancies in a popular singles complex on the north end. After taking the tour, I convinced myself that my oriental flower-print sofa would offset the orange shag carpet, so I signed a year lease and put up a sign for a roommate on the bulletin board at the club.

Athena Sawicki was a southern sorority girl whose enthusiasm, bold fashion choices and funky Polish name far outshined her looks. Her athletically thin frame and big curly hair couldn't compensate for her small eyes and pointy chin and nose. Though I'd learned to avoid friendships with girls who were less attractive than me –they could be resentful and subversive – Athena was social, independent, and made a daily point of complimenting my aerobic routine. When she asked me to happy hour at the trendy oyster bar where she waited tables, I jumped at the invitation.

It was her day off and she secured free drinks and hor d'houvres. "I can't believe you've already been married," she said, legs crossed on the barstool, in a pleated plaid mini and saddle shoes with pink anklets.

We munched on the raw veggies and dip.

"It was a way to get out of the house," I said, careful not to disclose more. Nana had warned me the last time Jeff and I'd broken up not to tell people that I'd already lived with a guy. It pissed me off. *I didn't murder someone. I'm not going to be ashamed that I had a boyfriend.* Now that I was older, I could see her logic. My experiences could be misunderstood and I might be perceived as damaged goods. Until I knew someone, it was best to keep things superficial.

"I can barely get a date with anyone I like enough to waste my Friday night on," she said. "Besides, I'm a Catholic. If I ever get married, it's for life." She moved her clutch to make room on the bar for the cheese puffs. "It's not like I go to mass anymore, but I'm brainwashed," she said.

The bar filled up, people maneuvered for space and we scooted closer to each other.

"I'm not the slightest bit worried that divorce will send me to hell," I said, over the noise. I didn't believe in the church. I could care less what some *man* –and really, that's all those priests were– decreed about God. Mommy was dead. My marriage was over. The worst had already happened. Was there another fiery place I'd be sent to from here? "Sometimes you've got to cut your losses," I said, cheerfully biting into a molten grease ball.

Some guy reached over us to get his beers. He handed the bartender a twenty, stared at my cleavage, then said, "Excuse me," as if he suddenly remembered his manners.

After we got our second round, Athena and I flirted with a dentist who's tan and lean muscles made him look more like a professional tennis player, and his well-groomed realtor buddy who didn't bother to hide his gold wedding band. "You girls should golf with us sometime," one of them said.

"When we retire," Athena said, laughing at them. "We'll stick to our bikinis for now."

She was right. We belonged at the beach, not some stuffy club with a bunch of aging jocks. "I like your attitude," I said. We clinked our wine spritzers, turned away and giggled. She was fun. She seemed dependable, never missed her morning work-out, even when she worked until midnight. "I found a cute two-bedroom at Seaside but I need a roommate," I said.

"How much?" she said, bright with interest, crunching on the calamari.

"Three fifty plus," I said. She had to make good money, the restaurant was packed. I was beginning to think I should work there.

"I could do that," she said, licking red sauce from her fingers, waving down the bartender for another round.

"Cool," I said, hopeful in a way I hadn't been in a long time.

Chapter 16

Athena and I took Sunday off to enjoy one of the few remaining hot days before the gloom of winter descended.

We got free Kahlua Frosts at the Hilton pool bar and sand chairs from the beach attendant. The concessions would be closed by the end of September, and the hotel, like the rest of the Strand, would be empty.

"He's coming. Look. Look. What did I tell you," Athena said. The beach guard shined with suntan oil, zinc covered his nose and his thick mop of sun-bleached hair bounced as he walked. "Cute, right?"

He was, but he knew it, and I wished she would stifle her enthusiasm. I could see why she said she had trouble getting a boyfriend —as with all her emotions, her eagerness seeped all over the place. "How old is he, thirteen?" I said, adjusting the string of my bikini.

"I've had a crush on him all summer," she said and flushed as he strutted up.

"Hey," he said, practically ignoring her as he wiped a sandy hand on his red trunks and extended it to me. "Scott," he said.

Athena's face cramped with the same disappointment she was unable to mask when I won the coin-toss for the master bedroom. But she composed herself and hugged into me. "My new roommate, Robin," she said with an adorable pitch in her voice. "Scott's one of the guys I was telling you about who's going to Park City for winter," she said.

"Do you ski?" he said to me.

"No," I said, sitting on the lounge chair.

"You'll love it," Athena said. Her hand fluttered at me, more girly than usual, but her eyes fixed on Scott. "We're planning to go this winter, too."

It was the first I'd heard about it but I went along. "Can't wait," I said.

"Come to Utah, you can stay with us," he said to me, then ran to the water and waved in some swimmers.

Athena was giddy all afternoon, even though Scott barely paid her any notice, and it made me uncomfortable. But to keep my roommate happy, I closed my paperback with each of his interruptions and smiled politely through the small talk, making a point to bestow little more than good manners.

After awhile, I took a long walk to diffuse the tension and slowed my return until I saw Scott's red lifeguard shorts far from our chairs.

"He thinks you're gorgeous," Athena said with a mix of envy and satisfaction that was hard to read. "You should go out with him."

"But you like him," I said, feeling the high school silliness of it all. I'd made the mistake at Wilson of dating an ex-boyfriend of a friend who swore she was completely-over-the-guy. She wasn't and I was the slut. "Besides, he's not my type," I said.

"There's a big party tonight. We can meet him there," she said, packing up the magazines and Bain de Soleil.

I couldn't believe it, Scott made her blush like an eight year old with a new Tiger Beat magazine, now she was shoving me at him. But I knew what she was doing, using me as bait would keep him close. I shook the sand from my beach towel, folded it then stuffed it in my tote.

"He's got tons of friends, he'll get totally jealous when he sees me flirting with them," she said, sensing my reluctance, her hands clasped in prayer to exaggerate her I'm-too-sweet-to-deny-me pout. "You'll only make me look good."

We rinsed our feet at the freezing deck shower.

It was stupid and felt like a trap, but she was so excited. "Who can say no to a party?" I said.

She squealed. "God, we're going to be so popular together."

Chapter 17

I ignored the stack of unopened bills and crashed face down on my bed in the plaid skirt I wore to my secretarial job. My bartending shift started at seven and the uniform khakis and pink oxford were in the dirty clothes pile on the floor. They'd need to be ironed. The clock read five-thirty.

Three months, three jobs. I wasn't bringing in enough money. The day gig barely covered my half of the rent. The tips from Drew's went from a hundred a shift to thirty when the season ended, and I only continued to teach aerobics so I could work out for free. The car, insurance and credit cards remained unpaid.

I was coming down with a fever. I had chills.

I stared at the blinking light on my answering machine. I didn't dare to listen. Since Jeff went back to Canada, the credit card companies had only me to harass. I wanted to kill Jeff for sticking me with the messy remnants of our marriage. But I deserved it for ruining his life, didn't I? God, I resented him. He'd been so brutal and unforgiving, predicting my failure.

I called Ed.

"You don't sound good," he said. Surprisingly, his familiar lazy drawl afforded me some comfort.

"I'm sick." I dug in my bedside drawer for a Tylenol and I swallowed it with my spit.

"I can scrape up five hundred," he said, when I asked him for a loan.

I appreciated that he didn't cross-examine me. Despite his allegiance to Jeff, he'd been my only real friend in the end. When Jeff left, Ed loaded up the U-Haul with my things and drove them to me so I didn't have to go back to the house. "I owe you the world," I said. I'd figure out how to repay him later.

"It's on the tab. I'll slip the check in an envelope under the door," he said. "Call when you feel up to it."

I crawled fully-clothed under my comforter.

Too weak to cry, I moaned instead.

Athena came home and found me rocking like a baby. "Are you okay?" she said.

"Maybe Jeff's right," I said.

"You talked to Jeff?" She threw her purse on the dresser.

"I don't know how to live." I wiped my face on the pillow. Foundation streaked the periwinkle case.

"What did the fucker say?" she said, pushing me aside with her butt as she sat next to me.

"Who? Nothing."

She pulled a wet strand of hair off my face. "You're burning up," she said. "I'll get you a Diet Coke."

"I can't. I can't do it," I said.

Athena returned with a can. Lifted my head to drink. She picked up the phone on my bedside table. "The number for Drew's Deli," she said. After she talked to my boss, she went into the bathroom and washed her hands. "I better not get sick," she yelled over the running water. "My sister invited us to stay with her in Tahoe for a couple months," Athena said, tossing her hand towel to the floor.

"I don't have the money," I said and pulled covers over my head.

"We have three weeks before the rent's due, we'll sublet. Get jobs there," she said. "It's ski season, girl. You said you wanted to learn how, didn't you?"

It sounded like a perfectly logical plan. I'd look good in tight black ski pants. "OK," I said, before I passed out.

Chapter 18

Athena and I first skied together at Kirkwood, where her sister and husband had their season passes. After a couple runs, Athena was bored and wanted to go to the summit. I'd only skied twice before when we stopped in Park City, on the drive to California. I was fast to pick up the basics from the ski instructors who fought to give me free lessons. One of them took me on the intermediate slopes and taught me how to parallel my second day out.

Now Athena was convincing me that I'd learned enough to go on the expert lift. Fed my ego, said I'd easily caught on. "Keep at what you've been doing, all the way down," she said.

The chair had hit me square on the butt and knocked me flat. The lift stopped and the long line of skiers groaned behind us.

Athena laughed relentlessly.

It was cold on the way up, I gripped the metal arm rest.

Athena skied with the guys we stayed with while in Utah. I allowed her to ditch me because she was a real skier and I'd felt her silent contempt toward me for drawing all the male attention.

"Go left when we get off, there's an easy place to cut in," she said, pointing at the ridge.

Always so assured, like she'd been when she paraded me in front of Scott, the lifeguard she had the summer crush on. But her game –Robin's my best friend; I can deliver her –backfired, because I'd slept with him in Park City and it sickened her.

I wondered if she was thinking about it right now. I'd taken mercy on her, barely told her a thing about how Scott had waited for me in his shared cabin room with the thin walls. His eager warm hands as clumsy as the jocks I'd fooled around with as a teenager. It was too quick, too staged. Bored with his inexperience, I left unsatisfied, not knowing why I'd expected more. Athena's irritation with me on the drive to Tahoe only magnified the futility of the act.

I'd made her look good when she couldn't hide her desperation. She'd been obsessed with Scott and thought she could settle for living the experience through me. She'd persuaded me to give in to him, and I went along. But in the end, she couldn't handle the reality and we'd stopped trusting each other.

Above the tree line, the air felt thin and the terrain looked like a wall. I tried to control my nerves with slow, deep breaths. Athena on the other hand, seemed at ease for the first time in a week.

At the top, numbing gusts made it hard to stand. I leaned over the edge of the precipice looking for a way out. It had been a light snow year and the base had diminished, leaving patches of ice at the wind-beaten higher elevations.

Skiers jumped over the lip. I heard them slide and scrape the icy face.

"Just plant your pole and turn," Athena said from the run below me.

I peered down at the vertical drop. If I fell, I'd make an ass out of myself, but anything was better than taking the lift back down.

She was getting back at me. Up here, it was transparent. Real friends didn't want to see you in traction. She was showing me up on the slopes. But I wasn't competing, I was the exhibition.

"What are you going to do, Robin?" Athena taunted.

I jumped into the run, made one turn, then wiped-out. My skis popped off, poles went flying, and I rolled screaming down the mountain. I picked up speed until two guys mid-hill snatched me by my arms. My goggles were askew and my nose packed with snow. I lost my hat. My ponytail was deranged and I had hair in my mouth.

"Nice form," one of the guys said, handing me back a ski. His blond hair shot up over his headband.

Athena skied down with my poles and my other ski. "It's only her third day out," she said.

"Better not take her up there again," the other one said, brushing the snow off my back.

"Thanks," I said, embarrassed.

"We saw you get on the lift," the blond one said. "We knew you'd be worth watching."

I caught my trashed reflection in the guy's Vuarnets when he pulled me to my feet. "I hope you got your money's worth," I said.

"You were definitely entertaining," he said, rubbed zinc on his nose and he zipped the tiny tube into his jacket. "I'll talk you down the rest of the way," he said.

Athena threw a glance of approval my way and held me up while the guy used his pole to tap the snow off my boots.

The base seemed miles away. "I'm OK," I said.

Too angry to be scared, I made it to the lodge while Athena and the guys watched me like a child, then I gave the cute one my number before he took off.

Chapter 19

I sat in the executive offices of Harvey's Hotel and Casino, feeling obvious in the "borrowed" cocktail uniform. I picked Harvey's because Athena's sister said I'd have a better chance getting in at a local place. If I hadn't bragged to everyone before leaving Myrtle Beach that I was going to work in a casino, I wouldn't have even been there. I'd have settled for the Italian restaurant where Athena's sister got her a job.

I'd already waited a half-hour and kicked myself for coming at lunchtime. I shifted on the itchy Herculon to avoid creasing my bare thighs. I skimmed a year-old ski magazine, an article about freestyle, the kind of skiing Athena's brother-in-law did for the U.S. Ski Team. The magazine would have called him a hot dog. Knowing these tidbits kept me from sounding like an idiot when talking with the locals.

A gray-haired guy in a brown suit walked through the waiting area, noticed the empty office and stopped. "Is anyone helping you?" he said. His name tag read Food and Beverage Director.

An hour earlier, the Human Resources lady had told me that because the money was so good, there was a waiting list for cocktail jobs. She offered me a hostess position instead, explaining that after four years, I'd be eligible to move to another department. I could have a medical degree in that amount of time. As it was, I hadn't planned my life beyond the end of ski season.

Once I left Human Resources, I took my rejected submission to the security station. Harvey's wasn't hard to navigate. The skinny guard was flipping through *Truck Trader*. I told him what I needed, indicating the employment office behind me and he sent me to wardrobe. Since I didn't have a requisition form, I did some charades for the non-English-speaking woman behind the counter. She returned with a choice. I picked the skimpiest.

I handed the man in the brown suit my application. "I'm here for the cocktail waitress job," I said.

"None of those posts are open," he said and stared blankly at the paper. "Who gave you that uniform?"

"I figured if you met me, you'd see what a find I am," I said.

Instead of throwing me out, he opened his door and sat behind his desk.

His shoulders were sprinkled with dandruff, like snowflakes on dirt and I wondered why no one dared to point it out. I tugged at the velvet turquoise mini-dress and let my corseted boobs enter the room first.

He didn't allow his gaze to linger below my neck and reached for my application, glanced over it. "How did you get past security?"

"They didn't seem to mind," I said and gave my best pageant smile. "You can see I have a lot of experience. It'd be a shame to waste my talent in your twenty-four hour café."

He looked at me like I was the break from his boredom he'd been waiting for. "You've got nerve young lady," he said, and it prompted me to sell harder. Pictures of his children lined the credenza behind him. His wife. The one who should've brushed off his shoulders before he left in the morning.

"I've wanted to work at a casino since my father took me to the opening of Resorts in Atlantic City," I said.

He leaned back in his chair, took me in. He had kind eyes. I could tell he liked me. "I just fired one of the girls from our rooftop restaurant. Swing shift. Four to midnight," he said. "You'll have to get a Sheriff's Card."

I'd figure out what he meant later.

Chapter 20

I spent two hours getting ready for the date with Evan the skier from Kirkwood, the guy who saved me when Athena tried to kill me. "It's a date," he'd said when he called. *Date.* I hadn't had one I looked forward to since Doug Jenkins. All the others were time fillers. Free dinners. Eye rollers.

It was hard looking sexy when the temperature outside was fifteen degrees. I borrowed Athena's tight pink ski jacket which zipped diagonally up the front.

"You sure clean up well," Evan said at the door, his words steaming white into the cold.

The warmth in the cab of his pick-up reminded me of Jeff. How I'd hated those winters in Canada. But I didn't feel trapped and bitter here. Like any vacation, this would end.

We ate pizza and played pool. Evan cradled my body while he slid the cue stick between my fingers. He smelled like snow and Herbal Essence. After dinner, he took me to Caesars where he was a blackjack dealer. We drank free Margaritas and he passed me an envelope of coke. I did some in the ladies lounge. We did the rest at his place, an A-frame he shared with a friend who ski-patrolled at Sierra Ranch.

I disappeared into the warmth of his bed. His body was smooth, strong on top of mine. I came almost as soon as he entered me.

"I'll get us some water," he said, then covered me with the heavy down.

When he returned, he rustled under the warmed covers, his skin cool from the drafty house. I slipped under his arm, rested against his chest. He kissed my head. We stared silent at the long shadows on the wall. "Where have you been, beautiful?" he said.

It was Evan who was beautiful, a Sea & Ski ad. But I'd had plenty of that. Since Jeff, I'd picked the boys like I'd been sampling the buffet. Going to their place, so I could leave when I was done with them. So I didn't wake to the harsh mess of it all, so I didn't feel humiliated.

Evan touched my hair, turned my face to his and looked at me as if he saw beyond my face, with an almost reverence. I wanted to hide from his gaze and the corniness of how it made me feel. But there was something natural, even vulnerable in his desire for me, and he didn't shy from it. I climbed atop of him, kissed him with the intent to stay, time removed, inside the dream.

In the next weeks, I left Evan's only for clean clothes and work. We fell into a rhythm. Work, ski, fuck. When he told me he loved me, I said it back.

Athena was the consideration, the tug of responsibility that kept me from total immersion. Also, it was her Renault we'd driven across the country and I was at her mercy for rides more than once, reminding me of that summer I lived with Melanie. But I deflected her attempts to make me feel guilty. I expected her to buck up, find her own diversion.

Two months later I'd spent the night, like most, at Evan's. He'd gotten up early to ski the powder while I sat alone in his living room wrapped in a down comforter eating Fruit Loops, enjoying the solitude.

I'd barely had a moment alone in Tahoe. It was March and Athena was pressing me to go back East. She was leaving in a couple of weeks and she was peeved with me. The boyfriend had cut into our playtime. "We've only had two nights together," she'd said. And she wasn't wrong.

The snow fell heavily and the matte landscape was blinding. I pulled the curtains shut.

Athena was in San Francisco with friends, ticked I didn't go with her. "When I return, you've better decided whether or not you're coming home with me," she'd said before leaving.

Here in Evan's house, where I'd been protected from making any hard choices, Athena's demands became unavoidable. The calendar screamed spring, whether I liked it or not.

I was torn. The Evan thing worked for the winter, for the whole escape, but starting a life with a blackjack dealer had no appeal. If Athena left without me, I'd be stranded in the Sierras, banished to life as a casino cocktail waitress. And the image of clinking coins and strobe lights, the dangling cigarettes from the mouths of wrinkled women seated at the slots didn't make the prospect of staying anymore appealing.

The window was drafty, making the room colder than was comfortable for me, I stood hostage at the floor radiators, absorbing the heat on my ankles.

Athena and I came with our winter clothes, left an

apartment full in Myrtle Beach. Up to this point I'd been on vacation. If I stayed, at the very least, I'd need to return with Athena, get my car and file for divorce.

Evan was an acceptable choice for someone else, not me. Let another girl stay for the flannels, Sorrels and sensimilla. I'd crossed that kind of contentment off my list. I planned to travel, meet a millionaire. Evan wasn't going to show me Paris. It'd hurt to tell him, I'd leave with Athena.

I snuggled into the couch, wrapped my feet tight in the blanket, flipped through the TV channels, tried to ignore my nerves.

I'd been self-centered to let Evan believe I wanted more and I'd allowed us to go on too long. I hadn't considered the consequences of being careless with his emotions.

On the TV, the Skipper was yelling at Gilligan again. I put down the remote, tried to listen but I was sullen. Then the fear I'd had when I left Jeff crept in: there will never be another one who wants me. But I'd only been separated seven months and proved that theory wrong.

I heard the lock turn. Keys on the counter. The stomping of snow-covered boots. Evan bumped through kitchen, found me in the living room.

I avoided the kiss. "We need to talk," I said.

Chapter 21

I'd dropped Athena at the restaurant and was on my way to Harvey's when the car skidded into the back of a Jeep. The daylight had given way to street lamps subdued by fresh snowfall. I banged my knee on the dash, ripped my Sheer Energy suntan pantyhose. Waited in the biting dusk for the tow truck. The guy drove me home. I called Athena.

"I told you to be careful," she said, like I crashed on purpose.

"I slid on the ice," I said, "on that hill."

She'd been selfish with her car all winter. It was the privilege she bestowed when I was good. When I asked nicely. When she felt benevolent toward me. When I acted grateful. Melanie, five years later, déjà vu.

One of the reasons I'd hung out with Evan so much was the freedom he gave me to drive his truck, but since telling him that I'd return to South Carolina, we decided to cool it on seeing each other every night. I was back to depending on Athena's random best-friendship, but I should've thought about that before I parked my car for the winter. Now with two lousy weeks left, I had to smash her wheels.

"I'm going to pay for it," I said, fully aware restitution would extend beyond the monetary kind, she'd embarrass me with the mistake anytime it was convenient.

I held the receiver against my shoulder while I unwound the tangled phone cord.

"It has to be fixed before we leave," she said. "Did you tell the body shop?"

I took offence with her superior tone. I could've stood some compassion. The knee throbbed. I rubbed it. "They said it'll take two days," I said.

"I'll get a ride home tonight," she said, and hung up without saying goodbye.

I rummaged for food. Peanut butter. I put bread in the toaster and called Harvey's. "I'm lucky I wasn't killed," I told the hostess.

"We worried when you didn't show up," she said. She was sarcastic. Sceptical.

The bitch had been a problem from the beginning. I wanted to tell her to fuck off. I was allowed sick days, could probably milk a couple more, but I needed to work these last two weeks. The damage for the headlight and bumper would cost over three hundred and I needed travel money. I had no intention of relying on Athena for a loan. "Tell them I'll be in tomorrow," I said.

Chapter 22

The Top of the Wheel Restaurant —roulette not wagon–was on the top floor of the hotel and served Polynesian food. The room had floor to ceiling windows and the view of the lake was breathtaking. The cocktail lounge was a tourist attraction where customers happily waited two hours for their table, drinking flaming bowls of fruit-laden pineapple juice and rum concoctions called Monsoons.

The uniform was a shiny purple leotard with a white and purple flowered polyester full-length skirt, slit to the hip, complimented by pantyhose and strappy shoes. Far from the cute little number that I stole to get the job.

I made it in early the night after my accident. The three other waitresses on my shift were distant and whispered among themselves.

I skewered orange and maraschino cherries with the hag who cornered me on my first night with an accusatory, *which department did you come from?* Her perm was tight. Frosted. Her blue glitter eyeshadow met her over-arched eyebrows. "If you aren't going to take the job seriously, you shouldn't be here," she said.

"Take it up with management if you have a problem with me," I said.

From the day I started at Harvey's, the girls had ganged up on me, not understanding how I got the job when their friends were in line for the spot. The sick day gave them ammunition to peck at me like I was a crippled chicken, but I was over their squawking, over kissing up.

When I turned my back, I knocked a stack of ashtrays over and they fell with a loud crash. One of them landed on my ankle and broke in half. Blood poured over my foot.

"I'm bleeding," I said to the bartender.

He was short and chubby and had difficulty seeing over the bar. He rushed from behind the counter. "Give me a rag," he said to the other waitress, who stared motionless.

When the blood didn't stop and I became faint, paramedics took me to South Lake Tahoe Medical Center.

I was made to wait on a gurney in the hall with my leg elevated. The smell of alcohol and bleach made me nauseous. I hated the sterility of the place, the sense of impending death, needles and blood. Past the swinging door an old man was smoking through a tube in his throat. I shuddered.

I was sure my little fuck-up caused a gossip frenzy at the Wheel. Those witches were having a heyday. I'd have to suck it up. If everything was OK with my ankle and I had a couple good nights, I'd have about a thousand to go home with.

A nurse took me to a curtained exam area, took my blood pressure and temperature. The plastic mattress crinkled beneath me. The pasty doctor wasn't worth flirting with. He shined a light in my eyes, put a butterfly suture on my wound and sent me home.

The bill was two hundred and fifty dollars.

When I got back, the house was empty but for a message from Harvey's. They'd no longer need my services.

My heart sped to keep pace with my thoughts. Where was I going to get the money food and gas or next month's rent? God. I was useless to care for myself. Worst, Athena would gloat. *If you'd have been responsible. Saved. Worked more, played less.* Really what she'd mean is, played less with Evan. The car and ashtray were accidents. So why did I feel guilty?

The windows whistled from an outside gust. Any other time, I'd see the purple glow of the moon-filled darkness as magical, but now it only made the plowed street and snow-laden trees appear lonely and menacing. Frightened, I shut the curtains then hid behind my closed bedroom door.

March 1984

Chapter 23

It was early at Club Jacks, and the crowd was thin, many of the same faces. Athena and I had returned to town only a few hours before. My objective for the night was to *run into* one of my previous conquests, sleep with him and then hit him up for some cash.

I was down to my last dollars after the drive home. Tahoe had put me in the hole. After the hospital stint, I had to endure a responsibility lecture from my grandmother so that she'd Western Union me two hundred.

Jack's was the obvious place to grub for a loan. It was the only private club in Myrtle Beach, allowing its members the exotic privilege of drinking in a dry state past two in the morning.

"Same thing?" the bartender said. He was sexy in a long-haired-English-rocker sort of way. Tall, thin. Eyes like onyx beads. I wondered why I never slept with him. We'd certainly done enough blow together.

He slid me a kamikaze and I left a five that I didn't have on the bar.

"Look what the cat drug in," I heard from behind. I didn't need to see my ex-boss Joe McClure to distinguish his particular drawl. A mix of sleaze and condescension.

I spun on my barstool and tossed my hair so he could get a good look at what a woman I'd become. "Hey, baby," I said.

He stroked his finger up and down my arm, sipped his scotch, checked me out. "Where've you been?" he said.

"Skiing in California." I said.

He was unfazed. "You're not with that guy still."

"My husband?" I said, taking a draw off my Virginia Slim.

"Yeah, him." Perspiration formed on his upper lip.

I looked around the room, hoping to see Buddy Farmer, or Big Fun, as his personalized license plate said. Hoping to capitalize on the insufferable crush he had on me, I was sure I could squeeze rent from his rich chubby fists. If I settled for Joe, it wouldn't be boring, but I'd have to find the courage to ask him for a loan.

"Your girl over there," Joe said. "You party with her?"

Athena was at a table talking to an insurance salesman and a real estate broker. She was animated; they were rapt, laughing, touching her leg. "Never," I said.

"There's a first time for everything," Joe said, combing his head with his hand.

"Give me a bump," I said, deciding not to wait for an invitation. Insulting him was impossible. "Don't even say you don't have any. You're hopping around like a cricket."

He peered over his glass while he downed the last of his drink and scoped out the bar, then dug his hand deep in his khaki pockets. "Take this," he said, handing me a vial. "Why don't you and your friend come to my house when you're done here?"

"I'll come by myself," I said. Athena didn't need to know what I did with Joe McClure. "Where's your wife these days?"

"She left me," he said, then disappeared through the back.

When I got there, Maggie was pouring drinks in the kitchen. She was the local beauty with the bad reputation.

"You're here," she said, welcoming me as if I was a long lost pal.

It was the first time I'd seen her since we'd been caught making out in the bathroom at Club Jack's Christmas party. "Hey," I said, playing off my embarrassment, hoping I hadn't turned red.

The gossip about Maggie was rampant. People stared, whispered whenever she came into the club. I thought she looked like an angel. Someone said she was a hooker. A *hooker* in Myrtle Beach? I had been curious. Not judgmental. Why would someone so stunning need to be a prostitute? Did they mean she had a pimp like Huggy Bear in *Starsky and Hutch*? I wondered what people said about me behind my back.

At the Christmas party, after a few too many drinks, I'd followed her to the bathroom. She fussed over her hair in the mirror. Our faces glowed pink in the blinking colored light from the miniature tree on the sink. We didn't shy from eye contact. In the stall, the hook-and-eye on the back of my dress was a problem. I asked her for help. We closed the door. She was strawberry-blonde. I wanted to touch her neck, her arms. I knew that every man in the place felt the same. When she kissed me, I kissed her back. Took in her taste of bubblegum, her scent of fruit punch. We were lost in it until the latch of the metal door gave way; caught together by some lady in a red suit washing her hands. The moment was scandalous.

When we left, one at a time, the stares were obvious. I acted like nothing happened.

I never saw her again until now.

I did two lines cut from a pile of coke on the bar before taking the sweating drink from Maggie.

"I've been asking Joe about you forever," she said, picked up the straw, did a hit.

It made sense, her hanging out with Joe. He loved beautiful girls, the subversive. I wondered who knew they were fuck buddies. Surely he wasn't paying her, he was too cheap, too devious. And I doubted he let her drive the SL around the way I had as a teenager, she was too notorious.

I had a good buzz already but downed my drink, thirsty from the coke. I lit Maggie's cigarette, then mine. We smoked on the couch and watched Joe dance.

"A nice surprise, huh, girlies," he said. "Robin used to work for me."

"Many years ago," I said. Our history made me feel oddly superior to and unthreatened by Maggie. I decided to stay for awhile, blew smoke at the ceiling, stretched out.

It wasn't too long before we moved the party to Joe's bedroom.

I was jealous of Maggie's perfect body, and she said the same to me. Even with the drugs, talking was superfluous.

We picked up where we left it in the ladies room. Kissing was only the beginning.

Joe didn't mind that we ignored him. He was on the phone. Taking a shower. Doing lines.

At daylight, half-dressed in a mess of linen, smoking, sipping vodka and orange juice, I asked Joe for money. "I'll pay you back once I get settled," I said.

"You know I want to help, sweetheart," he said. "But I have divorce lawyers and accountants examining every penny I spend."

I wondered about the long gated driveway, if it kept people from seeing girls coming and going, if the petty cash covered the drugs. "What about a job," I said. "You could say I'm your secretary."

"Secretaries like you are grounds for divorce," he said. He wrapped the sheet around him, did a line off the dresser. "Who wants a drink?"

"Ask him about this weekend," Maggie said. "The golf tournament in Charlotte." She did a bump, gave me the straw.

"What golf tournament?" I said. I hoped it wasn't an event Daddy could be involved with, but I didn't remember him ever going to anything in Charlotte.

"There's some big one starting tomorrow," she said, chewing her bottom lip, eyes wide.

"You're working there for him?" I said, trying to figure myself into the equation. I bent over the mirror for another hit.

"Not for him. For myself," she said, fumbling to light two cigarettes at once.

"A trade show?" I said. I'd heard that you could work for boat conventions or car shows for a hundred a day.

"Ew. No. They couldn't pay me enough," she said. She handed me one of the smokes then leaned close, looked at me playfully. "You know, Joe's *friends*."

Then I understood. Joe was going to fix her up with some guy for money. Joe could fix me up with someone, too. How bad could it be? Some rich man. It'd be more worthwhile than the nobodies I screwed for sport. He'd probably be old. Most golfers were. But who cared? Joe was old. I could handle him. And no one would know me in a different state.

Joe brought in three splashing glasses of booze, spilled some on the wall-to-wall, on the bed. I didn't want to be around when the maid showed up.

"What about Charlotte?" I asked.

He shot Maggie a look. "That's not for you," he said.

"Oh, come on. You can find a friend for me, too," I said and I pulled my mussed hair into a ponytail.

"That's not what it is."

"Then what is it?" I asked. "Maggie's going, right? You'll be there. It'll be fun. No one will know."

"No one *can* know," he said.

I pulled one of Joe's blankets around me. It was soft, the color of butterscotch. Expensive. I thought how I didn't even know where to buy something so luxurious. "Will I make enough to pay my rent?" I said.

"And then some," he said.

I'd never been so high. I'd never sunk so low.

Maggie and I started doing bumps before we left for Charlotte and continued through to the next day. We drank vodka tonics from the mini-bar in the airport Sheraton. Stayed drunk. Nothing happened the way I imagined it would, but I didn't have a reference for what *it* would be. Would mean.

The first men arrived around five, after the tournament, two at a time. Who scheduled it? Where was Joe? At the bar? We never saw him. Silent in the background. Absent from the crime, the one I was about to commit on myself.

I wore a white silk camisole and matching tap pants. I *dressed* for it. I pretended to know what to do. I thought I knew what I was doing. I did what Maggie did. She was in the next bed. I closed my eyes when the first man stuck his dick in my mouth. I thought, I don't deserve this, what I inflicted on myself. I decided it was easier to let the next one fuck me, get it over quick. It'd be done without any work on my part. But the work wasn't physical, it was mental. When it was over, I'd lock the bathroom door. Shower.

I watched Maggie prance around in pink panties and a cowboy hat. I felt self-conscious that I wasn't as adept as her, though. I didn't want to be. I hated myself for caring. I told myself *not* to hate myself. I was doing what I needed to do. It was about handling my shit. Getting it done.

More booze. More drugs. A sandwich bag full, the size of a quarter pound of pot, but it was blow. I'd never seen so much. Who brought it? Who paid for the drugs, the room? Was it Joe? Was it the balding man with the Carlton cigarettes?

And the cash came. A hundred here, two hundred there. Here's a couple of C-notes, someone said. After the first night, I had enough to flee, but I didn't have the will. I was fucked up. Scared. Who'd be with me when I came down? Where would I go? Not back to Seaside, to Athena. She thought I was at a trade show. *Working for the weekend.* I couldn't predict what I'd feel like afterward. I'd stay with Maggie until it was over. Truly over. Sober. Clean. After sleep. In Myrtle Beach. Then I'd go home. Pay my bills. No one the wiser.

A tall man with a cigar said we'd each get another thousand to go to this house. A bachelor party. Was someone getting married? We were the gift. I did another line. Maggie said yes. Our flight was leaving at four, she said, our ride to the airport from wherever would cost them extra. We got dressed.

A car ride. The daylight hurt. I saw powerlines. We drove far away from the real world to the inside of some garage. There were men behind the door, but we weren't in a house; it was more like a workshop. There were tools on the wall, cabinets, harsh overhead lamps, and I smelled grease through my stuffed up nose. Two boys, eighteen maybe, shot pool. Too young to get married, I thought. I'd never meet them in my life outside of this hole. I'd eaten the pill, followed the rabbit, fell in.

We went down a hall; it was dark compared to the place we left. I held Maggie's hand until we entered a bedroom. The men pushed Maggie and me together on a big bed. Our bodies tangled, imitation wanton sex. Music. Was it Molly Hatchet? Money was thrown down. I thought of the scene at the end of the *Deerhunter,* the men screaming, dollars clutched in their fists, Christopher Walken with a gun to his head. I suddenly understood how he was able to pull the trigger. One of the boys was laughing, then Maggie went away with someone and I was alone with the laugher. My jeans were still on, my bra tossed aside. He jerked off. Let me come on your tits, he said. I wiped it on the sheet.

The man who had driven us there was still wearing his overcoat. He brought me a glass pipe. Freebase, he said. Lit it with a torch. Great show, he said. *Whatever.* I took the hit.

It was almost dark by the time we landed in Myrtle Beach. Maggie drove us in her beat up Mustang from the airport to her place. We never stopped doing the drugs and I didn't plan to until I passed out. We chain-smoked, did more lines, drank beer. Hallucinations in the bathroom mirror. Dark blue blotches dripping down my face. We took turns peering out the little rectangular window on the trailer's front door.

Maggie had a "roommate," a pretty brunette with long legs and high heels. "Where have you been," she said to Maggie, while looking at me.

"I told you I was going to Charlotte," Maggie said and kissed her cheek. They fought while I covered my eyes on the couch. The roommate slammed her bedroom door.

When I woke, I was sick to my stomach. I needed food but I only wanted to hide.

The roommate brought in McDonald's. Double cheeseburgers, milkshakes. She was productive; putting out plates, opening curtains. She tolerated my presence like she didn't have a choice. "Feel free to use the shower and anything in there," she said to me. She gave me a towel and then stared at Maggie, forlorn. She probably loved her.

I would've felt sorry for her if I had any sorrow to share but I needed my misery for myself. I ate the cheeseburger and made humble requests: Do you have any Tylenol? Can I borrow a t-shirt? I cried behind the bathroom door, I scrubbed my body with a washcloth. Steel wool wouldn't have made me feel clean.

Maggie's trailer was the first I'd ever been in. It looked like a house inside with beat-up secondhand furnishings. I wondered if they rented it that way. We were near the Air Force base. A-10's rattled the walls on their fly-bys. *A trailer park.* At least I wouldn't run into anyone I knew walking to the car.

I sat on the edge of Maggie's bed, moved the pillow with the cheap nylon flowered sham and called Joe. I needed to be consoled and he was the only one to turn to. "I'm so disgusted," I said.

"You made money, didn't you? Nothing to feel bad about," he said.

I sat hunched, my elbows on my knees, teardrops landed on my red painted toenails. "You should've told me what I was in for."

"I did you a favor," he said.

I rolled my forehead on the heel of my hand, the phone cord entwined in my fingers. Could I forget this? I let out a soft wail. "I feel like I'm going to die," I said.

"You're fine," he said. "No one's ever going to know. It's between you and me, kiddo. OK?"

"I want you to come and get me," I said, sobbing. I wiped my nose with a McDonald's napkin. It was rough on my skin. The tears closed my already swollen sinuses, forcing me to breathe through my mouth.

"I can't, my wife's on her way here. Maggie'll take you to your car," he said. "Get some sleep and I promise, before you know it, it'll be like it never happened."

I searched for a wastebasket and settled for a chipped white dresser. Teddy bears and dolls lined up in front of the streaked vanity mirror. The room looked like a little girl lived in it. "What about Maggie?" I said.

"What about her?" Joe said, irritated.

A plastic doll with a green-crayoned face stared at me. I turned its head around. "You'll call me tomorrow?"

"Yes," he said. "Hey babe, I did you a solid, right?"

"I'll try to see it that way," I said.

Maggie's Mustang rattled. Azaleas and dogwoods bloomed in the sun. I watched the new green of the trees as we drove, my face turned to the window that rolled down only halfway. I couldn't smell the spring air; it'd probably be days before I'd be able to do that again. I'd tell Athena I was sick and then pull the shades, go to bed.

I'd been complicit in my own rape, but I would put it away.

We pulled in the space next to my car. "Maybe I'll see you around," Maggie said. She was sweet. Genuine. We hugged good-bye over the shifter.

The Datsun was airport parking dusty. Seeing it reminded of the person I had been. *Between you and me, kiddo.* I'd start fresh. A new job. A good life. A happy girl.

Chapter 24

Athena and I agreed to go out together on her only night off, so we went to Drake's because she had a crush on the bartender and she said he owed her plenty of free drinks.

Things between us hadn't changed since returning from California, only that we'd grown more distant. We weren't our pre-Tahoe selves because we stopped trusting each other. Maybe it was because I couldn't talk about what happened with Joe. Maybe it was because she reminded me of someone I wasn't anymore.

By the time we arrived, the restaurant was filled with tourists who shelled out for the thick steaks, au gratin potatoes and thick sliced cheesecake. Looking around, I was grateful for my job. Serving Pina Coladas and Strawberry Daiquiris in a bikini on the Hilton pool deck with a ten to five schedule had its benefits –free nights, a dark tan and more than enough money to pay the bills. But Athena was back at the oyster bar six nights a week.

"Ya'll look ready for fun tonight," the bartender said. He was lean with white blond hair and colorless eyes, cute but dorky in his bow-tie and vest. Straight. Just my roommate's speed.

"Bo is a golf pro during the day, right?" Athena said, a qualifying note in her description –as if bartending couldn't possibly be enough for this gem of a guy who was merely stopping by on his way to save the world.

"I work the tournament circuit," he said, shrugged as if it were no big whoop.

"Exciting," I said, though I couldn't have imagined anything less so. I gave the room a quick glance, worried I'd run into a waiter I'd had a drunk make-out session with at some club the week before. He'd left unreturned messages for me on the machine every day since. I'd have to stop giving my number out.

Bo slid napkins in front of us. "Finally, I get to treat," he said to Athena. They laughed. "What'll it be?"

"You know I like Kamikazes," Athena said, enthusiastic and bright.

I could see that Bo didn't have a clue about her likes, but he said, "Of course," and shook the shots, strained them into chilled martini glasses.

Hanging out with girls from work had been easier. There was tension with Athena and she made me feel chaperoned. I'd been sleeping around, and when I wasn't getting laid, I was doing coke with this one or that one until five a.m. I kept that part to myself because, for Athena, getting shit-faced drunk was just dandy, but she was judgmental when it came to drugs.

"It's the owner's birthday. There's a party here after we close," Bo said. "You two should come."

"Definitely," Athena said, all doe-eyed. She'd never mastered subtlety, but then I wasn't sure that was entirely the problem. She signaled that she was looking for something steady, and in the middle of summer, there wasn't a guy to be found interested in that.

I knew Athena would take it personally if I didn't devote the entire night to her escapade so I decided to eat the embarrassment of facing the waiter I'd dissed.

"To a wild and crazy night," Athena said. She raised her eyebrows and glass to mine and we threw back the drinks.

Bo followed me to Drake's bathroom, looked at with me hunger, whispered, *I want to spank that sweet little ass of yours.* So incongruous with his clean-cut image. I was a drunk fish snagged by the lure and gave into my curiosity. Animal instinct. Temporal moments. Take, partake. What the hell. I'd given up enough when I didn't want to.

I went to his place, let him ravage me, in all the nasty, kinky, satisfying ways I thought he would. When daylight brought reality, I was through with him. I'd never be comfortable with someone who thought he had control over me just because he knew I liked filthy talk and my hair pulled; because I let him rope me to the bed with his Brooks Brothers ties. Someone who knew how I wanted it. I took out my keys when he pulled into Seaside.

"What are you doing tonight?" he said.

It was always this way in the end. "I'm busy," I said; my hangover beat against my temples.

He held onto my hand. "When, then?" he said.

I tried not to look at the veins on his forearm through his pale skin. "Athena likes you," I said, as if that even mattered now. I should have remembered that before I torched what was left of our friendship.

"She'll understand," he said. "Come on, we'd be fun together."

"More fun than I have time for," I said and got out of the car.

It was a damp morning. The azaleas bloomed pink and white along the sidewalk. The landscaping was one of the benefits that attracted Athena and me to rent in the complex. She'd seen us leave the party together and guilt crawled into my stomach up to my throat with each step closer to our confrontation.

She was in her room, stuffing boxes with clothes, shoes, hot rollers, refusing to look at me. Her suitcases were half-filled on the bed.

I leaned on her doorjamb. "He's not a serious person," I said. "Hardly interested in the things you want."

"Shut up, Robin," she said. "It wasn't for you to decide."

I marched to my room, stripped and pulled on a t-shirt. "You've been working on him since before we left for Tahoe," I said from my room. "If he wanted to ask you out, he would have."

"You couldn't let me have one guy," she said, her eyes full of rage. "You didn't even *like* him."

She was right. I didn't find him appealing in the slightest. He was too white, too preppy. Wore pullovers and docksides. *Golfed.* "You had plenty of openings," I said.

"I'm not like you," she said.

All I wanted to do was pass out but my adrenaline kicked in. "How's that?" I said. "Being virginal hasn't gotten you anywhere but alone."

"He was going to ask me out," she said.

That I'd willfully hurt her was too much to concede. "When a man wants you, it isn't a secret," I said.

"You said yourself you thought he liked me," she said.

I'd said that. "I was wrong to egg you on," I said.

"Now that you've fucked him," she said.

I convinced myself that she'd have done the same to me if given the chance. But she didn't waver on the thin line of integrity that I did and I despised her for her innocence.

I brushed my teeth for the second time.

She continued packing while she shouted at me. "You better think about how you're living because it's not right."

A nice girl act to mask her prudishness. It was why she was passed over, why she had so many buds but no dates. "You should apply your moral judgment to your jealousy," I said, rubbing the residue mascara from my eyes with baby oil and toilet paper.

"You're not my friend," she said. "You don't even know what one is."

"I know it's not someone I have to constantly downplay myself for so she can feel good about herself," I said.

She'd been allowed to be the entertaining, clever one, the better dancer, more athletic. The ruse became exhausting. I was tired of fighting and didn't want to take care of her anymore. She wasn't my father, my sister, my husband, my equal. I didn't want to have to answer to her or protect myself anymore from her resentment. She'd helped me move on from Jeff and I'd outgrown her.

I wanted to sleep.

"I've found another place to live," she said without looking up. "I hope he was worth it."

I'd done this, been reckless with my needs, my loyalties. "I'm sorry," I said before I closed my bedroom door.

Chapter 25

Saturday nights at the Mayor's House was the new hang, but I'd never even heard of the restaurant until Philip Baines showed up, sending me bottles of Dom Perignon whenever he came to Club Jacks. He had the standing weekend reservation and I'd gotten used to being spoiled.

I was seated next to him at a round table of ten. He was stout with a bowl of a head covered in thick straw-colored hair and an acne-scarred face that looked like its parts belonged to another human being. His audience sat expectant, listening to his every utterance as if he were a leprechaun who promised prosperity with the snap of his fingers.

"You've never been to New York, Miss Daniels?" Philip said.

"Not the city," I said, afraid of sounding unsophisticated. I speared a snail from a bubbling, greasy shell.

"Please let me take you for the first time," he said. The spaces between his teeth revealed poor childhood dentistry and reminded me of a jack-o-lantern.

I chewed the rubbery meat, searched the faces of my fellow dinner guests for a cue.

"You'll have a private suite, of course," he said.

No one at the table seemed appalled. Philip did have his own jet and I'd always wanted to see Manhattan. If

I had a separate room, then at least it would appear that I didn't have to sleep with him. "It shouldn't be hard to trade for the days off," I said.

When Philip sent a limousine to take me to the airport. I was all no-big-deal, as if it was perfectly normal to be ushered around town in a black stretch. I used the phone, left a message on Donna's machine. *On my way to New York City for the weekend.* A movie star. I smoked behind cat eyes, turned up the music.

The driver delivered me to the runway and the waiting jet.

Philip was talking with his pilot but stopped when he saw me. "Miss Daniels," he said. The sleeves of his Members Only jacket were pushed up like he was a young man; he wore mirrored Aviators, took my hand, his touch was soft, inviting. He led me up the steps. "You're in for a real treat."

He was hideous in the way his features seemed to blur together into his short blob of skin, the manner in which he licked his lips searching for moisture after each sentence. I wasn't sure that without the company of his group, I could overlook it. But his enthusiasm put me at ease.

I sat, rubbed the leather armrests of the swivel seat. The steward handed me a flute of champagne and served caviar with toast triangles on china plates.

"Sit back and enjoy the flight, Miss Daniels," Philip said, leaning out from behind the cockpit door. "If you'll excuse me, I have a plane to fly."

We arrived two hours later at a jetport outside of Princeton. The humid New Jersey summer smelled of cut grass and gasoline; gnats swarmed. We took refuge in Philip's air conditioned Porsche which awaited us on the runway and headed down the Interstate.

"I would've flown into Teterboro, it's closer to Manhattan, but I couldn't resist driving you in from the south," he said. "Besides, I want to show you my office."

We passed acres of metal buildings off the highway, then pulled into the driveway of Baines Chemical. He used a remote and the chain-link gate rolled open. We entered one of the gray buildings and walked through a series of locked corridors.

"What goes on here?" I said.

"Private-label chemicals, Miss Daniels. Bleach and detergent for chains like Safeway," he said. "I'm proud to say we're the largest privately-owned chemical company in the world. Meaning, this all belongs to me."

I understood none of it except that it was wealth I couldn't comprehend. Philip got cash from a safe and checked his messages. Just as I was getting antsy he said, "Let's not squander any more of our precious time together. The Four Seasons awaits."

To my surprise, we spent the night at the hotel in Princeton where Philip had a three bedroom suite. "I've lived here since the separation," he said, as if I should already know the intimate details of his life.

Philip strutted through the parade of staff nods and smiles and hellos. He was Castro and this was his Cuba.

The apartment was sumptuous, with canopied beds and tulips in crystal vases. The sheets were white linen and piled with starched pillows, the sink in the bathroom adorned with luxurious sundries and plush face cloths. I set my purse on the desk atop the engraved stationary.

Princeton. Laine lived here. And this was how she lived. Gold crests, perfumed comfort. I'd gone home with her for Thanksgiving that year I was at Pratt. The trees had been bare, throwing shadows on the covered pool. We'd walked for miles freezing in our school sweatshirts through woods padded with wet leaves. Holding hands, kissing on a fallen log until dark. We'd taken the truck at night, got drunk on Boones Farm.

She might have taken a job in Manhattan or in the Peace Corps, but her family would frequent a place like the Four Seasons. I'd die to run into her after so many years –she with the Senator waiting for their car at the hotel's valet, and me, stepping into a Porsche with some old toad.

"I'm beat," I said to Philip. "Can we order room service?"

"Miss Daniels, I urge you to have dinner downstairs," he said with a hint of desperation. "I promise it will be an unforgettable culinary experience."

I looked away when he folded money into the bellman's hand. "Let them know I'm coming," he said to him, his manner respectful, so used to getting his way that only a whisper was ever needed.

The bellman tucked away the bills with the nonchalance of someone who'd witnessed this rich geezer with a pretty young girl set-up a million times. "I'll freshen up," I said.

Philip confessed over the Chateaubriand how he'd once gotten a girl pregnant and she'd had an abortion. "You have to understand, I'm Catholic. It's a mortal sin," he said, carving himself a bite, pausing for a beat to savor it. "That's when I made a promise to God to remain celibate."

I ate a glazed carrot, watched the man at the next table dip the sleeve of his navy blue blazer in the au jus when he reached for his water glass.

Catholic guilt. Athena toyed with the gold cross around her neck like it meant something. The whole thing irritated me. Their same God killed my mother and replaced her with someone cold, prim and unforgiving. No amount of his giving up this or genuflecting that was going to change a thing. Sparing an unwanted baby was, in my opinion, a virtue, not a sin.

But God worked here in my favor because I wouldn't have to peel Philip's graceful little paws off of me.

The captain returned with an opened bottle of something red and I nodded when it was offered.

"The beef's magnificent, isn't it, Miss Daniels," Philip said. His cufflinks were gold, his shirt unbuttoned in casual elegance.

"Everything's perfect," I said.

I fell asleep alone to a re-run of Monty Python, and I sailed up, a kite on a string, the sidewalk and the playground below, fearful I couldn't land. But I kept going higher into the stratosphere above the turning earth and clouds and water and land and I thought I'd fall and burn on re-entry but it would be OK. Then Laine was there, wearing a school sweatshirt. We ate sand with a plastic shovel and I awoke with a dry mouth and stomach full of sadness.

I took time getting ready, I wanted to look like

perfection, but Philip kept knocking on my door. He'd ordered breakfast and the table had been set when I joined him. He looked me over after putting a napkin in his lap, sighed. "Such a flower you are," he said, shaking his head as he picked up the fork and plundered the cream soaked eggs.

His compliment died alongside the others he'd squandered on me. He'd never illicit any sentiment from me, no matter how delicious the freshly squeezed the juice or how fragrant and pink the roses.

After breakfast we were back in the Porsche heading for the city. I toyed with the radio. Barry Manilow came on. *I made it through the rain.*

"I love this song, don't you, Miss Daniels?" Philip said, turning it up, humming along.

Jeff detested Barry Manilow, but I'd said, how could anyone hate *Mandy*? I smiled, remembering the arguments we'd had over pop versus rock, as if they were mutually exclusive. I'd listened to the Bee Gees on my own time but Jeff forgave ABBA. Canadians. Another life. Jeff and I'd taken road trips like this, but we'd stayed at Holiday Inns. If he heard this song now, would he turn it off in disgust, or would he stop, think of us?

"The Verrazano - Narrows. When it opened, it was the longest suspension bridge in the world," Philip said as we drove over it, as if he designed it himself. "You were just a baby," he said.

Staten Island. The endless row houses, reminded me of Buffalo. Was all New York outside of Manhattan as dismal? I stared out at the concrete and power lines, grimy against the horizon.

Traveling was how I saw myself. Away. Further. Could it only be if viewed through the window of luxury? I looked at my escort. Maybe not.

I gripped the rail of the Staten Island ferry, breathed in the dirty air, as we passed Liberty Island. The Statue that I had only seen in movies rose in front of me now, and I was reverent. I'd missed the Wilson senior trip to New York, taking pictures in front of postcard scenes. Daddy and Cheryl had their city weekends alone while Melanie and I stayed behind at Nana's. I'd been cynical about how none of it meant anything to me.

"You see, I'm right, Miss Daniels," Philip said, as he watched me. "This *is* the only way to see New York City for the first time."

The sight of Manhattan made me want to cry: I already knew I belonged there.

It was late morning when we disembarked and Whitehall Street was deserted.

"It's Saturday," Philip said, excusing the quiet.

I looked up. Up. South Street, Wall Street. *Wall Street*. The height of the buildings pulled at me like the downhill of a rollercoaster. I craned my head through the open window and wanted to get out of the car as it continued down the thin streets of downtown. "One day I'm going to live here," I said.

"Of course you will, dear," Philip said and patted my knee in condescension.

He didn't believe me —we'd see about that.

The entrance to the midtown Hilton was a swarm of yellow taxis, the lobby massed with people. Our bags were wheeled away. The concierge on the 45th floor said, "Welcome back, Mr. Baines," before showing us to a tower suite.

"Not like where you work, is it, Miss Daniels?" Philip said.

I'd suffered similar pronouncements throughout the day. I'd have to pace my smiles for a weekend of his aren't-you-a-cute-little-bumpkin remarks.

The afternoon was a fairytale. We ate hot dogs from a vendor on the way to the theater. "Come on, Miss Daniels, try it with kraut," Philip said.

Mesmerized by *42nd Street*, I clutched my Playbill like precious art. On our walk to the Plaza, we stopped at a stand on Sixth Avenue and Philip bought me a pair of white sunglasses to match my outfit.

The Palm Court was a movie. The harpist played *Canon in D*. Women wore hats. We were delivered finger sandwiches and poured tea in bone china.

"This is Amanda," Philip said, taking a photo from his wallet as we walked down Fifth past Rockefeller Center, Saks. The picture was of a red-haired girl with the features of a doll in a green satin dress and emeralds. We turned into the Helmsley Palace. Lush red carpets, bronze statues, gold leaf, chandeliers. "This was our favorite place," he said, his eyes regretful. His hand lingered on, almost caressed a marble pillar.

We stopped in front of a closed jewelry store. "They

know me well here," Philip said. "I purchased a new piece for her each time we stayed."

I'd had enough. Why were we at the Hilton and where was *my* jewelry? "I need time to get ready for dinner," I said and marched for the exit as Philip scurried behind.

At Tocana, Philip said Amanda had been twenty when her mother sent her to stay with him, and I thought: her mother sold her. He rambled about their famous excursions. Italy, the Kentucky Derby. I studied the room. All these people were somebodies. Bankers, editors, violinists. The woman at the next table had black hair to her waist, gloves to her elbows and a cigarette holder. She swayed to the beat of the disco that permeated the room. I wanted to take her hand, disappear with her to the dance floor.

"You know, Miss Daniels, I can afford you a very nice lifestyle," Philip said, wiping his mouth, replacing the napkin on his lap before washing down his food with his Pepsi.

Apparently he'd done this and more for his Amanda, but at what price? Public humiliation in fashionable night spots and posh hotels, to start. I hadn't thought beyond having a good time and now I knew this was not how I wanted to spend a free weekend –embarrassed, self-conscious, worried about the outside chance I'd run into someone I knew, even in Manhattan.

When I didn't respond, he said, "All I want is to please you the way you've pleased me today." His face sagged while he insinuated intimacy between us with his eye contact. "If I could only taste you," he said.

Surely my wince did little to mask the nausea on my

face. *Taste me.* Who says crap like that? Catholic my ass. He thought that long as he didn't actually stick his dick inside, he'd be ready for judgment day. I stared at the palm trees and birds etched in the frosted glass partition. Between the Caesar salad and grilled Turbo, my magical day dissolved. The food no longer tasted special. I was grown up, but so naïve.

I emptied my champagne, signaled the waiter for more.

"You're going to love the disco," he said, pretending that he didn't just ruin the weekend.

Was I more embarrassed by my stupidity or the notion of letting him have his way with me? Really, would it be so appalling? Hadn't I already let men I didn't even know violate me? Old men. Was Joe McClure any better, and wasn't Philip at least kind? Gentle, in fact? But there was nothing *nice* about his manipulation –the professed chastity: the lie is what disturbed me. Not only his but the one I told myself, that I could be interesting beyond what my body had to offer.

Philip got us a booth close to the dance floor. More champagne. He kept after me. "Shall we dance, Miss Daniels?" but I wanted to be invisible.

All the pretty people who belonged here and their counterparts. The blue wash that switched to red when the song morphed into something Latin.

Philip watched the scene eagerly. Someone who'd missed the revolution, the polyester, the casual sex. He wanted to fit in a different way than I did, to capture the party. They were all here, still dancing, but the drugs had changed from Quaaludes to coke. It was all bullshit now, more money, less sex, and for the time being, I could live with, even like, the anonymity of it.

That summer before I'd run away, when I'd been a teenager, playing at love and still believed in happy endings, we were all doing it. Everyone. Sex was feminism, orgasm was defiance.

Philip wanted in on that, but he'd missed the train. He was old and looking for a partner in his quest for what was already history. And I was in for a good time, but not with him.

I stubbed out my cigarette. "Can we go back to the hotel now?" I said.

He was hopeful and I was smashed. The limo was waiting.

Back at the hotel, I spun drunk and half-naked on Philip's bed with his head between my legs. I didn't have the will to fight him off. "Excuse me," I said, through the bile pooled in the back of my throat. I made it to the bathroom before the entire day of food and drink came out my nose.

"You OK?" Philip said from the other side of the door, all sweetness and light.

The whirling had stopped, but I stayed on the cool tile, my eyes closed in protection against the burning ceiling light.

Philip tapped again. "Miss Daniels?"

My legs shook while I rinsed my mouth. Mascara rings. I didn't care. The hotel robe was suffocating as I wrapped myself in it and pushed past him. I didn't owe him a thing.

"Call me Robin," I said, over with the pretense of his formality. I staggered through the open door between our rooms, locked it and passed out on the gold-foiled chocolates left on my king size bed.

I wore the *I Heart NY* t-shirt I'd purchased in the gift shop, belted over a mini-skirt for the flight home and nursed my hangover with caffeine and saltines. Philip tried ever-so-hard with polite nothings. Muffin? More coffee? Too bad about the weather, isn't its? I nodded from time to time but I was through with the congeniality.

The drive to Teterboro was interminable. The sky said rain but the meager droplets only smeared the windshield. I wanted to nap like a child on a trip to Grandma's. How magical to wake at your destination. No time lost. No boredom. But magic wouldn't whisk away the creepy old man watching me while I slept.

Philip talked with his secretary or some other subordinate on the car phone, his voice competent, effectual. But that kind of respect, even with the millions to back it up would never be enough for him. He yearned for what he'd never have: to be looked upon adoringly by a beautiful woman. To conquer her heart. But he wouldn't get it without dragging her by the hair into the cave.

And I'd only be regarded for my fleeting good looks. My heart, desires, would remain inconsequential. My authority, non-existent.

The city skyline retreated through the back window of the car. I'd be back someday, under better circumstances.

Philip hung up, touched my knee to acknowledge my quiet presence, then looked out into nothing, in thought –maybe about his grown children, his un-divorced wife.

The church wouldn't tolerate that, right? Perhaps he was planning his next selfish extravagance.

The road was slick where it had rained. Water drained foamy with pollution over curves in the road, and I thought of home for the first time in forever. The turns of the Schuylkill on the way to visit Nana. A flash of melancholy.

I felt duped. That nice lifestyle Philip dangled had been nothing but bullshit. Except for the cheap sunglasses, he hadn't bought me a thing, hadn't even offered to pay my rent. I hated him, but hated myself more for not being smarter.

The airport was rinsed clean but only until the sun steamed it up again and the fuel re-greased the runways. It was the typical northeast summer, those rare days I'd experienced, squeezed between school and camp. They'd been sad, sometimes dangerous, but never lonely. We'd get out of Cheryl's way, find friends, waste the day until dark. One afternoon, Roxanne Mullin and I rode our bikes in the rain all the way to Nana's. *How on earth did you get here?* Nana was shocked, angry, but then she made us peanut butter with honey sandwiches, poured Fresca, and I was grateful when she didn't turn us away.

Philip's plane ascended through the clouds, blue skies now over Teterboro. The private jet, I could get used to. I reclined, eyes closed, head against the soft leather. All this, the jet, New York City, the magazine lifestyle that I wanted, was out there and I knew South Carolina wouldn't cut it anymore.

I pulled my cigarette case with the hand-painted peacock

Jeff had given me one Christmas from my purse. I'd juiced up the matching lighter for the trip. Virginia Slims were thin enough I could almost fit the whole pack in the flat jeweled box. I lit one, drew deep.

I'd have to leave Myrtle Beach, the same as Tahoe, but this time, alone, without a roommate. One more month left of the season. California, maybe. Or Miami. I'd be brave. And like always, I'd be fine. New place. New job. New friends. End of the summer.

I dozed and dreamt of an old painting —faded brush strokes of wings, maybe angels but the faces were blurred. I held a triangle-shaped frame. Who bought this, I kept saying to no one.

The familiar bump of wheels on the runway woke me and Philip emerged from the cockpit. "Welcome to Myrtle Beach, Miss Daniels," he said, a bashful child. "I mean, Robin."

I barely nodded but thanked the steward as he lowered the steps.

Philip followed down, but he'd never get as much as another dinner out of me. Still, I wanted more from him than expenses and some lame souvenirs or I wouldn't forgive myself.

At the limo, I turned, tall in my heels. Lifted my funky sunglasses, looked down at him, opened my palm. "I'm low on funds, will you help me out?" I said.

He pulled out his money clip, peeled off five one hundred dollar bills.

It would never be enough.

Chapter 26

At five o'clock, the marble-floored bar filled up with bored office workers making an attempt to be social and I was grateful theirs was not the life I'd chosen.

Charlie's Pub was inside the mall. I was there to see Daddy and I specifically asked for a table with a view of the parking lot. He was late as usual. I summoned the waiter for a Dewars and water.

Another dreaded reunion. My stomach hurt while I smoked. All I'd eaten was cocktail fruit from the pool bar. If Jocelyn from work's father hadn't dropped dead of a heart attack, I would never have had the courage to call my own. I covered her shifts so she could go to the funeral. She hadn't returned since.

Though I clung to moments when I'd known my father's love, guilt ruled the memories. When he wasn't violent, he was endearing, funny, charming. Everyone thought so. But they'd never seen the monster. That was family business.

When I'd called, my throat closed like an allergic reaction to his voice but I powered through the nerves with a rehearsed speech. I just want to talk, I'd said. Let's not waste time with blame —though it was him who'd dumped me on the street when I needed him most. When he didn't hang up, I said I loved him. And like long ago when Jeff forced me to phone my father before we'd left for Canada, I'd gotten more than I asked for.

He'd be in Pinehurst, then Myrtle Beach at the end of the week.

I chugged my drink, lit up for the second time. My hand shook. I'd left work early so that I wouldn't be rushed, spent the week obsessed over what to say, and still I wasn't ready. The knee-length skirt and blouse, conservative enough?

Tick tock. I could run, say I'd waited, then had to go. Work. Yes. But I saw him get out of his dusty Caprice, the knock-around car he kept at the airport for his weekly business errands. I put the ashtray on the next table, checked my lipstick in the reflection of my butter knife. Marilyn Monroe had done it in a movie. Every hair in place, I waved.

He came to the table as if on a mission. Unsmiling. To remind me that I was the one who caused his anguish. If we got through this, we'd survive anything. I smoothed my skirt, he embraced me the way he always did, his arm circling my neck, my head pulled to his shoulder, face squeezed to his chest. Tears welled and I worried about my make-up on his polo shirt. So I pushed him away, swallowed the hurt.

"You look good," he said.

It was a scrap, but I craved it. "You too," I said, knowing I should've let him hug me better because who knew when I'd get held like that again. He'd lost weight, he was tan as usual, but his eyes were fatigued.

"What are you drinking?" he said, ordered an iced tea.

"Dewars and water," I said, then reached for my Bic.

When the waiter left he said, "Scotch and cigarettes are *not* a good sign at your age."

Of what? My suffering wasn't silent enough? I sunk in my chair. "It is what it is," I said, and lit up.

When the small talk and the food had come and gone I said, "It was you who told me to get out."

He stiffened and his eyes narrowed. "What?" he said.

"I only did what you told me to do. At the courthouse, remember? I was unhappy, so I got out before it was too late," I said, though I'd never quite understood what he'd meant by *too late*. Age, pregnancy? I dried my palms on my napkin, followed his gaze toward happy hour.

"Maybe I should have supported your decision," he said.

I reached across the table and squeezed his hand, but he didn't look at me. "You're everything to me but you can't go around hitting me anymore," I said. "I'm a grown woman."

He pulled away. "I've never laid a hand on either of my kids," he said.

No memory of how he smacked us senseless for not memorizing our multiplication tables, or how he belted us black and blue for closing the door too loudly on a Saturday morning, or how he yanked us out of the bed at midnight and threw us down a flight of stairs in a rage over a messy playroom, kicking us and shouting.

My love for him clattered with the din of the bar, then fell silent against my inner slideshow, and it was just me and him and the hands which nearly strangled the air out my lungs more times than I cared to remember. And I was frightened because if he really didn't know what I was talking about, then he was nuts, certifiable. And then there was no hope. You couldn't fight crazy. You had to accept it. But I wasn't ready to surrender my expectations.

"What are you going to do now? It's the end of the summer," he said, ignoring any bewilderment on my face.

The conversation was over.

"Maybe Florida," I said. There's supposed to be a lot of jobs down there."

"You know I have a condo in West Palm," he said, picking at the fries.

"No, I didn't," I said. I knew as much about Florida as I did about my father. My food had gotten cold, rummaged chicken, a bite of broccoli eaten. I refrained from lighting up when the guy at the next table dug a Marlboro out of his shirt pocket.

"I rent it to the same couple from Ohio every January to April," he said, casually scooping slaw with his fork. I was talking about a life change but to him we might as well have been discussing his golf handicap.

"That's nice," I said, wanting another drink.

"You can stay there until the end of December. It should be enough time to get settled."

This was beyond my expectations. A gesture to make it all up to me, I thought, and I would take it. He caught my look of surprise and I blushed but held his gaze until he abandoned me again.

He put his credit card inside the check billfold. "I'll send you the keys when I get home," he said.

It was something.

We walked to the parking lot. The scar that ached more every time I said goodbye to my father was wrapped neatly in the fear that I'd never see him again. Homesickness. But home was never Philadelphia, it was Daddy.

At his car, we hugged again and this time I let him muss my make-up. Then I stood in his parking space and waved until the car disappeared around the corner.

September 1984

September 1985

Chapter 27

Florida was hot, flat, vast. Interstates, railroad tracks, quiet concert halls. But quiet. Daddy's West Palm condo sat on South Flagler Drive, which ran along the Inter-Coastal Waterway. A doorman showed me the freight elevator when I arrived with a car full of luggage but it was as if all humans had boarded the spaceship and deserted the marbled high-rise.

MTV wasn't enough to drown the silence. I'd never truly been by myself. After Athena left, yes, but in a town where I didn't know a soul? The fifteenth floor balcony was like a drive-in movie of outside where you followed something happening on a distant screen. Palm Beach and three drawbridges extending to million dollar homes with silent boats docked, or en route leaving a lone wake.

A sailboat with a mast too tall to clear a viaduct waited while traffic stopped and the drawbridge lifted. I was that vessel waiting for passage to who-I'd-become and worried that no one but me was watching.

Lights up and down the water melded earth to the evening sky. I breathed the humidity, then slapped a mosquito chewing my arm and returned to air-conditioned safety inside.

The beige wall-to-wall and the stiff furniture, despite the sunny warmth of the palm tree wallpaper, weren't enough to distract me. I microwaved a popcorn dinner and munched the entire bowl upright in the corner of the sofa while watching Miami Vice. There was excitement somewhere in Florida, sure as hell not in Palm Beach. But I could rationalize that this was the off-season, one more month and this town would be teeming with the jet-set. *Cosmo* wouldn't steer me wrong. I'd find a job, make friends, and with no rent, I'd be secure through the end of the year.

I sang and danced to whatever played on the local station on the clock radio, shaking out my wrinkled clothes before lining them up on hangers.

I'd find a party or meet a rich guy. Alone meant no one to judge me, I could be as good or as deviant as I wanted. But I'd get the business of setting up out of the way, there'd be time for the rest.

The next morning, I drove around town. Nothing in the barren and dilapidated municipality of West Palm Beach had appeal. No concentrated areas of people, like a boardwalk or a strip of decent hotels. I couldn't even find a beach, so I headed for the island where I could meet a millionaire who'd take me to lunch or for a ride on his yacht but all I found was a sterile sherbet-colored town with walled country clubs and a few intimidating restaurants. I drove down Worth Avenue, past Cartier, Saks and a smattering of retired patrons in golf and tennis attire, but didn't get out of my car. I'd only get depressed looking at everything I couldn't buy.

What *was* this nightmare? It was like a retirement community on sedatives. No place for me. I didn't leave my marriage to end up in this well-maintained prison.

At Publix, I bought over-priced cans of tuna, granola, a two-liter bottle of Diet Coke and miscellaneous staples that would have to last until I got a job. But my reconnaissance turned up few opportunities for work; everything seemed closed, and even if they were open, they fell way short of the glamour I'd imagined or seen in magazines. Stodgy was the speed here.

Back in the condo, I flipped through the *Yellow Pages*. There had to be something I missed.

Donna had given me the name of a friend from boarding school. Ronny had gone to the University of Miami and moved to Ft. Lauderdale after graduation. When I called and he invited me down for the night, I couldn't get dressed fast enough.

Interstate-95 was congested, but the drive to Ft. Lauderdale took under an hour. Ronny's exit was Sunrise Boulevard. The tall lit buildings seemed so sparse from the highway, but became concentrated the closer I got to the coast and I was astonished to find Lauderdale such a big city.

The address was on A1A, the coastal route adjacent to the beach. Distant ships blinked on the moonlit ocean. The waves were close enough to hear and salt and seaweed filled the air.

The high-rise was similar to Daddy's, I assumed Donna's friend was also crashing at his parent's. I checked myself in the elevator mirror, nervous I didn't have a friend to tell me if I looked alright. Neon pink off-the-shoulder mini with a mesh tank and a wide black belt; hair in a spikey ponytail and bow, I looked good. I could afford to be more stylish here than the hick town I'd come from.

Ronny swung open the door, dressed in pastel-blue linen with a pale pink t-shirt, sleeves pushed to his elbows, an arm up propped on the jam. His hair was shoe polish black, his cologne wafted. "Donna told me you were a babe," he said, his teeth gleamed.

He was confident I'd jump in the sack with him, but there'd be no sex with this guy who reeked of conceit.

He grabbed a *Wham!* cassette and we took his new white Supra to dinner, Ronny talked about his teller job while we drove, never asking me one question about myself. But I didn't care, I was happy for the company, and he was easy to tune out. He pointed to this place and that, the city was alive, he said, it never knew an off-season.

We ate at a happening restaurant on the Waterway; the crowd was young and the bar was packed. I was down to my last dollars and had no right to frivolity so I ordered pasta. I reached when the check came so I wouldn't appear presumptive. With older, more accomplished men, I had no problem expecting them to pick up dinner but I didn't want some guy my own age to think I didn't have my shit together or that I owed him anything.

"I'll get it this time," Ronny said and laid down his Master Card with a snap.

This time. Despite my relief of having enough gas money for the rest of the week, I was now completely turned off.

Back at his place, I declined his invitation upstairs, gave

him my cheek when he went for a kiss and told him I'd call him soon.

I was near sober driving home on the empty highway, thinking, that while Daddy's condo was free, West Palm Beach was too dreary a place to live, and so I decided to change my strategy. I'd look for work in Lauderdale the next day. It felt like the direction I'd been seeking.

Chapter 28

In Lauderdale it was balmy and clouds loomed for an imminent afternoon deluge. I drove to the waterway and stopped at the first fancy property I could find. The Yacht Club had a valet, but I parked down the street.

The interviewer said I could start immediately. I'd been confident walking in, knowing I presented myself well and that my previous hotel and restaurant experience looked impressive on the application. Thinking about how I'd stolen that outfit in Tahoe and landed that casino gig put a smile on my face that I took into the room with me.

The location makes this place one of the busiest in town, the guy said. The tips would be good, $100 to $150 a night during the week —more on the weekends with the champagne brunch.

In the car, I cranked the Miami dance station. My new uniform lay on the seat next to me. Things would work out.

I handled the commute from West Palm Beach for less than a week before I found a roommate in Lauderdale on the break room board. Laura was a petite ex-flight attendant from Minneapolis, with pale skin and a black bob, who claimed she'd slept with Prince. She blow-dried her hair standing naked before the living room mirror. Too stuffy in my room, she'd say. She worked across the Causeway at Carlos & Pepes, a hopping Mexican joint that served nachos and pitchers of Margaritas. The best part is I can wear shorts to work, she said. I went there after my shift, hung with her workmates, ate chicken quesadillas and drank for free. We'd all come from someplace else, which gave me a sense of ease.

Lauderdale was not only young, it was gay and most of the waiters I worked with were. I gravitated toward them because they were the most fun, complaining about the polyester uniforms, calling me Marlene like I was serving up breakfast at a diner, calling, Sling the hash! behind me as I delivered Early Bird specials. One of them swooped up his orders and swung his hips like a super model while the line cooks heckled faggot. There were even queens living in my apartment building.

The gay clubs –Backstreet, the Copa, the Alley, became my favorite after-work hangs. Since Athena, I was guarded from getting too dependent on my roommate and was mindful to carve out my own separate scene. But I craved the protection I'd always felt from being around men. I'd learned, though, with male friends there was that inevitable tension unless you fucked and got over it. I was trying not to repeat the messiness of Myrtle Beach, so it was an easy solution to surround myself with boys who wanted nothing from me but to be my girlfriend.

The day I met David Cardona, I was assigned the window section, which meant I had to arrive early to cover the gap through to dinner. I was five minutes late when I made it to the floor.

The lunch guy slapped me with a check and pointed to the window. "Table 22, have a nice day," he said.

"She's in a good mood," one of the queens said. We laughed as we punched our time cards.

Table 22. The two middle-aged men had already received their drinks. The one wearing a hooded sweat-jacket and jeans gave me the up and down. Golfers. I disliked them immediately, and worse, I detected Canadian accents when I took their order. I'd thought I was immune to thinking about Jeff, with all the Ontario snowbirds I'd encountered, but for a moment I was stung by sadness.

When I returned with their food, I noticed the man in the sweat jacket had a diamond stud in his ear and I questioned my previous assumption.

He caught me looking. "Do you like it? It's new," he said, his voice genteel. He played with his ear and never took his eyes off mine. "It's heart-shaped."

Something like a joke passed between us. His eyes were vivid blue, pretty. It was hard to shift my gaze to his ear. "So it is," I said.

He looked at my earrings in turn. "Tell me, how does a waitress afford those?"

I touched my diamonds studs. "Not that it's any of your business, but my grandmother gave them to me," I said, trying to cover an unusual shyness. "Enjoy your meal." I directed my smile at his dining companion, who'd already shoved a handful of fries in his mouth, dropping a couple on his polo shirt. Oil soaked in, turning the shamrock green to a forest pine color.

"You guys from Canada?" I said, when I picked up the empty plates.

"Toronto," the man with the earring said. "We're here to buy a boat, just looked at that one." He pointed to the hundred and twenty foot sailboat docked outside the window.

I smiled, not believing either of them could afford it. "I used to live in Canada," I said.

"What made you leave?" he asked.

"Divorce," I said, flirting. David's friend was bored. "Let me get your check," I said.

Half an hour after Table 22 vacated, the hostess told me, the gentleman at the desk wanted my number.

The Canadian with the earring leaned against the hostess stand.

The only person I slept with in the over two months since I'd arrived in Florida was the service bartender —long dark lashes, a chiseled face —but he could barely put two syllables together. I miscalculated, thinking he was saving it up for the bedroom. A dismal disappointment, and hanging out with my gay friends wasn't getting me laid. It was time to try something new. The Canadian was twice my age but he'd left me a forty percent tip. I jotted down my number. "Sure. Give it to him," I said.

I got a couple days off at Christmas to visit Melanie and her live-in boyfriend Chad in New Haven, but my New

Year's Eve was spent at work. I'd made a small fortune in tips off the prix fixe dinner with a band, and dropped a frozen strawberry daiquiri into a diner's sequined cleavage.

My roommate and I rang in 1985 together with her boyfriend and his shipmates, the crew of the Henry Ford yacht. We sang a Brit punk version of Auld Lang Syne and ran cannonballs from the front door of the apartment into the kidney-shaped pool.

It was four in the morning and everyone's door in the apartment complex was open. I sat poolside, wrapped in a towel, feet in the heated water. I didn't want more than this moment. I'd made things happen. I'd moved and changed and made money. Survived. And the only resolution I had was to lose the five extra pounds I'd been swearing off since summer. And to maybe get laid.

At four the next afternoon, I woke to the phone.

"We met at the Yacht Club. From Toronto. With the heart-shaped diamond earring," David said.

My memory was mud. "Yes, of course," I said, through a dry throat. I needed caffeine and saw nothing to drink but a lipstick smeared can of Diet Coke on my dresser.

"I'm at a horribly boring party and I was thinking of you," he said.

Flattering, to be an alternative to boredom. "Are you in town?" I said.

"No, in London," he said, "but I'll be in Key Biscayne next week. Why don't we meet?"

He was probably in Pompano, calling from a payphone.

But I remembered him as endearing, then cringed: *In a father-figure sort of way*. Good for a free dinner and a few laughs. "Call me when you get here," I said.

Chapter 29

If David wasn't to be in Miami for just two days, I'd never have consented to such an early date. Yet, for some reason, I not only agreed, but went to him. Maybe it was his playful dig — *You wouldn't be able to stretch your social calendar and squeeze me in, would you Princess?* Or maybe it was simply that spending the afternoon with a man who could make me laugh appealed to me, and a comfortable feeling settled in.

The sky had a slate blue-black clarity, then fat rain began to fall on the Rickenbacker Causeway. Key Biscayne was hushed beyond my windshield wipers. I parked in an uncovered lot and cursed myself for not being together enough to own an umbrella. I'd worn my rabbit fur jacket because it was winter-in-Florida cold, just enough to make your teeth chatter. But I wished I'd chosen the rain slicker. By the looks of the place, I was entirely overdressed.

The complex was on the Atlantic side of the island. Cooking reeked in the hallway and the carpet needed replacing; the dull yellow and burgundy tones were too traditional for the beach.

A man with thick white hair and large black-framed glasses opened the door to the second floor apartment. "You must be Robin. On time. A rarity among women. Vladimir Teodosie," he said. His voice had a hint of Edward G. Robinson. "Come in. The Prince awaits."

With a sweeping gesture, he extended his arm into the narrow foyer. "Prince! A cosmic beauty to see you," he said.

"What kind of name is Vladimir?" I said.

"Romanian."

"How Count Dracula of you."

"But it's daylight, sweetheart. I'd be in a coffin," he said.

I walked into a yellow glow. The gray day stormed outside the balcony door.

David sat propped on an elbow in jeans on the imitation antique plastic-covered sofa, peering over the top of the *Key Biscayne News*. He closed the paper, smiled. "Robin," he said flatly, patting the spot next to him.

He seemed unaffected by my entrance. I expected more, considering I drove all the way from Ft. Lauderdale, so I decided not to sit. "I see you're excited to see me," I said.

He got up. "Let me take your beautiful coat. You must be getting warm in that," he said.

My damp, matted fur seemed not to warrant a hanger and ended up slung on a dining room chair. I adjusted my bra and ran my hands through my hair.

He took my hand and kissed it. "Thou art more lovely and more temperate than a summer's day."

Was he kidding? I remembered a wrestler I'd dated at Wilson High and his love notes. It was my last experience with anything remotely connected to the romantic, and Jeff had been about as poetic as a stock car race. "Do women fall for that?" I said pulling my hand away.

"I just thought you'd appreciate Shakespeare," he said.

I mulled my option of leaving, stealthily glanced at my surroundings and shifted my stance in my heels. "It took me an hour to drive here, at least you could be ready to go," I said and searched for an ashtray to see if smoking was acceptable, but didn't see one. I'd have to suffer.

"I was hoping we could hang out a little and get to know each other," he said.

I didn't *hang out* and this place was a little too much like the apartment of someone's crazy aunt. But it didn't matter because I didn't care about him. Rain dumped outside. I took a seat on the sofa. "You smell good. What cologne is that?" I said.

"French perfume. Ombre Rose," he said. "I wear it because I like it." Then he said, "Glass of wine?"

Before I could answer he said, "Vlad, open that bottle."

His hair was longer than I remembered, curling at his neck. I refrained from twirling a ringlet in my finger. "Does he work for you?" I asked.

He laughed. "No. This is his place, we're good friends."

He had to be pretty cheap to want to stay here instead of a hotel, I thought. Maybe broke. "Why does he call you Prince?" I asked.

"I call him the Silver Fox. Doesn't he look like a fox?" he said.

"You may be right about that," I said and glanced at my watch, hoping he didn't hear my stomach growl.

"Still at the Yacht Club?" he said, facing me, one leg bent on the sofa. His feet were bare; his toes were neat, clean, pedicured.

I nodded. "Don't know why, but I took the day off just to see you," I said.

He smiled, as if he saw right through any game I wanted to play.

"I'll take that as a compliment," he said, working at eye contact. "We should get you married, get you out of that job," he said.

I'd thought about the boat he'd been buying, it was one of the reasons I agreed to see him –he might have a wealthy friend for me. "I've been married. That's the last thing I want," I said, emboldened by my own honesty. "I was thinking more of getting a sugar daddy."

"You're too good for that," he said, searching my face for something he seemed to think I was holding back, inhaling like he was breathing me in.

"Says you," I said. "I don't see you wearing a ring. Why aren't you married if it's so great?"

"I *am* married. I don't like rings."

I considered the pierced ear and had trouble picturing him with a wife. Was she keeping him in Ombre Rose? Maybe that was how he was buying yachts. "I'm sure your wife appreciates that," I said.

"My name is David Cardona, I'm forty-six, a business man. If there's anything else you want to know about me, I'm happy to oblige," he said, then turned serious. "But right now, I want to make love to you."

It was like ice water in the face, but I had to admit he had balls. He was hardly Mr. Universe, shoeless in Aunt Crazy's apartment. "Right, that's going to happen," I said, trying to cover my surprise. I looked after Vlad for the wine.

David touched my chin with his index finger, turned my face back to him. "Sweet beauty, you're not angry with me already."

I let his hold linger and smiled. "Does Mrs. Cardona know you romance waitresses?"

I took his hand, gave it back at him.

"We'll be dear friends, you and I," he said, as if he'd worked my answer over for me. "As Shakespeare said, 'A friend is one who knows who you are and gently allows you to grow.' That's what we can have together."

His manufactured attempt to get into my pants was oddly charming. I couldn't help but laugh. "I have enough friends," I said, giving him a shove.

"Why don't we get through the honeymoon before we start fighting," he said, never taking his eyes off mine.

Vlad returned with an open bottle and three glasses.

What did I tell you?" he said to Vlad. "Isn't she exquisite?"

I decided to try sex with David, though it was more like I let him have his way than my really wanting it. When he first kissed me, I attempted to beg off, remembering his silly Shakespeare romancing, then thought, what the hell? I did like him and he didn't live in Florida, so if it wasn't great, I didn't have to be bothered again. But, even so, if we got the sex out of the way, there was always the possibility that he'd eventually introduce me to the next Mr. Right, as I'd originally planned.

In the end, after lunch and a couple bottles of wine, we had a drunken roll in Vlad's guest room. He tried to satisfy me, but I was unable to concentrate, so I faked my orgasm to get the deed over with and left Key Biscayne all smiles with lots of see-you-again-soons.

Chapter 30

Ft. Lauderdale was the perfect place to be young and single. I found a whole new group to dance with. The Alley was the closest place to the Yacht Club and it didn't get started until eleven. After our shift, and with whoever was working, we changed and maneuvered through the crowd to the door where beefcake boys in a skin-tight tees let us in for free.

Chris was popular in the club and I always sought him out wherever he was with his gang. He invited me to his thirtieth birthday bash the upcoming Saturday night, I'd felt the same achievement as when I'd snagged the Wilson quarterback, or had the affair with Laine, or married the boss.

Chris was impeccably dressed, smoked European cigarettes and drank Absolute. He handed me a vial of coke and told me to do it out in the open, at the bar, like everyone else. So casual, as if we'd known each other forever and I used the tiny spoon and danced with him the rest of the night.

"Dump whoever you're dating, honey, because I have someone for you who's a lot better looking, with a ton of money," Chris yelled over the music.

When I asked him what I should wear to his party, he said, "What you have on is perfect minus the clothes."

Saturday night, I didn't even care that I felt fat. I wore the blueprint-blue Kamali with a neckline open to the bellybutton and chandelier earrings, and went fearlessly stag, coveting the event for myself.

Chris's driveway and street were filled with Mercedes, Jaguars, and BMW's. His house was a large Spanish-style on one of the canals off Las Olas. I hated that I had to park so far down the block; the walk was a pain in three-inch pumps and the low clouds made the sky starless, which meant rain was on the way. My perfectly made up face was already melting in the humidity but I was electric. About seeing Chris again, yes, but more, I wanted into his chic crowd and to meet his rich business partner. I already had myself living like a well-kept pet. I could easily slip into the comfort of a new car, get whisked away in a private jet like with Philip Baines, and anybody would be younger, less dreadful than him.

I worried about spending the right amount for the birthday gift. The Tiffany address book was store-wrapped in its blue box and satin bow. *Ideal for a new acquaintance on whom you'd like to make a good impression.* I trusted the sales girl's opinion.

Madonna drowned the clack of my shoes on the terracotta pavers. The carved wood door opened with a whoosh like a bank vault. "Who are you!" a blond boy said, pleasure on his face, gold around his neck. He air-kissed, waved me in, danced off.

Chris was in the kitchen handing a uniformed girl empty champagne bottles. This was what I wanted, a life surrounded by pretty things, parties with help.

"Keep the glasses full," Chris said to her, "starting with mine." Bubbles ran over when she poured, and he slurped off the excess. "Darling," he said when he saw me. He took my hand, spun me out to pose. "Stunning," he said, and his welcome felt to me like immediate belonging.

"Happy thirtieth," I said, handing him the gift.

"A robin's egg blue box, my favorite," he said.

Robin's Egg Blue. I saw the future as a pile of Tiffany boxes and white ribbons. Someone put a goblet in my hand.

"I adore it," Chris said and kissed my cheek. "Now come meet your new ex-boyfriend."

A new ex —the freedom it invoked. The old mistakes were just a normal part of the equation.

People fixed on the wedding-white carpet, a staircase led to a crowded balcony. Chris tossed aside two jewel-colored pillows from one of the large sofas. "Move your butt over and make room," he said to a man with gray at the temples.

Tanned skin, eyes almost black. He smiled at me with nice teeth, wearing a lot of gold and an onyx ring. Not really my thing, but he was sexy in his European-cut clothing and I thought how I could easily fuck this guy.

"This is the girl I was telling you about," Chris said. "Robin, my partner Niles."

I pretended I was the creature Chris wanted me to be for his partner. Classy, beautiful, worthy of a jet-set social life. If I played it well, maybe I'd get the boyfriend I came for. "Chris is so fun," I said, sipping my champagne, as if I'd known him a million years.

"Always," Niles said.

I crossed my legs and stretched an arm over the couch, careful not to spill the drink. Sophisticated was what I was going for, but then it was always about my body, wasn't it – hardly a tough sell, evidenced by his glance at my cleavage.

A girl with short crispy hair and a bright-patterned, shoulder-padded suit took a fingernail scoop of coke off the silver tray on the coffee table, sniffed it back.

Niles offered me a gold straw. Expensive cars, Cristal, plenty of drugs in the open. I did a bump.

I was turned on like a light, as if I hadn't been already. The outside, the past, the future melted away and I was only, drinking, talking with Niles.

He told me about the jewelry store he owned on the Galt Ocean Mile with Chris. How he was divorced with a twelve year old daughter who lived somewhere else. I mentioned my job, my roommate and how much I loved Florida. Flirting, I held a cigarette between my fingers and waited until he pulled out his lighter.

"Let me see that," I said. I took it from his hand. Cartier. "I like it. I lost mine," I lied. The one Jeff gave me wasn't near as nice.

"Then we'll have to get you a new one," he said.

He knew it was what I wanted to hear. "How about dinner with me next week?" he said.

I mulled the possibility of a new lighter, leaned over, almost brushing my breast against his knee as I tapped my ash into the crystal bowl, looked up at him. "Get my number from Chris," I said.

Chapter 31

The woman stared at me with arms crossed, but I caught the door despite her. I glared. I'd already slept here after my third date with Niles and knew the drill. I used the key with authority then pressed the button for the penthouse.

I'd planned to meet Niles at his jewelry store before dinner but Chris said he got stuck in Miami and handed me the keys to Niles's oceanfront condo. Have a drink. Relax, he said.

It felt good being trusted; I was already part of the group.

Standing at the floor-to-ceiling windows, I watched the ocean and debated whether a trip out to the windy wrap-around balcony would spoil my hair. I'd spent my day off shopping for something new to wear and worked tirelessly to look gorgeous, and decided not to ruin it all before Niles even saw me.

Things were going as planned. We'd slept together and I didn't feel used, I was in command of my emotions. I'd given him just right amount of horniness and I-could-fall-madly-for-you, and he was awed. It was obvious he already wanted me, maybe even to move in.

The sound of breaking glass and a high-pitched squeal startled me. It's the maid, I thought. But what if Niles was being robbed? Heart drumming, I tiptoed down the hall, peeking around the threshold of each room as I passed.

Splashing sounds came from the inner sanctum of the master bath. A beautiful frosted-blonde girl was immersed in the marble Jacuzzi. It was worse than robbery, this bitch in the tub.

"Watch out! Broken glass," she said. "Can you believe it? That's the third Baccarat I've broken. Niles is going to kill me."

She had nothing to worry about, I'd kill Niles before he had a chance. What an idiot I was, naively thinking he was fixated only on me. I surveyed the shards on the tile; the stem of the flute was intact on the thick-looped rug.

"You must be Robin," she said, carelessly plopping a sudsy bar of soap in the crystal dish.

Interesting. But who the hell was this nympho Niles chose to fuck just one night after being with me? "And you are?" I said.

"Leanne," she said, reclining. "He's right, you *are* pretty."

I forced a close-lipped smile.

"This must look so bad," she said, tucking stray curls back in her hairclip. "We're not sleeping together. I mean, not that we haven't, but that was a long time ago and we were totally wasted." She laughed at her own memory. "We're just friends now. I live down the street."

Great. That's all I needed. Her stuff was piled high on the chaise.

"We're not exclusive," I said.

"That's not what I heard," she said.

"Yeah? What'd you hear?" I said, taking a seat on the carved black-lacquered bench, embarrassed by how little it took for me to revert into the gossipy cheerleader.

"There's a new girl in Niles's life and he's in love," she said, all sing-songy.

"It's a little early for that," I said. "What's with the bath?"

"My bathroom's being renovated. The maid let me in." She reached into the adjacent shelf, upsetting the stack of neatly folded towels, and dried her hands with the corner of a bath sheet. "Do me a favor, hand me my purse," she said.

A long leather strap stuck out from under the heap of clothes. I handed her the bag and marveled at the menagerie she pulled out of it: a large bottle of Paul Mitchell Sculpting Spray, a plastic vented brush, an address book, two makeup bags, a beeper, a key ring the size of a Hula Hoop. She found her bulging wallet. Inside was a tiny Ziploc of white powder. "Would you like some?" she asked.

"Sure," I said. Partying with the enemy was probably a bad idea, but I thought it'd be good to have her on my side. I took a mirrored tray from the anteroom, cut some lines, rolled a crisp twenty dollar bill, and held the mirror for Leanne. "After you," I said.

I did my line, lit us cigarettes. Her hair color cheapened her. Niles couldn't possibly be more attracted to her than me. She tapped her smoke, completely missing the ashtray on the ledge behind her head.

"Where do you work?" I said, feeling coke-chatty.

"I'm an escort. I date men for money."

I was shocked by her candor. "Was Niles one of your

dates?" I asked.

"You're so funny," she said. Her perfect coral lipstick exaggerated her baking soda white teeth. "Hey, can you find a broom so I can get out?" she said.

We heard the front door slam and Chris's voice calling my name. The closer he came, the more urgent he sounded.

"In here," I said.

"My friend Leanne left a message," he said, catching his breath. "Doesn't matter, I got here first." He turned pale when he saw her.

"We've met," I said.

"Hey baby," she said pushing herself to her feet. Bubbles slid down her tan-lined body leaving a calico of soapy puffs dripping from her perky boobs and pubic hair.

"Please Louise, cover yourself," he said, throwing a towel at her. "She's got no shame. I'm sorry, honey, I had no idea."

He was protecting me.

"Relax, we're best friends now," Leanne said.

"Watch out for glass," I said as I passed him, nodding at the broken stemware.

"Not again," he said, surveying the mess. "Leanne, I've told you, use the plastic."

Chapter 32

Fun was all I was having nightly with an endless supply of coke and Cristal champagne. I thinned my schedule at the Yacht Club to nothing so that Niles and I could spend most nights together. We went out with Chris and their group to whatever club-of-the-night. We'd all retreat back to Niles's après hours. Leanne would join if she wasn't on a call and a various assortment of other friends rotated throughout the week. We'd pop Halcyon or Valium or Xanax to come down, sleep in. Niles left at ten every day to open the jewelry store.

I ran into my roommate on interludes between dress changes and it was clear that I had, for all practical purposes, stopped living there and we agreed to dissolve our agreement and Laura's boyfriend took over my half of the rent.

Niles wanted me there when the store closed at six for dinner and play. It wasn't hard to convince me to quit the Yacht Club.

My past dissolved and the present was rumrunners on the beach, shopping at Neiman's and lunches in Bal Harbour. When Niles bought me a Mercedes SL, I remembered when I'd driven Joe McClure's around Myrtle Beach, how I thought I'd have my own one day. Now I lived in South Florida, in a beachfront penthouse with my good-looking boyfriend.

Chris was my new best friend; we saw each other daily. I'd met his parents; we shopped and dined together. When Chris took me to Saks and Neimans, it was the sales he showed me, the *finale racks*. "Honey, you have a lot to learn," he said, pulling designer tops, dresses and pants for me. "Forget the tragic mall stores, you can buy the real thing here for less," he said and pushed me into the dressing room.

His implication was that I looked cheap. I'd wasted thousands on clothes and nothing I'd ever bought was a classic piece, or an investment, as Chris would say.

After we shopped we ended up at Chris's house. His dresser was covered with gold jewelry, his table with lacquer boxes filled with blow, Baccarat crystal. His closet was full of monogrammed French-cuffed shirts and Louis Vuitton.

"Honey," he said, "they used Louis to line the tires of tanks during World War II – worth every penny. You've seen the Great Gatsby –what does Daisy B. have in tow?" I sopped up the tidbits of knowledge as he flitted around.

I'd seen plenty of Vuitton at Pratt. Liana Doolittle, the redheaded mouse who roomed down the hall from me hauled riding tack in it. I thought it was ugly. Brown. Dull. But if it implied status, maybe I should reconsider.

"This came into the store and it's totally you," he said and pulled a gold cigarette holder out of his Cartier bag. Something from a black and white movie. I stuck a Parliament into it, lit it with the gold lighter Niles's had given me.

Him bringing me a gift, wanting me to have something special, *thinking* of me, felt like love. I hugged him. "It's nothing," he said, then checked the mirror, traced his lips with cherry Chapstick, stuffed it into his bag with his beeper and keys. "Are we ready? We don't want Niles getting jealous. You know what a brat he is when we keep him waiting." And we laughed because it had been that way —where Niles had become a scolding parent, but really he was the child.

Chapter 33

I was furious with Niles for no reason except that after six months of living together with no occupation other than to be beholden to his schedule, his whims, and his unrelenting sex-drive, I was over it. I wasn't in love with him, though I'd said so –because at the beginning, it seemed right in the moment, then I perpetuated the habit without meaning it. Now the cutie-pie talk irritated me and I found his mere presence grating.

He was leaving for his annual June trip to Bogotá to buy emeralds and I was going meet him afterwards in Panama. His friend Jorge Juarez, an important political figure, was hosting us there.

"Why am I bringing Leanne again?" I said, scrunching extra height in my hair for the fundraiser Niles had committed us to. We'd been to several similar events since I'd been living with him.

"Because Jorge wants her to come," he said, patting on cologne. We dodged each other around the double sinks.

"I just don't want to be stuck with her the whole time," I said. It was better traveling with a group, and though Leanne was usually entertaining, she was also disorganized, dramatic, and chronically late. I'd be the one expected to wait around for her while she got her shit together.

Niles filled his pockets: money clip, drugs, lighter. Always impeccable, always precise. "Jorge is one of my best customers," he said.

"And hers," I said. I'd met Jorge once before, attractive and charming, but there was something sinister in his remove that frightened me.

"Well, yes," he said.

"When did you become her pimp?" I said, combing fresh mascara through my lashes.

"There's no need to be jealous, you know I love you," he said, then took the Benson & Hedges from his mouth and kissed my shoulder. "I'd appreciate your help with this."

"Don't worry, babe, I'll do my part," I said. I was glad Niles was leaving before me. I was looking forward to having the place to myself. I'd exercise, take my time packing and have Chris and the rest of the gang over.

"And don't ask Jorge a lot of questions when we're all together," he said. He did a line in spite of the impending dinner party, then handed me the straw.

"I hate that sexist Latin bullshit," I said. I caught sight of myself in the full-length mirrors. Patent heels and panties, bent over the silver tray. "American women don't giggle politely with their hands folded in their laps."

"It's not that," Niles said. "He has a high position in his government and has to be careful with his associations." He took a seat on the edge of the chaise.

"You mean like Leanne?" I said. I threw my head back, cleared my sinuses, shook out my hair.

"It's best to keep things light," he said.

Niles's chauvinism was another thing I couldn't stand.

"Chris is going to drive you guys to Miami," he said, checked his watch and sighed.

I fastened the twenty-carat diamond necklace and matching drop earrings I'd borrowed from the store. "Thank God he's going," I said.

Despite my pouting, I was thrilled Chris was chaperoning us to Panama. He had the ability to wrangle Leanne like no one else and I could care less what Niles was doing whenever he was around because he could make balancing a checkbook interesting. It was going to be one big party.

I stepped into my red strapless dress. I turned my back for Niles to zip me, then repositioned the jewels on my neck.

"Those are gorgeous on you," he said.

I was stoned. We'd gotten rid of all our illicit drugs but smoked a joint in Chris's car. It was the first time I'd been high since Jeff and I felt like everyone was staring at us. "This is Jane's," Chris said, looking at Leanne's driver's license. We were at Miami International Airport.

"I know, but we look so much alike," Leanne said of her sister. "I couldn't find mine." She sat on her suitcase in the middle of sidewalk, forcing travelers to weave around her.

I lit a cigarette.

"We're all going to jail," Chris said.

"I'm not," I said, waving my passport. A bus fumed on us.

"Shit, my hair," Leanne said.

"You're going to have more to worry about than smelling

like exhaust," Chris said and pulled her to her feet.

"Jorge will handle it when we get there, he's like the president or something," Leanne said.

"Works for me," I said shooting Chris a look; I wasn't going to let Leanne ruin our trip. As far as I was concerned, it was her problem.

Niles's open shirts bothered me. He was exuberant, glossy with anticipation and dressed in pressed French cuffs, unbuttoned halfway, exposing his chest hair. The whole look was disco seventies. I reminded myself that we were in another country and it didn't matter what anyone thought.

"I missed you, baby," he said, kissing my lips.

Jorge was with him at the gate when we arrived in Panama City. He nodded to a uniformed man and we were waved through customs, then immigration. It was impressive and scary at the same time.

The humidity outside hit us like a wet towel, but the a.c. was pumping in the limo.

We drove alongside the Panama Canal on the single paved artery to the city center. The last of the daylight gave way to an unlit road. Through dense tropical brush, banana trees and black palms the business of the canal's locks lit the evening sky.

The driver passed us thirty-five millimeter film cases full of yellow cocaine. It was moist and flakey with a strong plant smell. Peruvian, Niles said. One bump was enough.

We arrived at the five-star resort, average by U.S. standards, with its mauve carpet, sea foam furnishings and potted palms. Not far from the entrance were the canal's locks where massive cargo ships loomed like dark ghosts.

We unpacked in connected suites, then headed downtown, energized by the mystery of the experience.

Tourists and young locals crowded the dance floor in the disco ball dinner club. When Jorge arrived, he called a Panamanian boy dressed in tight jeans and t-shirt to our table. He spoke in Spanish with the kid, who took a seat, then introduced him to Chris.

I wondered if Jorge had done the same for Niles the previous night with a Panamanian girl. Was it sophisticated that I didn't care? Niles had jumped me for sex in the hotel before leaving for dinner. I acted interested, but in truth, hadn't missed him one bit.

The party continued to Jorge's apartment. We sat on a modern sectional sofa that took up the whole room. Chris and the boy from dinner disappeared into a bedroom and Jorge passed a pipe filled with peyote. We smoked. Tripped. Everything blurred, like watercolor. Bodies in the room moved slowly, muted, as if through gauze. More people. A lot of hola, hola. I didn't care when the Panamanian girls kissed Niles.

Leanne and I woke up at five the next afternoon naked in bed together. Niles had left a note: 2:00 — Meeting Jorge. A message from Chris – Gone to town.

I peed with the bathroom door open.

"Those girls, I can't believe they wanted to be with us," Leanne said, perusing the room service menu. "I never would have done that if we weren't in Panama." And I wondered if is was true.

We'd left Niles at Jorge's after he disappeared behind closed doors and we brought two of the Panamanian girls back to the hotel. Not a word of English spoken between us. We had a foursome on the king size bed, legs and arms everywhere. It was an indulgence, not a performance.

"Niles was so left out," I said. "Serves him right for having them there in the first place."

"What time did he get here?" Leanne said, trying in vain to tuck her voluminous hair into a shower cap. "Do you think he's mad at us?"

"Oh please. Fuck him," I said, over my toothbrush. "What do you think he's been up to with Nic since he's been here? They probably had hookers around since he got off the plane, it's most likely what he's doing now. What goes around, man. I'm not his slave."

"Aren't you jealous?" Leanne said, splashing her face with water.

"No," I said.

"But you love Niles," she said, circles of suds on her cheeks, searching for a clean washcloth. There were none.

"I might've talked myself into loving him at the beginning but he's needy and controlling," I said, suddenly safe confiding in her. The trip had unexpectedly brought us closer. We were beyond tolerating each other and had become friends. "Niles is not the guy I'm going to end up with."

"But you get all that jewelry and he bought you a car,"

she said, drying off with the used towel that hung on the door.

"Would that be enough for you?" I said. Strewn pillows covered the floor; I threw them on the bed so I could walk. Remnants from the previous night's debauchery buried the tables and dressers: empty bottles, glasses, tiny lotion containers.

"Not all the time," she said. She picked up a stray lipstick and applied it out of habit.

"I didn't think so," I said.

We lounged on chairs in hotel robes with our feet up, ordered room service. Cheeseburgers, Bloody Marys, Marlboro Lights.

"Pretty cool that you haven't had to be with Jorge," I said, picking at a Toblerone from the service bar. "It's like you're getting vacation with pay."

"I don't know if he's going to give me the usual since we haven't, you know," she said through a drag of her cigarette.

"But you came here for him," I said, licking melted chocolate from my thumb. "Isn't that the deal whether you fuck him or not?" Leanne blew the smoke up to the ceiling, her thoughts elsewhere. "I have to know; how much?" I said.

"He usually gives me five hundred to go to the other room with him, get him off. Two thousand plus expenses is the day rate when I travel," she said.

Leanne wasn't free, but she was. She didn't have to put up with the daily bullshit of being kept, like me. She could do what she wanted and probably made enough to live on her own the way I did at Niles's, without the emotional maintenance. "I want to get paid like that," I said.

Ten a.m. the next day, the market was teeming, the sun's glare a reprimand for our sleepless night. Leanne and I bought matching pink sunglasses for a dollar and Niles and Chris stocked up on food, wine and pharmaceuticals. Niles had a jeep and, I assumed, directions to where we were going. Filthy children pulled at our bags, then stretched out their hands for money. We gave them dollars and they chased us as we drove out of town.

The city gave way to a clay-paved road and we passed cement shanties with cut-out holes for windows and tin roofs. We stopped alongside a barefoot boy with a back-breaking load of tiny bananas; Niles handed him a dollar for the bunch.

We all got uncontrollable giggles in the brutal heat. "Where's your new boyfriend," Niles said to Chris. Crumbs from a Chips Ahoy cookie sputtered from his mouth. Leanne sprayed Sprite through her nose. My stomach cramped from the lunacy.

"Shut up, I'm trying to drive," Chris said, pushing Leanne's feet off his lap. I felt bad that Chris had to be the responsible one but I wasn't in any shape to help him.

Ahead was a military checkpoint. We were stopped by uniformed men with machine guns and assault rifles. Our passports were demanded. "Jorge Juarez," Chris said with a shut-the-fuck-up look at our silliness, and the soldiers let us pass.

I felt the danger, despite my haze. What was I doing? Daddy and Melanie had no idea I was even out of the country. I could be kidnapped, murdered, disappear, and no one would know. Jorge would have any evidence of me erased and I'd be just another dead girl, a Central American statistic. Too messed up to think about it anymore, I pushed the idea out of my mind.

We woke twenty-four hours later at Jorge's heavily guarded ranch. Leanne and I were alone again. The last thing I saw before I went to bed was Leanne passed out on a rocking chair; her sunglasses on, with a Dorito hanging from her lip.

There was a note from Chris: Jungle with Jorge and Niles. Not back by dark call U.S. Embassy.

Leanne looked concerned. "He's just kidding," I said.

We guzzled Diet Coke and sat at places that had been set for us on the long dining table. The small woman who brought our breakfast did not speak.

"How did you start what you're doing?" I said, spooning salsa on the eggs.

"I waitressed at a topless bar," she said, eating a chunk of papaya.

I'd only seen strip joints in movies and pictured bookies drinking shots and bruised girls in a sticky, seedy, smoke-filled place.

"The nicest one in South Florida," she said. "All the dancers looked like centerfolds."

"Did you strip?" I said. Someone you knew could walk in and see you doing that. It was like posing nude; the pictures would eventually surface.

"Not at first," she said, "but I got raped and it changed everything.

The woman returned with warm tortillas, oblivious to our conversation.

"Some guy crawled into my second floor window in the middle of the night and held a knife to my throat. I slept on the floor at the foot of my mother's bed for a year after it happened," she said and sipped her juice.

I didn't want to intrude with further questions and was afraid to hear more. But I admired her honesty, was honored that she confided in me. Who else knew? I got up and hugged her. "I'm so sorry," I said.

"It was two years ago," she said casually. "We're suing the landlord for not fixing the broken window locks. He was told a million times."

Chapter 34

I was a nervous wreck. Melanie and her fiancé Chad were arriving at four o'clock. Melanie's vacation plans hinged on my providing them a free place to stay and I was eager to oblige. I actually missed her, hadn't seen her since I'd left Jeff and this was my chance to show off how far I'd come –glamorous friends, fabulous oceanfront apartment and new car. After I invited her, I realized my mistake, I'd set myself up for ruthless scrutiny. What she was going to think of Niles? Not only was he more than twenty years older than me, he was very European, not like the preppy guys she dated. I was sure she'd be snobbish the way she always was about anyone I was involved with. But I had to own it. Niles was at least good-looking, and I wasn't going to apologize about him ahead of her judgment.

I hadn't met Chad before, but I knew his stats: Yale Law School alum; clerking for a Supreme Court Judge in D.C.; future in politics; good family; conservative. Melanie sent me a picture of them together in tennis clothes, from their recent trip to Newport Beach, where Chad was from. He was handsome, tan and tall. Melanie told me he'd not only been a tennis pro as an undergrad, he'd also been ski patrol in Colorado for a season before law school.

Was the fact that Niles designed million dollar baubles interesting at all?

I stocked the guest room and bath with the best linens. The florist delivered fresh flowers —Chris's idea — and I had the liquor store bring an extra case of Louis Roederer. The maid made everything spotless.

. The minutes ticked away while I assembled myself in a sleeveless navy and white knit dress and gold jewelry. Hor d'oeuvres I painstakingly purchased were readied on platters.

"You look good," Melanie said when she and Chad arrived. We hugged around her carry-ons. She was thin, her hair was longer since the last time I'd seen her.

"You do too, love the hair," I said. Changes in hairstyle was how we measured our time apart, as if the outside transformation reflected our personal growth.

Chad and I moved through the hellos as if we already knew each other. Nice view, he said. He was confident with an easy smile. But I was focused on Melanie as she stepped around her luggage, assessed the place. She seemed pleased as she followed me to the guestroom.

I began to breathe normally by dinnertime. At Rick's Seafood on the waterway, Chad talked to Niles. It's so much colder in the Alps, I overheard, while Melanie and I caught up.

"Did he buy that watch for you?" Melanie said, examining my Piaget; finishing off my cigarette.

"To be fair, he got it wholesale," I said, needing to humble myself, taking a last sip of wine.

When I laid my after dinner cigarette in the ashtray,

Melanie picked it up and took a drag. She never surrendered to the habit enough to buy her own pack. "Chad hates it when I smoke," she said. "I only do it when I drink." She was quick with disclaimers about public vices, and for her, the private ones didn't exist.

We have courts downstairs, Niles say to Chad.

"He seems nice enough," Melanie said, watching them. It was as close to a compliment as I could expect from her.

"He is," I said, believing the affirmation would make her happy for me. My only hope was to show her a good time and it was working. She'd leave thinking I was doing well.

I stayed up with Niles until one-thirty, then prepared for bed. I needed to be an up-and-ready hostess in the morning when Melanie and Chad wanted to leave for the beach. When I brushed my teeth, Niles cupped my boobs from behind.

"Come on baby, party with me," he said.

I slapped his hands, wiggled away. "Get off," I said. Toothpaste sputtered from my mouth. "My sister's in the other room. We've got to get some sleep."

We had a deal. For one night I wanted him to behave. I gambled that his pride would keep him from embarrassing himself in front of houseguests. But he was determined to screw things up for me.

"I've been more than generous with you and your sister," he said, with emphasis on *your sister*, then he did a big fat line and handed me the mirror.

"I don't want any," I said, and in that moment, I realized that I hated him. I put on a t-shirt and crawled into bed.

"Go in the den if you can't sleep and turn off the light," I said and covered my head with a pillow.

I drank enough so I wouldn't need to take a pill to come down off the couple lines I'd done. I curled on my side and my body rushed as much as my mind –if I slept, all would be fine in the morning. I tried to ignore my paranoia. Valium, would make me foggy all day. Halcyon would knock me out for eight hours. But what if Melanie was up before me? I was afraid to look at the clock.

The bedroom lights came on, the covers ripped from me. Niles stood next to the bed and grabbed my wrist. "Get up!" he said.

I squinted through the unexpected brightness.

"Ever since we've been back from Panama, you're a bore," he said. He rummaged through the bedside drug drawer. He wanted sex but I couldn't entertain the idea of him touching me. "Stop being an addict," I said.

"You're the addict. Would you like it if I woke your sister and told her everything?"

It was the price of having a sugar daddy, babysitting for a roof over my head. "I'm calling Chris," I said.

"That's original." He did another line.

I didn't care that he was jealous. It was always a competition with him. I dialed the phone, dragging it around while I pulled on sweats and threw things in my oversized Halston bag.

Chris was asleep.

"Niles is attacking me," I said.

"What?" his voice was groggy, "Where's Melanie?"

"In bed. Asleep for hours. What do I do?"

"Get in the car," he said.

"I can't leave Melanie, when she wakes up, she'll wonder where I am and who the hell knows what this maniac is going to say," I said. Niles's stare was a combination of pleading and viciousness as he swirled Remy in a snifter. "I'm scared."

"We'll deal with Melanie in the morning. Don't worry about Niles, he'll be passed out," he said. "Put Niles on."

I grabbed underwear, make-up, hairspray. Checked my wallet –plenty of cash. Drugs, keys. I threw the green velvet box with my jewelry in the purse. High-maintenance. Ice queen, I heard Niles tell Chris, as his voice trailed from behind the bedroom door. I crept down the hall, my heart a marching band, as I slipped from the penthouse without saying goodbye.

I gunned the Mercedes from the underground parking, slammed on the brakes in front of the building. Two-twenty-six a.m. By the lobby's entrance, I could see the well-lit doorman, reading. Melanie. Oh God. Remain calm. Chris will make it better.

A thud on the pavement. I jumped. My Ralph Lauren riding boot. Then clothes fell from the sky. Every color of the rainbow in slow motion. My new silk Flora Kung dress, a Balenciaga bag, Reeboks. Niles disappeared and reappeared with more armfuls and dropped them over the balcony. A favorite Echo scarf hitched on someone's railing halfway down.

I ran around the driveway, picked up everything and threw it through the open roof of the car. Bras and bikinis slung on the flowering bushes. Pantyhose on cars. My Derapagé sunglasses. Scratched, broken. Bastard.

The doorman came out.

"My boyfriend is not taking his medication," I said. "I called the doctor." I offered him a twenty. "If there's anything I missed, could you hold it?"

Another pile came down. My rabbit fur jacket and hats. They floated like feathers back and forth. A white pillbox, a navy wide brim, the English straw with flowers I wore to church with Chris on Easter Sunday. Raining down my liberty.

I chased after it all, tossed things in the back, the passenger side, the trunk. There wasn't a lot of room in the sports car, but then I didn't have much to begin with. Not more than I could carry was my rule since leaving Jeff. By the time I found the mate to a pair of YSL shoes, Niles was gone from the window.

What a disgrace.

I sat in the driver's seat and tapped a cigarette on my case, lit and smoked. The full moon illuminated a navy sky. All the windows were dark. The building's occupants were retired, old. They'd missed the show. I couldn't help but laugh out loud. There would be no compromise, no regrets. Niles and I were over.

I was in a stunned survival state when Chris and I returned to Niles's at nine the next morning. By the time Melanie and Chad were finished showering, Chris and I had the coffee made and the bagels we'd purchased on the way over, sliced and ready to serve.

"Sleep well?" I said, cheerfully, but felt faint.

Melanie, in a sundress and bare feet, looked tired. "I'm not used to drinking like that. I think I passed out," she said.

"Well, if that's the worst that happened," Chris said, and I gave him a terrified glance when I handed her a mug.

Chris knew the owners of a boutique beachfront hotel walking distance from Niles's place, and he'd secured Melanie and Chad a suite for the rest of the weekend.

My plan had been, just to come out with it, but I almost choked when I said, "Don't be mad, Niles and I had a huge fight. We broke up and I moved all my stuff to Chris's last night," I said. I had my back to Melanie while I returned the cream to the fridge. "We got you a suite at the Surfrider up the beach –my treat."

"What happened?" Melanie said, only slightly annoyed, if not indifferent, while she scooped and stirred the sugar.

"I'll fill in the gory details after we get you checked-in," I said, as rehearsed, face strained behind my smile. "We can relax at the pool, play tennis, whatever you guys want," I said. I didn't have the luxury to languish in humiliation.

Chad bounced in wearing khaki and a crinkled linen button-down, the sleeves rolled unevenly, as if he stepped from the pages of a J. Crew catalog

"Coffee?" I said and handed him a mug. I busied myself, wiped crumbs with a sponge, spread cream cheese to appear hungry and waited for something from my sister.

"Robin's got drama," Melanie said, smirking through a sip. "Tell him."

After a blunt reiteration, I said, through inadequately-veiled shame, "I'm sorry for the inconvenience."

"I warned Chad to be prepared for anything," Melanie said. "As long as the hotel's nice, don't worry about it."

Again, I was an utter failure. And worse, Melanie expected it from me. There was nothing left to do but leave before Niles stirred.

The beautiful day did little to quell my mortification but I pretended that everything was well with the world.

Chad slept on the chaise next to Melanie. I was the one who needed to nap but didn't dare until I was done with the task of behaving as if was fine. I watched Melanie for signs of displeasure but she seemed content with their new accommodations.

"You want to order lunch?" I said.

"Yeah, when Chad wakes up," she said, hinting annoyance. "Look at him, he's such a bum. He'd sleep all day if I let him."

Everything was an achievement to Melanie, even her vacation. She'd lie in the sun for hours, turning every-so-often to ensure an even tan –and it wasn't enough to be in the sun, you had to be awake for it.

"Put more oil on my back," she said.

I did as I was told, familiar with the chore of keeping Melanie basted. "Remember Coppertone Butter?" I said and wiped the residue oil on my legs.

"That commercial with the lifeguards and the arm patch test," she said.

"I can still smell it," I said. We laughed. The comfort of our shared memory was something.

"Hey, thanks for being cool about everything. I don't want you to be mad," I said and touched her arm. "It's nice here, isn't it?"

"Yes. And free. Frankly, I'd rather not to have to be burdened with some boyfriend of yours. Besides, Robin, he was too old for you," she said, and slid People from her bag. "Better now than later."

Hardly loving support, but I was relieved that she didn't lecture me.

"What are you going to do now?" she said, flipping the pages of the magazine over the side of her chair.

"I can stay with Chris as long as I want," I said, wanting to appear as if I had value to someone who Melanie liked.

She ignored this, glanced at Chad. "Cute, isn't he?"

I hadn't found anything to despise about him yet, which made him wholly loathsome. "Absolutely," I said.

"And smart. He's clerking for an Appellate Court Judge in D.C.," she said. "It's been a hard commute, but when I'm done with Yale, I'll be looking down there."

It was at rare times like this, when Melanie shared her plans with me that I felt she cared what I thought. "One day I'm going to be able to say my sister is a U.S. Senator."

"Stop living your life through me, Robin" she said, without looking up.

"Why is it a crime to be proud of my sister," I said.

"Because you compare yourself with me," she said. "Get your own life."

Her words stung, but I let it slide. I couldn't take losing another fight; I'd had enough disappointment for one day. I wasn't upset about Niles, just embarrassed. I watched a couple of tourists rinse sand off in the foot shower. I'd hardly walked on the beach once since living here. I slurped the rest of my iced tea and wished it was a bump instead, that this pain was over, that Melanie and Chad were on a plane and that I could disappear.

Chapter 35

I understood comfort food. The way real butter and cream made everything taste even better, the aroma of sautéed onions and the crackle of meat as it hit the grease. I'd lived with Niles in a world of skipped breakfasts, Chablis lunches, stone crab and cocaine dinners, and I'd missed cooking, eating, so I made Chris a meal to thank him for taking me in.

I hadn't wanted to cook for a man since I'd left Jeff. I'd been so adamant about distancing myself from domesticity, as if the mere idea of grocery shopping would send right back into a cage.

Fried chicken was on the menu; crispy skin, the hypnotic smell of it sizzling in Crisco. Disappointed when I hadn't found a real cast iron pan, I improvised with a copper-bottom skillet.

I cut up a fryer, soaked it in buttermilk, the way Jeff's mom had taught me. I'd retained those recipes. I'd had a knack for the kitchen; a ham for Easter, a goose at Christmas, baskets of fruit marvelously transformed into preserves, wax-sealed in mason jars at harvest time. But that was when I smoked Vantage cigarettes, had house plants and thought Jane Fonda was God; when I believed that the microwave and a princess-cut diamond ring defined happiness.

I created an assembly line on Chris's counter, dredged the seasoned parts in flour, submerged the meat in the melted fat and covered it with a splatter screen. There was serenity in my movements. Each turn of a leg, a thigh, a breast evoked what I hadn't lost of myself; those memories that weren't conceived in pain.

Chris and I drank Seabreezes and did bumps in the living room while the food waited. We conveyed intimate snippets of our past to each other when we were alone. Chris had just finished with his high school first time with a "straight" football player story and now it was my turn.

"I only did it because Donna did," I said. "Sixteen. Brad Davis. And no, I wasn't in love."

Brad had been more of a first heartbreak, then a first love. Hey babe, it's over, we're history, was how he put an end to our short-lived dating stint. The next day, I saw him in school with his arm around Wendy Schlessinger's waist and was devastated.

I told Chris how, six months later, after Donna confessed in the smoking stairwell outside the cafeteria that she'd lost her virginity to someone else's boyfriend, I'd taken Brad's hand down Montclair Road and done the deed. I picked Brad for practical reasons: he'd been the only boy I'd gone far enough with where I'd been felt up under the shirt and over the bra. We walked the two blocks to his father's house without speaking. The silence of the neighborhood, empty, while kids were in school and parents were at work heightened the criminality of the moment.

"I can still see the enclosed junk-filled front porch," I said. The cold linoleum floor stained under dirty work boots. The worn yellow carpet over craggy stairs. The small single unmade bed.

My masterpiece of fried food still rested on the well-dressed dining room table. I dismissed my regret of not eating with the knowledge that chicken tasted even better cold.

I divulged how I'd read *The Sensuous Woman* and *The Happy Hooker*, which described in detail how to perform a blow job, and how Donna and I practiced putting Trojans on bananas with our mouths. But that day with Brad had not been an exploration, only consummation.

"It was the first time I'd seen a naked boy," I said and squeezed a Parliament into the gold cigarette holder Chris had given me. He reached over and lit it. I extended my hand and admired the perfection of my manicured nails.

I recounted the awkwardness. How the kissing had been intentional, not passionate. How Brad produced Johnson's Baby Powder and rubbed it on my back; white dust over goosebumps. How he apologized for his cold hands and was small enough not to hurt me. It was over in seconds. I said, is that all? –pushed him off me. I told him I'd call, but I didn't.

Chris sipped his drink and took out another Dunhill, elegant the way it slid from the box between his fingers. "He's probably still got a complex," he said about how I'd dumped Brad in the end.

I thought how cruel Brad had been breaking up with me. How I'd hugged the speakers of my stereo, crying in a fetal position to Jackson Browne for months. How I'd almost failed that semester. How, after all the depression, and by finally being over it, in the end I was satisfied with the knowledge that I'd inadvertently paid Brad back in Spades.

I did a line, handed the mirror to Chris. "Fuck him," I said, brushing off the tip of my nose as if to sweep the memory away. "He was an asshole."

Chapter 36

Leanne's madam Blair was serene and direct. She was tall. The lines of her face shed light on the possibility of beauty but she was plain. Her hair, neat but forgettable. She examined me from across the table. Leanne had driven me to the restaurant; I could see her on the payphone answering a page.

"The phone number on the card is private. Girls only. Clients have a separate line," Blair said.

"I'm available as early as tonight," I said. I adjusted one of the solid gold earrings Niles had given me. I'd worn the Von Furstenberg dress, just in case.

Leanne had been surprised when I asked her for the introduction to the agency. Once you do it, there's no turning back, she'd said. She didn't know about my past, how I was no stranger to the act. I need the money, I'd said.

"Collect at the beginning of each hour," Blair said. "The rate is $500, one third to the house. If it's an overnight or weekly rate, we'll tell you."

I drank Perrier –Leanne said not to order alcohol in front of Blair –and listened to the orientation as if for any job that wouldn't require me to ask of a client, Are you a cop? before commencing business.

Leanne joined us, dropped her bag on the table; dug for lipstick. "We have a call, Rita," Leanne said, calling me by my alias I'd thought up on the car ride.

"Good luck," Blair said as she checked her pager. "They'll get credit card approval for at least four hours; otherwise, what's the point of putting on make-up, right?" We all laughed at that.

A private home. Return customers. There'd be two of them.

On the road, Leanne said the rule was no drugs, but no one paid attention it. The best dates, she said, would be all night parties with lots of girls, tons of drugs, little sex and stacks of cash.

Leanne and I cleared security at a gated Boca Raton golfing community and wove through immaculate roads. A mustached guy in seersucker golf pants and a polo shirt opened the door to the ranch house.

"Ladies, entre vous," he said, taking a quick gulp of his cocktail. His southern accent cancelled the already lame attempt at French. The ice in his glass clinked as we followed him down the hall.

His friend shook my hand when we entered the mirrored rec room. I thought how formal the act was, considering we'd all be naked within the next couple hours. "And I see you've met my uncle," he said. The guys clapped each other on the back, practically giggling.

There was coke on the bar. Vodka was poured.

Leanne noticed the pool. "Is it heated?" she said. The guy who opened the door for us confirmed it was and Leanne squealed like girl at a high school pep rally. "Let's get in," she said.

The drinks helped relieve my anxiety. I took cues from Leanne. When she took her clothes off, I did too. I felt unexpectedly safe. It was nothing compared to what I suffered through in Charlotte with Maggie. And certainly not more out there than Leanne and I had experienced in Panama. The guys weren't much older than us and had plenty of drugs. We stewed in the Jacuzzi, played swap-and-feel between with the two men, then retired to separate bedrooms.

The one with the mustache picked me. I let my brain leave the room as I had before; it was as easy as I thought it would be. He was gentle, wanted to touch my body. Pretending at intimacy gave me control. It made the exploit my choice, relieved any guilt that I have might had. I probably would have let this guy pick me up in a bar if we'd met in another time and place.

When Leanne drove me back to Chris's two thousand dollars richer, there was no remorse.

Chapter 37

If I knew anything, I knew the best way to get over a man was to not waste a minute before finding another one, but I didn't have a lot of choices. The only men I'd met in Florida prior to Niles, I'd worked with, and most of them were gay. So I called David Cardona in Toronto.

"How about the Bahamas this weekend?" he said.

It was a wonder how he could drop everything. How he never seemed to work. I'd save my questions until I saw him. "Is the wife out of town?" I said.

"Very funny. Meet me Friday night at the Paradise Island Hotel," he said. "I'll leave you a ticket at Chalk."

I knew the drill with Chalk Airlines. The seaplanes took off from Port-of-Miami and landed on the water in an hour but my flight arrived late. Since David had dinner reservations, I hastily attempted make-up in the steam-filled bathroom, still sweating from the shower. My hair was dripping wet.

David stuck his head in the door. "You look better without all that stuff on your face," he said.

Men said that when they were in a hurry. "You sound like my father," I said.

"We're late," he said.

Nothing annoyed me more than being rushed. I didn't even have a chance to unwind. "Easy for you to say, Mister I-don't-care-what-I-look-like, I'm-wearing-a-tee-shirt," I said. I pulled on a white sundress.

The beachfront bungalow seemed a mile from the main hotel. The moon lit the clear turquoise horizon. "Could we be any further from the action?" I said, struggling in heels to keep up on the stone pathway.

"I like privacy," he said. "The noise of the hotel is unpleasant."

Things weren't going my way. I hadn't expected to be subjected to an obstacle course every time I left my room, and I was self-conscious with wet hair. "Well, I prefer a little more excitement," I said.

"We have our own beach," he said. "You'll see how perfect it is tomorrow."

I hated mixing sand and suntan oil and I had no desire to swim; I'd have to wash my hair again. I'd rather be poolside drinking rumrunners, reading a paperback.

Vlad was seated at a bar inside the casino. "My dear," he said and kissed my hand.

"What a surprise," I said and hugged him.

"This is a woman who knows how to greet a man," Vlad said. "The boys are in the restaurant."

"Boys?" I said to David.

"Charlie and Aziz. They're in town for the squash tournament tomorrow."

So I wasn't the only reason David was in Nassau. But it didn't matter, I was glad we'd be in a group. It lessened the intensity between us.

Charlie and Aziz were brothers and professional squash players. I'd never seen it played and wasn't interested. Racquet sports bored me. Aziz, the good looking one, reminded me of Jeff.

We ate at the Steak House, drank bottles of wine. Got hammered. Vlad nicknamed me Contessa. The name stuck. It felt good to be around a group of straight men. It felt natural. I missed the unthreatening, underlying sexual attention that came with being one of the guys.

Dinner was expensive. I watched to see who picked up the tab. When David paid in cash, I wondered again where he got his money. He dressed like a hippie, didn't have a job but seemed to always have more than enough for traveling and pricey meals. His wife had to be rich. "What do you do?" I asked as we walked barefoot back to the room.

"This and that, not much," he said.

"Too vague," I said. "If you're a criminal, just tell me. I don't care."

"I'll keep that in mind," he said. He put his arm over my shoulders, took a drag off my cigarette, blew the smoke up to the sky.

"Do you have an open marriage?" I wasn't sure why it suddenly mattered that I knew more than I did.

"God, no," he said. "I'll tell you what, I won't ask you about your relationships and you don't ask about mine."

I thought about the date I went on as Rita. My exploits with Niles. Nothing I wanted to recapitulate. It was an acceptable compromise. "I can do that," I said. We staggered toward the beach.

"My friends are entertaining, eh?" he said.

"They are."

"And what about me?" he said.

The night had been unexpectedly fun. Being with him was effortless, like we'd been together for years. I gave him a squeeze. "A blast," I said.

It was almost noon when I woke. David was in a hotel robe and boxers wearing a tiny plastic shower cap, his curls protruding from under the elastic. He was cheerful, considering the amount of alcohol we'd consumed before passing out. He sat on the bed, swept the bangs from my eyes. "I thought you could hang out here while I went to the tournament," he said.

I was relieved; all I wanted was to lie in the sun and seeing David's buddies meant hair and make-up. "You're not trying to get rid of me are you?" I said.

"Never," he said.

I liked him, we were easy playmates. I wanted to be attracted to him, he had the right qualifications. He lived in another town, another country for that matter, so he wouldn't get in the way of my new occupation. He paid for everything when we were together. And married cancelled out the danger of romance. I was suddenly sad at how I'd changed. How I'd become separated from my heart. How I no longer dreamt more for myself. But David seemed to enjoy my pragmatism. At least he hadn't revealed otherwise.

After breakfast, he led me to the bedroom, pulled down the strap of my chemise, went for my neck. "You're a goddess," he said, then kissed me like a lover.

Goddess was a cornball word and the kiss had more intimacy than I expected. The daylight and sobriety were ruthless, turning my surprise into awkwardness. I looked at the ceiling fan. Its slow rhythmic motion and the breeze through the open French doors did nothing to encourage my involvement. I closed my eyes, tried to relax while he savored my body and let my thoughts distract me: How he'd talked at dinner about a trip to New York, how I only had a couple more hours of good sun left, how my flight was leaving too early the next morning. I groaned with fake enthusiasm until he was finished.

Chapter 38

The beauty outside held no allure for Chris and me. It was two in the afternoon on a Sunday and we had just finished breakfast, left the kitchen a mess and were now holed up in the den, the daylight glinting from beyond the blinds. Chris opened mail and sorted his bills and while I weeded through the train case I'd dragged with me from one place to another.

"Here's a picture of me from that time," I said, handing the picture to Chris. In the photo, Jeff and I leaned our smiling faces toward each other over a plate of barbeque, the forsythia behind us bright yellow, in majestic bloom. We looked happy, but I knew when that picture was taken, I had already made the decision to leave him.

"Good-looking," Chris said.

My habit of picking handsome men effectively covered the way I felt below the surface. The men I chose weren't grotesque; it was me who was the screwed up one, the one who wasn't worthy. Survival was maintained if the shell of my life appeared intact. Sadly, I'd changed only my zip code.

"I actually cooked a lot back then," I said.

Chris stretched out. "It's hard to see you as a housewife."

"Yeah, who is that girl?" I said and moved closer, under his arm, snuggled in. Our time alone together was precious. Chris was dealing coke now, mainly because he had the funds to buy an ounce at a time and distribute it to our friends. But because of it, there was a continual influx of people stopping by after work. At home or the jewelry store, the little gram bags would disappear every day by seven o'clock. But we'd partied the night before, fifty people until dawn, and for now, the usual addicts were at bay.

Chris and I had become a couple in an odd way. I went out at night for loveless sex and he did whatever he did with his adoring fans; it wasn't something we discussed in depth beyond the joke of it all. We were content to be a home base for each other, where none of that other stuff infected us.

Chris flipped through the channels with the remote.

My situation with him was indefinite but I had no game plan. At the moment, I was making good money. I'd gotten used to my beeper vibrating with calls from the agency. I saw regulars now, which made it easier to make plans with the gang. I shopped when I wasn't hung-over, took excursions with Chris to Key West or the Bahamas, so I felt like I was enjoying the money I made. Everything had been light and airy but I knew there had to be an expiration date. This was not the end of the road, just a very comfortable way station.

David and I spoke at least once a week when he called from his Toronto office. I'd become strangely attached to our conversations and his humor about my aimlessness, as if he thought my lack of intention and perpetual recreation was perfectly adequate for a girl my age.

I was cozy in a blanket, sipped my coffee and gave into the laziness of being in my sweats all day.

It'd been months since I'd heard from Daddy. All he expected from me was to be self-sufficient enough so I didn't affect his world. Silence was all that was required from my end to satisfy him. As for Melanie, who assumed the worst from me, as far as she was concerned, it was an achievement that I wasn't working at McDonald's. For my part, I was simply relieved to be left alone by them both.

Like Normal People was on the TV. Shawn Cassidy played a retarded guy in love with a retarded girl. They wanted to get married to each other against the consent of the custodial powers that be. I laughed. Any momentary guilt I felt at my insensitivity turned to irritation with the realization that even retarded love stories had to end in marriage.

Chapter 39

Philip Baines asked me to Chicago. He'd send the plane for me. We'd fly from New Jersey together, then he'd return me to New Haven in time for Christmas with Melanie and Chad. As always, I confided my plans to Chris.

"It's going to be minus zero there," Chris said. "Get him to buy you a mink."

"He's a nice man," I told Chris. "We didn't have that kind of a relationship."

We were playing with the Lancome at Neimans. All I needed was mascara. We'd done enough damage to our wallets for the day. A velvet Valentino halter with a rhinestone clasp, a red pillbox from Bonwit's, a Vuitton duffel from Saks, a Limoge inkwell from Tiffany's for Chris. Puilly-Fuise with lunch, coke with dessert. The day at Bal Harbour had been our Christmas gift to each other.

"I'll take this in black," I said to the powdered saleswoman. Her nearly bald eyebrows had been drawn in with a brown kohl pencil.

I slung the flowered Bonwit's bag over my wrist. Carry these, I said, handing a cluster of bags to Chris. I wanted to carry the hatbox; it made me feel so Holly Golightly.

It had been a year and a half since I'd seen Philip. We'd stayed in touch but I hadn't agreed to visit again, I was still sour about New York. But he practically begged me to see him. The chef is from Paris, a menu not to be missed, he'd said. And I consented though couldn't help thinking about how he should rightfully pay me for my time. I was a professional now. He didn't know it and wouldn't, but I did and I wasn't interested in giving away freebies. But still, I didn't think I had the nerve to ask him for a fur coat.

"Besides," I said to Chris, "when are Philip and I going to have time for shopping?"

"You don't have to be mean about it," Chris said. "Just tell him you don't have any winter clothes and he'll have to take you to Marshall Fields." He checked himself out in a mirrored pillar, lowered his Ray-Bans.

He was beautiful and I was overcome with gratitude that we were living together, that he was my confidant, my best friend. I wanted him to feel the same about me, to think I was amazing. And he did. I linked his arm in mine. "So, I guess, once I have him in the store."

"Exactly," Chris said.

We entered the esplanade. The December sun winked through the palm trees, it felt good on my face. "Do you dare me?" I said.

"I don't have to dare you, darling," he said and kissed my cheek.

I was a different person from the girl Philip took to New York, and he sensed immediately that I didn't have the patience for his being cheap with me. But he was full of compliments and hand-kissing and all that refined nonsense he'd thrown at me before. He must have had fond memories of the night he'd taken advantage of my naïveté.

Like Chris said, it was cold. The wind in Chicago ripped like ice through to the bones. I'd definitely need more than my Burberry lined trench, so it wouldn't be a stretch to complain.

In the suite at the Four Seasons, waiting on the credenza next to fresh cut lilies, was a jewelry box with a solid gold bangle inside. "It's beautiful," I said. "But unfortunately, you'll have to take me to Marshall Field's, this raincoat just won't do. It's freezing."

"But we have reservations," Philip said.

Chris's words gave me unusual courage. "Change them," I said and smiled sweetly.

At Marshall Fields, I went straight for the fur department.

"I know someone in New York if this is what you want," Philip said.

"But we're not in New York," I said. "I need it now."

And just like that, the credit card went down. The saleswoman said she'd wrap the tags and I waltzed to dinner in my new full-length mink.

Philip stayed to meet his family in Chicago for Christmas, so I traveled alone the next day to Tweed, the private jetport in New Haven. It was gray there and dirty with remnants of the previous snowstorm. Melanie picked me up and gave me a raised eyebrow when I deplaned in the new fur. I ignored her condescension, climbed into her Saab and gave her cheek a peck.

"Cute car," I said. "Did you know the cops in Aspen drive Saabs?"

"Yes," she said. "So what day do you leave?"

Could it have killed her to act happy to see me? Or to even acknowledge that I'd just stepped off a private Lear?

"The twenty-sixth," I said and felt a tinge of guilt that I'd made the flight for only two days later. At the same time, I knew that our civility had a short shelf-life.

"That's good, because we're meeting Chad's family in Vail for New Year's and I'll need a couple days to catch up with my work before then," she said.

The airport hangars and gas stations gave way to homes with barren trees and icicles hanging from porch eaves. Christmas lights had come on in the early winter dusk. I was reminded of Cheryl's tree, the one we were never allowed to help decorate, the perfection of tiny colored lights blinking from the living room's giant plate-glass window.

"Where's Chris?" Melanie said.

"With his family in Boston," I said. Florida was a place you fled from during the holidays to other places that you considered home. As if it was a purgatory that you returned from annually to receive your mandatory rationings of love.

"It's too bad he couldn't come. He's such a great guy," she said.

Despite her disinterest in me, her saying something positive about anything that concerned my world was a reprieve. The tiniest of affirmation was all I ever needed.

"The turkey's in the oven and Chad's already home," she said. "We have cider, too."

Those touches made me believe that our habit of Christmas together wasn't just the obligation we'd fallen into since we'd left Carpenter Lane. We knew Cheryl and Daddy were visiting her parents in Harrisburg, though they never shared their plans with us. But that check always came with Daddy's efficient block penmanship in the Daniels business envelope.

The windows were fogged with our breath and obscured the dismal day, but not the feeling of Philip's soft hands, reverent as he traced my body with them. I'd let him have me because of the gifts and the door-to-door jet service. It'd been a choice this time, and I thought I was satisfied by the transaction, but I shuddered, disgusted by the memory. "That cider's going to be good," I said.

Melanie was at her mirror, French braiding her hair. I'd never had the knack for it and always felt clumsy watching her precision. I sat on her bed. The room was outfitted in Ralph Lauren; her balloon shades matched the bedding. The warm air smelled of bayberry and roast turkey.

"He didn't even call me on my birthday," I said. Though we tried to avoid it, we always ended up talking about Daddy.

"I don't care as long as he sends a check," Melanie said.

"He always does," I said. I'd told my father this time to keep the check, buy me a one dollar card and put a stamp on it. I'd be much happier. He said, now I know why they call women bitches and hung up on me.

"You never knew how to play the game," Melanie said.

"I stay out of the way and call with specific requests. I don't need his attention."

I hated when she said that shit. I was defective because I had feelings. Because I cared.

I looked through her shoebox of pictures. She had all the good ones of Mommy. Of her. Some of me: in a playpen, crying on Nana's lawn, on the beach. Never smiling.

"Sometimes I still wish Mommy was here," I said.

"You're too sensitive," Melanie said.

"Easy for you to say," I said. "You remember her."

I put the pictures away.

Melanie took a mint green pullover from the shelf in her closet. There were neat rows of clothes, like in a store, price tags still attached. "Isn't this cute?" she said. "Loehmann's. Twenty bucks. I got it in every color."

The clothing would be held captive in Melanie's repository of material acquisitions until she purged them. Then items would be exchanged, returned or wrapped in a gift box for someone else. Her Christmas gifts to me had no store tags, size extra small. Her size. In my stocking was a Yo Yo Ma cassette. I had no idea who the hell it was, and so insultingly, without the cellophane. Open, used.

We were meeting Chad at the movies to see The Color Purple. I rifled through Melanie's make-up case and stopped at a tube of Chanel lipstick. My Brilliant Red lipstick. The lipstick I'd misplaced and had been searching my luggage and her house wildly for since the day after I'd gotten there. She snatched the bag, zipped it and threw it in her dresser drawer. "Hurry up," she said. "We're walking out in five."

Chapter 40

The white cardboard sign read: Daniels. The barrel-chested chauffeur driver seemed burdened by his girth as he took my carry-ons. He delivered stale deference with the congenial smile of one who'd been doing the same everyday for twenty years.

It was late February and New York was cold and gray, reminding me of what I didn't miss about Northeastern winters. I was pleased, though, to have a reason to wear the mink. I maneuvered over gutters that were full of filthy ice, then had to laugh at myself when I slipped in my pumps, nearly falling into the back seat of the Town Car.

We took the Triboro. The skyline, though dingy with winter, thrilled me the same as it did the first time I saw it. David put me up at the Helmsley Palace, one night. I was jet set, satisfied to be returning to New York in such a grand way. Finally staying with someone I wanted to be with, and, at the place that was deceptively dangled in my face during my previous visit with Philip.

I called David from the in-house phone. I was escorted from the lobby to the fiftieth floor of the towers by a stiff white-gloved attendant who addressed me with eye contact and shifted on his heels to ease his eternal deportment. The ceiling of the elevator was painted with blue sky and clouds, like up was heaven At the double doors of his two bedroom suite, David's benign embrace covered me in soft shelter. My trepidation of what I meant to him, my meticulous wardrobe choices, my fervid trip to Saks before I'd left where I purchased myself the bottle of Ombre Rose, fell away —it was only easy.

Dozens of pink roses in vases made the room cheerful despite the ugly weather beyond the heavily draped windows. The suite was crowded with suits, lawyers, bankers, accountants, I presumed, closing files, packing up briefcases. And David in jeans. "We're done now, aren't we, gentlemen?" he said. The men collected their overcoats, said their goodbyes.

"You don't even dress for a meeting?" I said.

"A little lesson in business, dear," he said and hung my fur in the closet. "The one in the least impressive clothing is usually the boss."

We saw I'm Not Rappaport at the Booth Theater and ate dinner at Cote Basque.

"If I lived here I'd want to see a Broadway play every week," I said, sipping the 1975 Château Lafite-Rothschild Burgundy David ordered in perfect French.

"If you lived here you'd take it for granted," he said, rubbing bread crust in the butter on his plate. He made extravagance feel normal, in the entitled way that said he'd never known hunger. I aspired to affect the same airiness, but knew former deprivations would never permit the charade.

I let him order for me without looking at the menu. I knew he'd pick something right. I didn't feel the need to assert my independence but I couldn't pinpoint why. Really, what had he done for me? Except that when I was with him, my life wasn't in fast forward. Time stayed in the present. I didn't want whatever I was doing with him to be over so I could get to the next thing.

Back in the room, David kissed me as if I was the drops of water that quenched the tongue of a parched man. He inhaled my perfume –our perfume –pulled me into his lap. I didn't tell him that I wore it every day. "The smell reminds me of you," I said. Then he undressed me with a blend of tenderness and passion that felt simulated, pretentious. He didn't give way to lusting savagery and hadn't the apologetic desperation that came with inexperience –I'd grown accustomed to those kinds of men –he was romantic and it beaded off me like water on wax. But being touched by him felt natural enough, even necessary.

I didn't want him to please me, to allow it was weakness. Real pleasure could mean love, and love had torn me to shreds. Physical need for me had become humiliation –I only came if my thoughts were degrading. The orgasm was submission, punishment. To love and lust for someone in equal parts was a hazard I could no longer chance. Death was on the other side. And though I kept that secret, it didn't fool David.

"You've never enjoyed yourself with me, have you?" he said.

Of course, I lied. My brain was heavy with wine. I needed sleep. I wanted to wake up again with David and I wanted to go back to Florida.

In the morning, the car company rang, signaling that our time together was up. David got my coat. I felt small when he folded me in it. A sad child, foolish in the fur I'd convinced myself was right for me. When would we see each other again? My eyes welled and I wanted to smack myself. The trip next month to Antigua, the boat, was too far away. I'd miss him, I said. I hated the way it sounded coming out of my mouth.

"You always do this," he said, wiping my cheek with his thumb. I was horrified by my transparency. I didn't love him. He leaned out the door and watched me with a paternal eye until I stepped into the elevator.

Chapter 41

I thanked the Lord for my Anne Klein sunglasses and my good fortune to be driving North, not East into the sun. It was daybreak and I was fucked up. The turnpike was, as usual, swarming with Florida State Troopers. I'd need to be careful for a couple more exits. What was Donna going to say when I walked in? I'd left in the middle of the night while she slept off the jetlag. What was the time difference from Milan? I couldn't remember. So hard to think. I'd have to tell her everything.

Donna returned from Europe without the boyfriend. She'd been upbeat about this being her plan all along but I suspected there was something more going on. It seemed like I wasn't the only one with shameful secrets.

It was my luck that one of my new regulars had called. At a grand an hour, the money was too good to pass up, and if not for the drive to Coconut Grove and the client's paranoia, the job would have been easy. Bob was a rich base junky, which meant that he always had another pipe for company and a bottomless supply.

Last night he was scary, answered the door with a gun –his Rottweiler jumped and barked, sniffed my crotch but was OK when he realized he knew me. Bob was on a two-day binge. He sucked on his pipe, paced torch-in-hand, kept peeking out the drapes.

A job like him required a lot of nodding. I listened for three hours to his delusions about the bad men and never asked a question. I didn't want to know about the people he talked about. Sometimes I thought it was the FBI, other times maybe the people he was in business with. Either way, the less I knew the better.

I sat in my bra and panties and set myself up another hit –little white rocks sizzled in the bowl under the flame. The rush of smoke to my brain, it was the only way to handle it. I'd have hated to be there if he ran out. Not that it would happen, there were always a couple kilos stashed nearby. For the money, it was easy, no sex. When I dressed, Bob went to a suitcase, took out a stack of bills. Five grand. A tip.

"Come back later," he said. "Bring a friend."

"Page me," I said.

I intended to get home before Donna woke up. It wasn't fair to leave Chris with the task of explaining my disappearance.

I parked the SL in Chris's driveway, the house blocked the sun's glare. Cars drove past, front doors closed with normal neighbors leaving for work. Inside, Chris and Donna were asleep. I tiptoed, got the Absolute out of the freezer, mixed a drink, chugged half of it. I'd tell her the truth. It's what best friends did. I took a long drag of my cigarette and caught a glimpse of myself in the hall mirror as I exhaled. My makeup was still perfect.

I turned on the shower, dropped my clothes on the floor. The combination of steam and tobacco was sickening but I ignored it. To choose between the nicotine and a shower at this stage was impractical. I climbed myself into the tub for ritual decontamination and left the burning cigarette on the edge of the sink. I quickly scrubbed my hair and everything else, too wigged-out to linger. Not that any effort would make a dent in washing away all the chemicals I'd ingested, all that I'd smoked.

Donna's voice startled me.

"What time is it?" she said while she peed.

"About seven," I said. The tiled walls were claustrophobic. The toilet flushed and Donna retreated –my cue to get out. I held it together but my hand shook as I pulled the towel from the rack. The butt left a brown stain on the sink's edge –I'd need to clean that before Chris saw it. Wrapped in a towel, I swiped a wet hand across the mirror so I could survey the damage. Mascara rings. My nose wasn't destroyed because we'd been basing. I used toilet paper to blow it as reassurance that I could. I dried off, finished the vodka and got my second wind.

It was easier to stay up than to force myself to sleep. I cut lines on a mirror, then told Donna all I'd been doing since my break-up with Niles.

"I'm an escort," I said. "A call girl."

Her eyes bugged when I threw the cash on the bedside table. "I'd be scared I'd get hurt," she said, took the straw, did a hit.

"I've never heard about that happening," I said and held my wet hair back while I did a bump.

"Can't you get busted?" she said.

"You're supposed to ask if they're a cop when you get there, but I never do, it's too low class," I said. "I only see regulars anyway."

I spilled the rest about the clients, the money, why it didn't bother me. Why it was excellent, even fun work.

How good things were, living with Chris. She believed me, she didn't judge. No worried lecture followed.

We dressed for the beach between catching up, bumps and drags.

Donna confessed how she'd left her cheating, drunk-ass boyfriend in Italy.

Rolfe was a fashion designer and Donna modeled his stuff, as did a parade of other chicks. She'd fallen into it, not that her beauty was in question, though she wasn't particularly tall and she'd never had any aspirations to the life. She'd learned the catwalk and acquired some haute style by osmosis. She'd sent me pictures, magazine ads – *editorials* she'd called them; some I'd framed. I was proud of her.

I never liked Rolfe. He criticized Donna's weight in front of me and monitored her food intake. I'd even caught her putting on lipstick before he woke up so he wouldn't see her clean-faced. What the hell are you doing, I'd said, mortified. And I'd felt guilty because, though I meant to condemn Rolfe, it sounded more like I was blaming her. But maybe I was. I expected Donna to adhere to higher standards than I could. Self-abuse was a choice, but woe to the man who tried to belittle me without my authority.

"I'm going home until I figure things out," she said.

"You can stay here if you want," I said, having learned the hard way that support was all that was warranted in these situations.

In the kitchen, we poured drinks.

"God, you two starting already?" Chris said. He joined us fresh from the shower and rested for work.

"Continuing," I said. "I went out last night."

He glanced at Donna to gage her reaction.

"Don't worry, I didn't drag her with me," I said. "She got plenty of sleep."

"Maybe you should, too," Chris said laughing and grabbed a granola bar for the road.

"I can sleep when I die," I said, it was Athena's joke for when we'd stayed out late and had to work the next day, but it didn't feel funny in light of all I'd just been through.

On the way to the beach, Donna and I stopped at Federal Express. Melanie was in trouble with some credit cards and needed two thousand. Nothing was ever how it seemed. How imperfect Melanie was, and I bailed her out without question. That she even asked me for help and I could provide it was enough to make me feel like I was doing something right.

I addressed the triplicate carbon label on the gray Formica.

"I saw Matty when I was home for Christmas," Donna said, tugging at her bikini under her shorts.

Matt was Donna's high school boyfriend. He dressed in beat military jackets and worn jeans, dealt pot, and worshipped Donna. They'd been the perpetual couple, dramatic break-ups, hunger strikes, obsessive sex, though Donna had other guys in between.

"Did he try to get back together?" I said, sliding the cash into the cardboard mailer.

"I reminded him of what we were allowed to talk about —no *I can't live without you baby's*," she said, giving me a drag off her cigarette while I rummaged my wallet for a twenty.

"Which didn't leave much but weed," I said. We laughed.

"He asked about you," she said.

I'd always liked Matt, we'd been friends since seventh grade Social Studies. He'd changed a lot from that thick-haired quiet Italian boy who wore white sailor pants the first day of school. "And you told him I'm doing great," I said.

"I asked him if you and he had ever gotten together," she said, hugging herself against the freezing air-conditioner.

"I haven't seen him since graduation." I'd hung out with Arlene that week. Driven Jeff's Lincoln back to Philly. I'd worn high-waisted Chic jeans and a turquoise tube-top with sculptured red nails. Matt had an extra Van Halen ticket because Donna was still at boarding school –it was something to do.

"I meant, if you ever slept together," she said.

"I can't believe you just said that," I said, stunned that Donna had questioned my loyalty all these years.

Donna climbed in the car. I started the engine and put it in reverse before she shut her door. "It's just because Matty always thought you were a fox," she said.

"Just because a guy thinks I'm cute, I have no say?" I said. "Matty was your boyfriend."

"It's not like you haven't slept with someone else's boyfriend before," she said.

Bitch. Finally, it was out –not even Donna let me live down my big high school mistake.

"Kelly and Frank were broken up, she was with Mike

Chasen," I yelled.

"But he was her first, they were in love," Donna said.

The school had been ablaze with the gossip that Frank and I were hot and heavy, and Kelly never forgave me, though she'd claimed to be over him. She didn't want Frank, but nobody else could either. From then on, I never treaded the sacred road of discarded boyfriends. Donna had always, at least to my face, defended me and to be accused so many years later of having slept with Matt, it was incomprehensible.

"I was fifteen," I said. The traffic light turned green and the car behind me laid on the horn. I floored it.

"It's only that Matty made it sound like you had," she said.

The tires squealed when I turned onto A1A.

"I'm the one who introduced the two of you. If we wanted to be together, we'd have done it long before you came into the picture," I said. "I thought you forgave my mistakes. Now I feel like I don't even deserve the safety of one real friend."

I screeched to a halt in front of the Surfrider Hotel where Melanie and Chad had stayed and we'd planned to spend the afternoon. "I'm really hurt," I said, taking the valet ticket.

Donna took her time following me through the lobby. Our connection snapped like an over-stretched rubberband. And I knew that our friendship would never be the same.

Chapter 42

I met David in Antigua in March at the St. James Yacht Club –a swank island resort with white sand, striped umbrellas and a marina.

"Come see the boat," he said and I followed him down the dock that serviced its vessels of grandeur, their names splashed in elation across the sterns. Winnie's Cloud, Troubador, Knotty Dog.

Anthem was a sailboat, with a crew of four and a chef. We had wine in crystal and a candlelit dinner on white linen. I'd been on plenty of yachts with Leanne but none equaled David's in its simplicity, its luxury. Understated, the way real wealth behaved. Like Laine's family. This is how David dealt me glimpses into his world, and I understood now why he never talked about money, why he downplayed everything. Despite our time together I was an outsider. I needn't be privy to his personal matters; he thought he should protect himself from me, and I felt idiotic in my previous assumptions. I knew I should hate David for treating me like a sycophant, duping me with his modesty, that I should rank him with the other men I'd been seeing, but instead I craved the refuge and wanted his approval. To what end, I didn't know. But leaving Florida, if only for the weekend, felt like temporarily stepping off the recent merry-go-round of drug fueled all-nighters, the incessant pager, and the parade of bloated, impotent, narcissists with credit cards and penchants for two minute blowjobs.

The thing was, David only knew a shard of the prism that was me, but it was the sliver that I held back from everyone else —my vulnerability —so, more precious, more deadly. And he didn't warrant this knowledge, did he? But he hadn't hurt me, not yet, anyway. And maybe he didn't have to.

We left Antigua by moonlight and sailed to St. Barth's while we slept like stowaways in the captain's quarters. David said it'd be the best sleep I ever had, and it was. I woke up to an empty bed, without knowing how long the boat and I'd drifted, how hard I crashed. Maybe I'd exhausted myself more than I knew, or maybe I felt safe hiding out on the Atlantic, untouchable, unreachable, as the bed rocked my dreams with the ocean.

I dressed in a bikini and washed in the bathroom. It was larger than most I'd been in, though, like in all boats, cup holders were bolted, latches kept cabinet doors from opening, mirrors were braced. I'd been on speed boats and yachts that were docked or cruised the Inter-Coastal, but never for any length of time in the vast empty blue. I felt confined by its trappings and bored with the silence in general. The cabin pitched, despite the craft's hundred and thirty foot length, and I steadied myself on the sink.

I hoped I'd missed most of the journey and wanted to emerge on the deck with our destination in sight. I splashed water on my face, dousing my chest and dripping on the carpet. I figured that was the norm, given the roll of the boat, though I hated being messy. I brushed my teeth and took in my rested reflection, then thought, with sinking pity, that because of my alleged self-righteous freedom, I was ashamed of having accomplished nothing. Each day seemed to fold into the next without movement. What the hell was the use of collecting massive piles of cash if all I did was buy things and travel so I could teleport out of my own existence? I wanted to do better but didn't know how. I'd buried any recognizable fraction of myself and now I was biding my time. Until what, though? I wished someone would tell me what was next.

If Mommy were watching, would she be horrified? Would she let me know, would I hear her? I'm OK, Mommy, I said to myself, and I gulped down the tears the way I taught myself to do when I had these frequent surges of insignificance. Wait for clarity. It'd come. I was still young and I could always start over. Again.

I peed. Leave it to David to have all the comforts right down to the normal-sized commode. I leafed through the luxury for sale on the pages of an abandoned Robb Report. My self-consciousness about taking a crap in the confined quarters made me aware of how even my compulsory bodily functions had become spaces and dashes.

What I'd been doing with Leanne wasn't going to last. I couldn't continue to put my life in danger with free-basing drug dealers, or dress myself for hire every other night to party with girls who didn't have a brain in their head for anything but waxing the hair around their cooches. And I had to admit I was a lazy call girl. I never primped or wore my best expensive lingerie for clients. I showed up in cotton g-strings and t-shirt dresses and expected whoever to consider themselves lucky they got to touch my flawless, dewy skin. I'd gotten to the point, and it hadn't taken long, that I'd initiate the proceedings by pulling my clothes over my head, get the guy off, wash off the assault and collect the money, all within fifteen minutes. Mostly, though, the only calls I'd answered lately were the drug kind where I was able to avoid any tangible physical contact. It's what I chose but it was burning me alive.

I put moisturizer on my face; I looked remarkably good for the damage I'd inflicted on my body. David couldn't tell what an empty suitcase I'd become. I was an unflinching actress; everything effortless, life was daffodils.

When I surfaced, we were anchored between two islands. David was reading a money magazine over breakfast and he rose to greet me. He nodded toward the larger, distant land mass. "That's St. Maarten," he said. I hadn't realized we'd be so close.

The steward or first mate or waiter or whatever, dressed in navy deck shoes and white tennis shorts, poured me coffee. His polished American smile was pleasant, his hair as neatly combed and parted as a Ken doll, his presence unimposing.

"The crew will sail her to the south of France, we'll meet in Cannes next month, then I'm there for the summer," David said breaking our uncomplicated quiet.

It was odd how people referred to their boats as her or she, like cherished loved-ones and it sounded peculiar coming from David. I bit into the warm blueberry muffin, a glob of butter melted onto my sliced strawberries.

"Glamorous," I said sarcastically, but I wanted to go. There was always that better party I hadn't been to yet. Being invited fit with my image of what I thought things should look like.

Then he said, "You can come."

I turned my face into the wet breeze, it blew my hair into soggy tangles and the salt settled in my lungs. Low swollen clouds would let loose an early shower, but the sun was pressing through and we'd land on one more beach, and another day would be taken for granted. "What about Mrs. Cardona?" I said.

David leaned on the rail and took in the calm of St. Barth's with its few early risers strolling through the petite town, packs of dogs, and boats embarking. He looked over his shoulder at me, smiled in his way that implied, my darling, you know nothing of the world. "You'll meet me in London first," he said.

I wondered what better I'd intended for my summer and couldn't come up with anything. "What makes you think I don't have plans?" I said.

"How rude of me," he said, "of course, if you're too busy." His tone was playful, ironic. I wasn't offended that he thought I was silly. I allowed myself the notion I had something to look forward to, that David was granting me a fixed end to my stint in mindless purgatory. I went to him, and after a lingering hug, he led me back to the stateroom.

Chapter 43

I drove with the top down and cranked Pat Benatar – *love taker, don't you mess around with me,* to drown out the ear-aching noise of an incoming plane. The clinging stench of jet fuel pissed me off more than the hair-whipping wind. Being marginally disheveled was part of my fuck you in the face of the pageant I was about to perform.

"I'd only send my best to this one," the phone girl said, pandering. She'd probably said the same thing to all three chicks she called first. How hard could it be, really, to be her *best*, when hair color was the primary criterion by which one was usually requested? "An easy two hours," she said, like my suicide was a holiday.

I turned down Dania Beach Boulevard, then onto a dark, neglected street. The house was set back in an overgrown yard. There was a 70's model tan Buick the size of a bus in the driveway. I shuddered at the thought that large insect eyes were blinking from beyond the unlit Florida brush. I walked at a fast clip and caught a heel on the edge of one of the flagstones. I shook the willies off on the landing. A dim lamp swarming with mosquitoes lit a screen door that looked like scrap from the junkyard. I yelled hello and banged the rickety frame.

I thought how I'd kill that ambushing phone bitch, with her "he's a good tipper" song, and ignored flashes of a cleaver-wielding murderer. Next time, I'd stay at dinner with Chris.

The whir of metal, rubber and motor. A glow backlit the wheelchair. Winsome eyes, sloped at the corners, looked up in submission. His wheat mop of hair was long and unkempt. His hand moved a lever and wheels whirred in reverse. Faded newspapers were stacked against the wall, cobwebs cradled dust that obscured the table light and the sofa's seat cushions sunk unevenly into broken springs. I tried concealing my shock with peppy chatter but ended up sounding more professional than I intended –smiling mechanically, overdoing the eye-contact.

"Could I get you some tea," he said, his composure deflecting my skittishness.

I wanted a drink. He had Chablis in the fridge. My heels sounded ridiculous on the cracked tile. He whirred to his Frigidaire with the cumbersome pull-handle. Whirred to the dingy white and gold-speckled Formica table. I sat in a wobbly vinyl chair, fluorescent-lit like a criminal, drinking a jelly jar glass of tart box wine. It went down fast. I thought of Jeff's friend who'd come back from Vietnam paralyzed, he drank a case of beer a day and sharpened his hunting knives –the war his excuse for being an asshole. I tweezed a knot of lint off my black miniskirt with my red acrylic nails and pictured the head of the phone girl dripping with blood on a spike.

The cripple said he'd called for just company, but I knew he wanted more, didn't they all? I wanted to know what happened to him, what he could feel, what it was like, if he despaired. I wondered if he pitied me, too, and I wished I could do my phony naked dance without exposing my self. I flirted and gushed and stroked his arm.

"What do you do when you're not doing this?" he said, like he saw me.

And I succumbed with frankness while he actually listened. We talked for hours like friends and he tipped me double. He'd seen through my clutter, and I knew that he was a compassionate man, that my time hadn't been wasted on him and, at the same time, I hadn't left unscathed.

Chapter 44

Chris and I stopped at a water-front restaurant in Key Largo on our way back from a Key West party weekend. We'd stayed near the beach in a kitchenette apartment that one of Chris's friends lent us but spent little time there because of the amount of bar-hopping we'd done.

The seafood joint was salty and decorated with fishing nets, buoys and shells, like every other place on the highway, though this one had fancier cars parked out front. We saddled up at the shellacked wooden bar. The place was dark in contrast to the bright open-air, but we kept our sunglasses on. I ordered a cheeseburger, and Chris, the fried Grouper with Bloody Mary's. The eating part was a formality before we'd finally hit the bathroom and get to the drugs we both carried. It was something we joked about daily, but it was becoming less funny.

"Did you give that hairdresser your number?" Chris said. "You were all over each other."

In a town like Key West, the only anonymous recreation I was going get was from the girl's who were down there for the same reason the boys were. I shot him a *yeah, right* look over my shades. "Not a lesbian, just a tourist," I said.

The drinks arrived dripping from the fresh stir of horseradish and Lea & Perrins. No Mr. & Mrs. T's mix at this roadhouse, but the specialness was lost on us. We drank them without celebration.

"I didn't mean that the way it sounded," I said.

"Yes you did." We laughed.

Laine surfaced at times like this, when I was between the forgetting. I wondered if, after everything, I'd end up with a woman. Would it be that much of a stretch? I certainly wasn't close to anything deeper with a man.

"I thought I might be once. In another life. Before Jeff," I said. "Gay."

"Please, honey," Chris said, his fag-bag vibrated and he pulled out his beeper, checked it, rolled his eyes. "Niles."

"No seriously. I never told you about Laine?" I knew I hadn't, I never told anyone about her. But she'd always lurked there, tucked neatly in my memory attic. "We met in prep school," I said.

"Never even told me about prep school," he said, crunching a leafy celery stalk. "And here I thought I had all the dirt on you,"

Odd, with our parade of true confessions, we knew so little about each other.

"Who has time with all our drama? The saga before the saga," I said. "My dad sent me there junior year. Anyway, she was my best friend."

"Laine, huh?" he said.

"Short for Elaine. I guess her family nicknamed her that and it stuck."

Laine, who'd only known me separately from that confused girl I'd been and left behind at Carpenter Lane. The clean slate me, the pure me. No history, no future, in a strange, suspended time. In a dream. "Whatever. I like dick. The second I hit summer break in Myrtle Beach, I was back to my slutty ways," I said.

"Knowing you, she was probably rich," he said.

"A Senator's daughter," I said, giving out her status helped to justify my actions. Money equaled OK. I always did that, dropping those little gems, while prancing around with my frivolous friends. But Chris was different and so was Laine. And I suddenly regretted flaunting her like a show horse. She'd meant more to me than that.

Chris saw my wistful face. "You loved her," he said, more revelatory than prodding.

Gulls fought over something discarded on the dock, their squawking intensified the throbbing at my temples. "No, I was just lonely."

Maybe it had been love. We'd been like children pretending to be grown-ups. A couple who snuck into each other's dorm rooms after dark to make out and explore each other's wanton teenage bodies. I'd chalked it up to having been sent to an all-girl's boarding school. Where would any vital, daring girl let herself go when faced with the option? Laine had been the first person to look at me with that kind of honest unconditional regard. I'd soaked it up like a drowned flower does its first day of sun. I'd never felt that total sense of abandon with Jeff –that combination of lust and love. But how would that translate back in the real world beyond Pratt? It wouldn't. The diversion was meant to be over when school was. Had Laine thought so, too? I'd never know.

Chapter 45

Airport hotels made me feel like a hooker, but one of my regulars got bumped from a flight and had called the agency. It was an easy two hours and the rest of the night still lay ahead.

Exhausted flight attendants and pilots rolled little black suitcases through the hectic lobby.

I stepped into the lounge to buy a pack of cigarettes. The leather booths and round cocktail tables lit by votive candles made little dent in the functionality of the joint.

"Parliament Lights," I said to the bartender in a low, authoritative tone that meant don't small-talk me.

An instrumental version of Rocket Man piped through the speakers. A couple drinking wine from cheap stemware sat without speaking, three guys on barstools wearing shirtsleeves and generic ties checked out a group of foreign coeds and a man sat alone with his briefcase wearing khakis and docksides. I recognized him; the slump over his rocks glass, the slope at his crown molded by his flat, colorless hair. *Joe McClure.*

My pulse quickened. First with fear; I wanted to duck from my past. But anger held me trancelike. There'd been no emancipation from the shame that had become the dreary nuance of my existence since he'd left me floundering after that distant weekend in Charlotte, when he'd pimped away the last of my innocence.

I grabbed my smokes, took the chair opposite him. "Look what the dog drug in," I said.

The stupor drained from his face and he lit up as if he beheld the grail. "Robin Daniels," he said. "What the hell."

I ordered a Sea Breeze and we dispensed with his you-look-amazing-where've you-been business, all the while me noticing how below average he was in his modified golf attire. He was now a regional salesman for Ocean Pacific, hence the briefcase. Was that supposed to be a step up? Had he sold his company and the club, had his profits gone up his nose? I didn't give a crap; I didn't want or need anything from him.

The polyester office brigade had made their move on the tourist girls and were now seated at their table. The girls laughed uncomfortably at what I could only imagine were brainless jokes, while Joe stared at me affectionately as if he'd been reunited with an old army buddy.

I resisted the urge to shudder. What a gargantuan presence he'd been when I was merely a child. And it wasn't that long ago, was it? But it'd been centuries, really. Now he only looked oily and tired. I almost pitied him.

He inquired about the state of my current vocation.

"It pays for the Mercedes," I said with pleasure, and despite my umbrage with him, I relished the brief escape honesty afforded me.

"Come on, you can't be making that much," he said, chewing on the end of his cocktail straw, his voice excited, as if he were being let in on the particulars of a sure-fire grift.

I didn't have to justify myself but I couldn't help it. He was the fugitive carnival barker who'd corrupted me and

I wanted to make it clear that I was now, and always had been, above him.

"Five an hour, minimum two," I said. "Five grand a night." I blew smoke in his direction, surprised by my memory of how he barely tolerated cigarettes. "But what would you know. That's the city, babe," I said.

"High class," he said, the words *high* and *class* a contradiction coming from his mouth.

Then he said, "You must know where to get some blow."

"Not here," I said, fighting the compulsion to brag about the stash in my purse; I'd given him all I ever would. I checked my Rolex without actually registering the time. "Besides, I'm off."

"Aw," he said, pouting for effect. "I'll buy you dinner."

His expectation was contemptible. Always the salesman.

The music changed, some nameless disco, and two of the European girls got up and danced tableside on the corporate carpet.

I took my last drag and sip, dug for my keys.

"I'm here a couple times a year," he said. "Give me your number."

"Please," I said, standing. "You can't afford me." Then I left without looking back.

Chapter 46

Chris's parent's spacious retirement condo held memories of an entire life. Ornate middle-class Italy-inspired furnishings with gold velvet fringed throw pillows and a framed gallery of Chris, his sister and the grandchildren on the marble mantle of the unused fireplace. Sunday night dinner with the Rossis had become a regular thing. Sometimes Leanne would join, or others from our crew, but for me, if I was in town, it was sacrosanct. The pasta was plentiful and Chianti a staple. Vince and Sophia welcomed me and made me feel temporarily accepted. Once again, I allowed myself to be taken like a stray into the fold of the most normal situation available and handed over custody of my soul to the next willing guardian.

I cleared the dishes from the table. "Chris says you're going to Maine for the summer," I said, taking a towel to the dishes that Sophia had washed.

"Every year," Sophia said. Her smile lingered on the photo of Chris's sister Doreen and her children stuck by a magnate to the fridge. "You know I can't stay away from those scrumptious little ones."

"Not so little anymore," I said, handing her a dried platter.

"I know," Sophia said, arranging the cabinet. "All the more reason not to miss a minute."

I knew the kids, Jerry was eight, Riley was ten. Chris and I'd gone to Disney World and Epcot with them. They'd adored me. I dressed in neon mini-skirts and mouse ears, we'd taken pictures with Goofy, spent a whole day at Wet-n-Wild. It was the first time in years I'd felt normal.

It was a grandmother's right to gush, hadn't my grandmother done the same? How distant we'd become, how far I'd traveled from those innocent days. I'd felt ashamed I hadn't called her recently. I'd do so before I left for France.

Chris came over with a green plastic watering jug, reached the long spout over the sink into the potted herbs. "Poor starved things," he said, sarcasm in his smile. "Sophia, you have to *water* them."

She laughed. "This one," she said, giving his arm a love-pinch. "He doesn't let me get away with anything."

I'd never once called Cheryl or Daddy by their first names. I'd heard friends occasionally address their parents in this manner but always with an air of subordination. And I still cringed at the memory of how Jeff had addressed Daddy. But here, Chris's respect for Sophia and Vince was implicit; it only felt right.

Sunday night was the only time I saw TV these days. 60 Minutes was on and the four of us watched together, lined up like cardboard targets at a firing range on the firm gold striped sofa. The upcoming trip to France couldn't have come at a better time. I needed some perspective. The novelty of the fast-life had tanked and things were slipping from my control; I was more guilty and polluted than lucky these days.

I'd been free-basing with Leanne until noon only two days before in a gated mansion in Miami with two guys who paid us ten thousand each in cash taken from the trash compactor.

I leaned into Chris, as if touching him could zap the image from my head. He knew my exploits and still, he loved me. It was times like this, when I was depleted, when I felt momentarily safe, that I didn't care he was gay; I could envision a life with him.

Vincent and Sophia watched silently next us. Sophia had been so interested in my decoy job as a step-aerobics instructor, asking at dinner how things had been going. I'd told the truth when I said all was well at the Sunrise Club. She didn't know I only taught there once a week to facilitate a free membership. I kept up the lie because I knew when I did, the wholesome girl inside me shined through. With her eyes, I saw my way out. It's what kept me from disappearing into the abyss.

When the 60 Minutes clock ticked into commercial, I broke the numbness of moment and went to the powder room. The pink-veined marble was dressed with paper hand towels and flowered guest soaps with dried suds. I was light-headed. I'd recovered from the previous day's ruin and had abstained from doing a line. I figured Chris and I would wait until we drove to the Alley.

June 1986

Chapter 47

The sun made me squint when I emerged on Hill Street. I was glad to be out of the dank apartment. It was June, for godssake, and I was wearing a sweater. I didn't care that I was staying at one the most expensive residences in London, it was damp and cold. The lift creaked like the knees of a cripple. I thought it was cheap of David to put me up at his friend's place instead of the Dorchester which was only blocks away.

I walked down Audley toward Sherpard where there was an open air market. I wore ballet shoes for a day of comfortable tourism. David had left after breakfast for Paris and dumped me with his friend Stan Rhodes, the owner of the flat, who I'd never met but was coming in from San Francisco and taking me to dinner and a play.

A beige Rolls crept behind me. The ghostly beak-nosed driver wore a precise comb-over and sported a navy blazer with a fucking ascot. I was immediately self-conscious in my orange leggings and matching straw bowler, like I was wearing a billboard that said I didn't belong in the pristine flower-boxed neighborhood.

The passenger window rolled down, the geezer puckered his non-existent lips and blew me kiss.

"Take a picture," I said, because he made me doubt myself, because he made me feel at once all the judgment I endured at Carpenter Lane, at the parade of country clubs, at my string of jobs —that I wasn't welcome, that something was wrong with me. I was too enthusiastic, too outspoken, too pretty, too sexy —just intrinsically wrong. And, as always, it wasn't me. I had every right to walk wherever I wanted, in fashion's color-of-the-minute through corpse-town without being harassed.

I retrained my focus on the beauty of the day, the tea and scones being consumed at café tables, cut flowers in buckets. I thought how nice it would be to have a sunny window near a market like this, to once again grind coffee beans like I had with Jeff, have wine and Brie in the fridge, a Siamese cat maybe. I was angry with David for leaving me in London. *It's business.* I felt eerily alone.

Stan Rhodes held a slice of bread and smeared butter with the gesture of a medieval blacksmith slapping metal against oiled leather. He was muscular and youthful for his thirty-nine years but for his cornfield of wavy blond plugs. I wondered at his vanity, hair transplants were as obvious as toupees. If he'd let it alone, he'd still be a chiseled hunk. Still, I couldn't help imagining him cupping my entire breast with one of his brawny manicured hands.

"Me and David have done quite a few deals," he said. His Harvard air did little to disguise his beefcake frame hulking over the pressed table linen and floating gardenias. "David's a smart guy. But if I were you, I wouldn't get too involved."

We drank burgundy from radiant globes and I realized then what I didn't like about the expensive bottles I'd been downing lately —it was how grown-ups drank. Not the party crowd I liked, but the middle-aged, rich, bored. The somber establishment. I wanted marinated vodka in chilled shot glasses and sushi, instead of Châteauneuf-du-Pape and filet mignon.

Stan, of course, was oblivious, imparting the obvious to make himself seem more appealing.

But had I felt more for David than I wanted to? "It's not like that," I said. David had given me nothing. No money, no clothes, no commitment, dare I say, not even an orgasm, yet I was drawn to him. He was certainly an entertaining escape. Maybe I stayed around because I didn't know what was next with him. So why did I feel so empty when we said good-bye? Whatever it was, I was looking toward a good summer on the Riviera and I wasn't going to let Stan Rhodes put a damper on it.

His ice-blue eyes reflected the color of his pullover. He smiled at me and made yum noises in acknowledgment of his first taste of sizzling beef.

London hadn't been so bad. I sped through Westminster Abbey and Parliament, had my picture taken with the Nutcracker guard in front of Buckingham Palace, and sent gifts from Harrods to Melanie and Chris, all in one day. I'd gotten more done by myself than I would have negotiating someone else's agenda. But for the first time in forever, I wished for someone to share the experience with.

Cap d'Antibe was a huge bore. We'd been in France for a month and all David did was lounge in the cliffside castle. He read the paper, in drawstring linen pants, made interminable business calls, insisted on leisurely wine-paired three-course lunches, and then he wanted to fuck. It was fine for a week but the novelty wore off. I felt imprisoned being so far from Cannes, which at least had a pulse running through it. Though we went to Hotel du Cap most evenings, the crowd was snooty and old for me.

I explored during the day, pulling the Porsche over to take in Côte d'Azur vistas, but I felt lonely, and it became apparent to me what being a mistress meant: isolation, unshared recollections, wealth that wasn't yours.

Chapter 48

The day I met Helene, I'd gone to meet Charlie and Aziz for lunch in the neighboring village of Juan-les-Pins. The beach was crowded with lots of wide-brimmed hats and high-heeled sandals. I'd gotten used to the topless beaches and sunbathed in a white g-string. When I went to get a drink, Helene stood at the bar in a bikini with bottoms that puckered around her tanned boyish hips. Her light hair spilled out of a knotted bun and freckles like bread crumbs sprinkled across the bridge of her nose.

"You should cover up," she whispered to me in thick-accented English. "It is vulgar to be at the bar without the top."

I was instantly humiliated and looked at the hundreds of undressed women three steps away on the beach. I remembered I'd done this every day, and wanted to disappear. But I casually returned in my top, despite my faux pas, never allowing myself to be shamed by my ignorance. "I could die," I said to Helene, seated on a stool, watching soccer from the tiny bar TV.

"Do not be embarrassed, the Americans, they do it all the time," she said.

We sat on wrought-iron patio chairs outside her family's cafe not far from the beach, tearing at baguettes and pouring anise into tiny cups of steaming coffee as the low afternoon sun made everything look dipped in caramel. Our exchange was amicable —she pantomimed broken English, I butchered high school French.

I talked about my divorce, sexual conquests and how I'd refused the orderly walk to conformity. "We have fun," I said about David.

"But what about love," Helene said.

"Not now," I said, but as the words passed my lips, I thought, hadn't David finally convinced me of the scarcity of my alternatives? Wasn't I only aspiring to someone with David's wealth and laissez-faire to fall unreasonably in love with me and rescue me from my decline?

A pointy-chinned teenager slouched at the table next to us while his mutt licked his toes. France's charm definitely had its limitation. Things I'd heard romanticized I hated the most, like dogs in restaurants.

David taught me the French word for disgusting: dégoûter. I liked it. It fit.

"How long ago, this husband," Helene said, re-knotting her hair at the back of her head, exposing tufts of golden hair under her arm.

"Three years in August," I said, and thought about all that I'd done since walking out on Jeff.

"Time to leave purgatoire," she said.

There I was, on a treadmill of purgatory. Convinced I was experiencing life, but instead, with each capitulation, a bit of me erased. Now my confessor was this girl who barely spoke my language. "Things will be different when

I go home," I said, feeling the boost from the espresso, wishing it were something stronger.

"To Florida," she said.

I was instantly frightened at the thought. Florida wasn't the choice. Despite my pretending to the contrary, I'd failed to find happiness there. New York had always been where I wanted to go, since my trip with Philip, but I didn't know anyone.

Handmade saffron and blue paisley curtains ballooned from open windows in Helene's apartment. Wilted lavender in vases covered cluttered surfaces.

I felt sorry for Helene, that she didn't live in a nicer place but she didn't appear to mind; to the contrary, she was proud of her thrift store decoration. "I collect from rummage sales," she said and showed me a cracked mosaic-tiled bowl spilling loose dead rose petals on the beaten wood floor, the space between her two front teeth sweetening her smile.

Wind chimes played on the breeze from above the rust-stained kitchen sink, cutting the beam of dust-laden sun that projected shadows on the faded wallpaper.

I lifted her cat to my lap and rubbed between its ears while Helene read poetry she'd written from a frayed pink notebook. I heard something about love on the lips of boys in flowering fields. "That's beautiful," I said, not letting on that I really thought it sounded childish.

"We go to Eze tomorrow," she said, showing me a picture of a medieval village atop a mountain. "You must do more than the beach." She turned the page to a picture of an ochre bell tower. "Nietzsche lived winter here," she said.

Nietzsche was someone I only pretended to know about so I nodded while she showed me cobblestones flanked by olive trees, petite shops with arched entrances and stained glass. I imagined us exploring the narrow roads together and felt my open hand run along the ancient stone walls, my fingers riding over shrunken grooves of mortar.

I wondered why she was being so nice to me, but I loathed passing up invitations, afraid of missing something fabulous. "What time should I be here?" I said.

Helene made me feel like the France wasn't a waste. She worked nights in the café but during the day we toured the surrounding villages.

David didn't mind, to a fault. It was as if we were on different vacations. We ate breakfast on the patio under the trellis, the air fragrant with wisteria and rose. Finches chattered, honeybees buzzed.

"When do I get to meet your girlfriend?" David said from around the pink Financial Times.

"Not my girlfriend," I said, "and you know you have an open invitation to join us." I finished my croissant, worried about the amount of butter I was consuming on a daily basis. I felt fat but couldn't stop myself from licking the jam and grease from my fingers.

"You never need me to have a good time, darling," he said.

He smiled at my excursions like I was his niece on vacation, doling out etceteras —you can see why Renoir lived in Cagnes-Sur-Mer, don't miss the Notre Dame Chapel when you go to the lighthouse —to imply his interest, to insure that I knew he'd already been there.

The cream in my coffee had turned into a swirling film. I was meeting Helene at the Picasso Museum at noon and needed to shower.

David followed me upstairs. "Invite her to dinner," he said when we got to the bedroom.

His sudden attention was artificial consolation for his having been so absent. "She works nights, but I'll ask her," I said. I tied up my hair and shed my robe.

"Let me run your bath," David said. He did things like that, tiny pretenses of romance that kept me hooked, distracting me from my irrelevance to him. It was how I interpreted his random deeds as loving and ignored his ambivalence and unavailability.

I smoked naked on the balcony while I waited for the bath to fill and watched his boat anchored in the cove; the water glassy against a clear sky, the hillside bright with bougainvillea. David took the cigarette from my hand and snubbed it in the ceramic ashtray. He traced my collarbone with his finger.

"Let me brush my teeth," I said, but he was already poking his hard-on between my legs.

"Have you kissed her yet?" he said.

Fury rushed to my cheeks. "No," I said.

"It would be fun, the three of us," he said, kissing my neck.

There had never been a moment when I thought, hey, what I really need to spice up my rationed time with my non-boyfriend is another girl in the bed. Even if I was interested in Helene, the fantasy wouldn't include him. Men loved the idea of seeing two women together, but it was never about that. The second the kissing commenced, enter the dick. It was all put your tits in my face, let me see your ass, why don't the both of you suck it. If I went there with David, he might as well be a client.

"She's a nice girl," I said. I slipped from David's embrace and headed inside. "I wouldn't even ask."

"*You're* a nice girl," he said, holding my hand, pulling me back to him.

I was transported beyond disappointment to disgust. Up until that moment, I'd been convinced that we were doing something unique. But he'd spun me like a top, until our arrangement was my idea. *No ownership.* It sounded revolutionary. But at some point I'd bought into caring more about what he wanted, bowing to his experience like he was some kind of Buddha. And here he stood in his Alain Mikli's and boxers, proffering an ordinary middle-aged fantasy, it was everything I'd come to escape. But it was useless to convey my thoughts; we had nothing other than what we did.

Underwater I tried drowning the marching band of dread in my head. My hair swirled like Medusa's while I swam the length of the pool; my body suspended in the light. David had taken Helene on a tour of the house and all I could think of was how he wanted a threesome. He was going to make his move and I allowed it, like a pimp.

Maybe I would have objected more if I loved David. But hadn't I, in some sick way, loved him? Otherwise why would I have been so chapped about his wanting Helene? Because it wasn't about his penchant for deviance, it was that he couldn't let me have something benign without pissing on it.

I pushed up from the bottom; wiped the water from my eyes. Helene could handle herself, right? David wasn't a monster for godssake.

I swam the front-crawl, the stroke a memory, like a friend. I'd competed once, before my hair and make-up took priority. There was a person before this; there was a girl who'd lost her mother, not herself. And she swam and rode horses and won awards. I thought how offering up my friends like a sacrifice had, in the past, given me power. I'd cultivated it and I'd felt it was worldly, in vogue. But now it just felt tawdry.

I gulped breaths with each stroke, barely able to fill my lungs, my throat sore with restrained tears. So I swam and I cried, the relief of my moans muffled by water and I thought: who will save me? Dignity might have prevented this but I wasn't taught dignity. What little remained was like an oily rope I clung to, trusting I'd have the strength to pull it one day.

I hooked my elbows on the side of the pool, unable to appreciate the crescent moon or perfume of the night-blooming flowers. I only thought of who I'd become, if I could change, was there hope. Would anyone put their arms around me, say it was going to be OK? It was a senseless wish.

Helene descended the stairs like Cinderella fleeing the ball at midnight, her tear-wet face impetuous. She sought me out. I was wrapped in a towel, hair dripping wet. "He kissed me," she said, walking the length of the room to the dining table and back. "He said you knew." She stood, her arms crossed, eyes landing on me long enough to emphasize her disdain.

"I'm sorry," I said, and I was, because I liked her; still, I resented her high-attitude, as if I was beneath her. And I hated David for his disrespect, not of her, but of me. And I wondered how I'd let my being shamed become inevitable.

"My purse," she said, "where is it?"

I found her bag in the foyer and gave it to her. I knew I wouldn't see her again and she'd have a bad opinion of me, and I was humiliated and angry with her for making me guilty.

"This man, he is not good. I am sad for you," she said and left.

I watched from the door as she puttered away in her rusted yellow Mini. The girl had unselfishly lent her time and I failed at decency. I wanted to defend myself, to yell, How dare you judge me. But you have to believe what you're defending before fighting for it and I didn't.

Chapter 49

It was the end of July and I was ready to leave. David had fallen from his plinth like a delinquent angel; from whatever I made myself believe we had, and now I felt dispassionate and guarded about him the way I did about Jeff after he had betrayed me long ago. When I checked in with Daddy, he told me about my cousin Julie's wedding in Toronto and I used it as an excuse to end my European summer early.

David seemed unaffected by my choice, said only, "Too bad you're leaving so soon, we could have traveled together."

I was relieved we weren't. He probably thought I thought he was offering me his sincere regret; like just being in his presence was all I ever needed from him; his daily disregard, his lewdness, his commonness, all to be excused. But I'd already demoted him to someone I'd only keep around for what was occasionally needed: introductions, free dinners, theater tickets.

I was hesitant about attending Julie's wedding. We'd been close cousins before Mommy died but had been extremely distant since. Daddy never got along with his brother Mike and Melanie was utterly dismissive of them; she had no use for the sentimentalities of family bond. The invitation, though, felt like I'd been included; more so by Daddy and Cheryl.

Emerging from customs at Toronto International felt eerily familiar, and I thought of Jeff who'd been living there a year by then. It had been almost three years since we'd split, and the knot of remorse around those memories was still nagging, but the comfort I felt at the thought of him nearby was immediate, and I wished we could meet for coffee, confide, be close again.

The line in the restroom was long, everyone exuding the same distress of flight exhaustion mixed with the urgency to pee. While I inched along, I thought how easy it would be to call information, get Jeff's number, say hello. Surely, he'd forgiven me by now. We'd been best friends, loved each other for Christsake, we could let bygones be bygones. Maybe reconnecting with him would reconnect me to the good I knew that was in me; help me move toward the fresh start I imagined for myself.

I rooted through my bag for hairspray and eyeliner, gave my bangs a tease. My lipstick was the same pink as the scarf I'd purchased in Eze, which I'd tied loosely around my neck. A little Parisian flair. It had been over a year since I'd seen Daddy; I wanted to look my best.

A lone filthy yellow vinyl suitcase knocked around on the baggage carousel while impatient travelers checked their watches, as if doing so would make their luggage materialize faster. I went to the row of payphones and called information from the cleanest one I could find; Jeff was listed. Staring at the scribbled number gave my stomach a jolt. Jeff would be happy to hear from me after all this time, wouldn't he? I would be if he called. He had to be with someone else by now, maybe even had good news about his business, his family. I'd feel more grounded knowing these things, feeling as if we'd both been pardoned for being human.

The first bags rolled down the ramp, my flight's LED numbers blinked. I dialed through my fear but wanted to run at the same time, half-hoped a machine would pick up, but he answered.

"What makes you think I'd want to talk to you," Jeff said.

I was stunned, devastated, pissed off. "Jeff, come on," I said. "Despite everything, I still love you. We lived together for four years. I don't know why we can't be friends."

"I don't want friends like you," he said, his voice intimate and alien at once.

"I'm sorry to hear that you still feel that way," I said. Why did I think Jeff and I could be friends? Never in the time we were together did he forgive Christine. He only spoke of her in unflattering ways and I encouraged it, feeling superior to her. Why would he be different with me? But still, for him to be so caustic, after so long. I was assaulted and sad for him at the same time.

"Why would I associate with someone who does the things you do?" he said.

Seized with panic, I angled myself into the phone, as if turning my back on the day-bright terminal would make me evaporate.

He couldn't possibly know what I'd been doing. I hadn't even spoken with him since I'd returned from Lake

Tahoe. How could he have known about anything since? I wondered whether he was even aware I'd moved to Florida; certainly, he wouldn't have information about me. He was only still angry about the divorce, maybe about my reputation of having slept around in the following year, his idiotic assumption that I became a lesbian.

"What things are you talking about," I said, convinced his comment had nothing to do with the dumpster of immorality I'd been exposed to since our marriage.

"It doesn't matter. You left, that's enough," he said.

I was a pinball of humiliation, rage and doubt. I felt responsible for his bitterness. "I wish it could be different," I said.

"Well, it can't," he said.

He was being a prick because I'd wounded him. It was true, we were different people now, but our break didn't dispel the essence of who we'd fallen in love with. I hadn't forgotten his kind nature, his sense of humor, and I'd prayed we'd eventually relent from our resentments. Maybe I was wrong, maybe it was still too soon, but there was no way to say those things succinctly.

"I always want the best for you," I said, wanting him to say the same. I listened to his silence and tried to compose myself, despising my need for his exoneration. I regretted having made the call.

My Hartmann suitcase tumbled down the conveyor belt and fell in line with the others.

"Goodbye," I said, wanting more from him, hoping to hear something that would alleviate the sting. But the only thing I heard was him taking another drag off his cigarette before he hung up.

I felt Daddy's presence before I saw him. He and Cheryl were with Uncle Mike and another couple. I excused myself from the best man, distracted by what I detected to be simmering anger beneath my father's courtesy smile as I crossed the room to him.

My first thought was *what did I do*? Was I talking too animatedly, drawing criticism from my Uncle? No. Uncle Mike was delighted to see me. Was it because I had a drink in my hand; I'd never quite gotten the hang of adult behavior in front of my father. Maybe I should have waited to come to the ballroom with him and Cheryl, but he'd never mentioned that he wanted me to.

Cheryl stood out in the crowd wearing a Laura Ashley floral dress. She hadn't changed. She was laughing at something the woman with Uncle Mike had said. She could never speak to a stranger without overdoing her pretend interest; oozing her insuppressible postulation that she was superior in every way to the troglodyte she was enduring.

Uncle Mike received me with a squeeze. "Quite a girl you have here, Will," he said.

"Yes, quite," Daddy said, his expression contorted.

I kissed my father, then pecked the cheek my stepmother offered.

When Uncle Mike left to greet another couple, Daddy grabbed my arm and forced me to the dumbwaiter. My face burned.

"You look like a high-fashion model," he said.

"What's wrong with that?" I said, but my father's glower told me that everything was wrong with it.

"I couldn't get in the room without someone mentioning my beautiful daughter," he said. "Why do you always have to make a spectacle of yourself?"

I thought looking sharp was a good thing. It's what I aspired to. Hadn't everyone been complimentary? Hadn't Aunt Liv been proud to introduce me to everyone? If my mere presence was considered a transgression, I had nothing. But didn't I know that? I'd never been enough, I'd never been anything.

I saw Cheryl set her purse at a table. I knew I wasn't going to be invited to sit with them. This time the tears gave way. I went for the door.

Aunt Liv caught me in the hall. "I don't know what your father said," she said. "But whatever it was, don't let it ruin the night." She put her arm around me, turned me back to the party. "Let's have a good time." She must have known my father hated me.

The telephone rang from black emptiness like a locomotive. I plundered the nightstand for the receiver.

"Steve wouldn't happen to be with you, would he?" Julie said.

Steve. Yes. The best man. He was breathing next to me. I was in Toronto. I opened an eye, the clock glowed ten-eighteen. I pushed the receiver at him, climbed from under the cord. Stumbled into the heavy curtains, moved the shade. Sun pierced the room like the lid had been lifted off a tomb. I closed it.

We'd barely slept. It wasn't the blow, it was the sex. It had been too long since I'd wanted it like that.

I passed up turning on the bathroom light, peed with the door cracked, heard him hang up. If Julie knew to call him here, maybe everyone did. I'd gotten laid at my cousin's wedding and there was no hiding from that.

My eyes adjusted to the dark hotel room. The mauve dress with a heart-shaped neck I'd purchased at Eaton's for the wedding was inside-out in a pile on the floor. A more modest choice than the one I'd worn to the rehearsal dinner. Steve had fucked me in it, consumed by taffeta.

"I have to go to brunch, make a toast," he said, his voice a hoarse groan.

I hadn't been told about brunch. I felt ostracized but justified it as an innocent oversight. Daddy probably told Aunt Liv my flight was leaving early; it had nothing to do with the stud in my hotel room. But still, no *Gee I'm sorry you can't make it* from my cousin.

I brushed my teeth and rubbed at the residual mascara. This guy fit me like a wetsuit. At first I dismissed the connection as drug inspired; I hadn't partied since I'd left for Europe; but he kissed me like he meant it, forcing me to do the same. His strong hands made me feel vulnerable and protected at the same time. It took me to a time when I knew who my type was, and we were immersed for hours. How love was supposed to feel, hadn't I felt it before?

Long before David, before my clients, before Niles. Never in Florida. Maybe in Tahoe. I'd gotten lost in Evan for a while, hadn't I? But I'd denied myself those precarious indulgences. I didn't want to fall in love; I didn't want to be married. Wasn't that the danger? I'd be right back where I started.

I went to Steve, the naked curve of his torso like sculpted bronze on top of the crumpled sheet. I'd shunned such beauty and I'd missed it. I pulled him into me, inhaled his scent of sweat and lust. I needed to get back inside the feeling. Suspend myself there because I didn't know when I'd permit it again.

Chapter 50

Melanie stood at her kitchen counter eating brownies from the pan. She could eat chocolate three meals a day and never gain a pound. "It's not that bad," Melanie said. "We've gotten used to it."

Now that she moved to D.C., into the first floor of a Georgetown brownstone, Chad was working on some Senatorial campaign and on the road most of the time.

"But you're finally living here," I said, sorting a hamper full of our co-mingled clothes. I intended to make use of the shared laundry room downstairs, as I always tried to be helpful when I visited Melanie. I never wanted her to accuse me of being a burden. "You must miss him."

"Not really," she said, sipping milk from the carton. "We haven't had sex in like six months."

"You're kidding, right?" I said.

I knew their careers had always been the most important thing but I didn't think a marriage could withstand that much time apart, despite the fact that they convinced themselves it worked. "Well, if your husband's not getting it from you, he's getting laid somewhere," I said, separating the hand washables.

"Not Chad," she said, "he's way too boring."

I wondered if David's wife thought he was too boring to go to France with another girl. "I'd keep an eye on him just the same," I said, then loaded the clothes into the basket. "Unless you want to get rid of him."

She stuck crumbs from the counter to her finger, ate them, licked her teeth. "I had a dream last night that I was in a raging river, struggling to make it to the bank and you were down stream yelling for help," she said, matter-of-factly. "I decided to save myself and swam away."

Melanie's disregard for the feelings of others bordered on sociopathic —I'd learned the condition: *a person who lacks a sense of moral responsibility and social conscience*, from my Psyche 101 class at Wilson, and it forever stuck with me. She considered empathy a weakness. "That's heartwarming," I said.

Later, I called Chris at the jewelry store collect from a payphone in Georgetown Park while Melanie did a second lap around the mall. I was beat, hadn't purchased a thing but a pair of foam shoulders pads, and the phone call was a good excuse to sit and have a cigarette.

"It's like telling someone you've been watching them sleep while you contemplate strangling them," Chris said when I reported Melanie's dream.

"Then, get this," I said, "My dad put two thousand in Melanie's account for us to share. You know I'll never see a dime of that."

"Why didn't he just give you separate checks, let you open your own account?" Chris said.

"It's his way of making Melanie feel she means more to him than I do," I said. "That she has better judgment, that she's more dependable than me." I knew my father was still punishing me for my birthday card comment and I felt like he was never going to give me another chance.

"Forget about her, what are you going to do next?" Chris said.

"Drum roll. I'm moving to New York," I said. "It's time. I'm going back to school." Some kids with Day-Glo dyed, gelled hair smoked in front of a Top Gun movie ad and ashed in the potted ficuses. Wannabe punks, ridiculous posers, unlike the ones I'd seen in London.

"I'm relieved," he said. "There's so much more you could be doing."

Chris was the only who could say that to me without it sounding like condemnation.

"I don't know which school or for what yet, but I'll figure it out," I said.

"David referred me to a real estate person. She's already looking for me. I'm taking the Metrorail up there tomorrow," I said.

"You have enough money?" he said.

"For a down payment," I said. I'd stashed twenty-seven thousand. I figured I'd be set for awhile. I organized my wallet, arranged receipts into one pocket, removed a wadded-up gum wrapper from the change purse. "If I need more, God forbid, I'll get a straight job."

"Are you ready for that?" he said.

"I have to be sometime," I said. Spending time with Melanie had only helped highlight my failures and her indifference to me made me feel invisible. I wanted to prove her wrong. "I can do without the jonesing myself to sleep every night."

"You weren't that bad," he said. "Don't be so hard on yourself."

Chris tried to soften the glare of my disintegration by coddling me when I was vocal about it. Melanie was steps away, checking out the Ann Taylor window for the third time. I thought how my life would be easier if I could despise her without exacting loss. "Here she comes. Big kiss," I said, then hung up in time to intercept her before she ducked into another store.

September 1986

Chapter 51

I'd been in New York since August and three weeks at a new waitress job. Café Mirabel was a happening restaurant near Nineteenth and Park. It was a perfectly fine place to start. I averaged one-fifty a shift, so the outlook for supporting my mortgage was good.

Most of the wait staff did coke, so it wasn't long before I was passing vials with the others on bathroom breaks and winding down with a group at one of the Thirty-Fourth Street pubs.

It was the end of one of those nights out after a long week when I hitched a cab uptown with Kevin the assistant manager. He was in his forties with a close-cut beard and had air of self-importance common to Food and Beverage lifers. He'd been girl-gossipy with the bar bunch and I chalked it up to the booze.

The cab turned up Sixth at Herald Square and cruised through the night quiet. A cigarette was poised between my fingers, but the breeze through the open window calmed me, and I didn't need to light it. The ride was quick through synchronized green lights.

Things had gone well. I loved my neighborhood and the restaurant. I felt like I'd rejoined the human race. I'd made the right move. Before long I'd be back in school. When the taxi stopped at the red light at 54th Street, I saw the Hilton and I thought how Philip Baines had patronized me years ago, the way he patted my knee when I suggested living here. It'd had been a long road but I made it and smiled in my accomplishment. Things happened the way they had, it wasn't perfect but now I owned a New York City apartment. I'd grown up.

Kevin had been talking shop in my ear the whole way –the usual complaints about scheduling and not enough time-off. "My wife's having a baby," he said.

"Congratulations," I said.

"Yeah, should be great," he said, with negligible enthusiasm.

I doubted that the wife was going to continue to be cool with his partying after work.

The cab stopped in front of my awning. "Do you mind if I come up for a little? I'm still amped," he said.

A presumptive move. Then I thought, why not? I'd been isolated, hadn't had anyone visit. And Kevin hadn't once made me feel he was interested other than as a friend. He'd be easy enough to kick out. He was the one with the blow and I wasn't ready to call it a night either.

"Sure," I said, feeling sheepish when my doorman let us in.

Kevin chopped some lines on my kitchen counter, did his first. "Nice place, but it looks like you could pack up and leave in a minute," he said as he surveyed my sparse decor.

But I was proud of the uncluttered room. Melanie had inspired my dumping the needless stuff. It felt fresh, like I'd cut off all my hair. "It's better to travel light," I said, sounding more intriguing than I intended.

I put a Pet Shop Boys tape on, poured some leftover wine, all I had, and we did another couple lines. After pointless coke talk with Kevin snarking about work and me babbling about how my failed marriage kept me from going to college, I was tired and bored. It was already three-thirty and I didn't want him around at dawn.

"It's late," I said. "I need to go to bed, so it's time for you to go."

I thought he was going to stand but instead moved closer. "Come on, don't make me leave like this," he said.

He was trying to avoid the come down. The last thing I needed was him freaking out in my place. If he thought he was getting some action to soften the edge, I had to dispel that notion immediately.

"I don't have so much as a beer in the fridge and everything's closed," I said, taking the empty wine glasses to the kitchen.

"I thought you liked me," he said and followed me.

"I do like you," I said. "But you're married."

I shouldn't have let him up in the first place. It was going to be harder than I thought to be a nice girl.

He took my arm; I pulled away, emptied the ashtrays.

"We work together," I said, trying another tactic while he lit another cigarette that I didn't want him to smoke.

"But we're having a good time, aren't we?" he said, removing his already-loosened tie.

He was getting comfortable. Now I'd have to be mean about it and he was my boss.

"We were," I said. "But now you're over-staying your welcome." I refrained from telling him how out-of-his-league I was. He had to go. I handed him his blazer.

He snatched it from me and threw it on the floor, with wildness in his eyes. I was thrown by the danger. He was too sure of himself.

I was worried about the doorman and neighbors in my new well-mannered building, for my new job, for my physical safety.

He yanked my wrists, pulled me to him and kissed my mouth. I felt the bruising already. I'd gone my whole life without this kind of thing happening, but how? Maybe I'd sensed the crazy, steered away from it. Why hadn't I caught it at the bar?

"Get off me," I said, wrestling him without apology. But he slammed me against the wall and my head hit hard. He laughed at my resistance with sinister satisfaction, a laugh under his breath. The fight turned him on and I didn't know what to do with that.

He was confident as he dragged me to the floor. He'd done this before. He was hard against my leg as he undid his pants, holding me down with one arm. He was going to rape me. Ridiculous. Ironic.

He yanked off my bra, bit my nipple, but I was too frightened to the feel pain. As strong as I thought myself to be, I was no match for a grown man. This man was going to hurt me; it was a question of how much.

His hand squeezed my throat. There was coolness in his brutality. How many girls had he done this to before me?

He ripped off my slacks.

I remembered what I knew about this: remain calm. Surrender. I'd get one of my mafia clients to torture him later.

He straddled me, sat on my arms, pulled the belt from his pants. I stared at his face. He wrapped the belt around his hand, like my father had done too many times. I braced myself.

"I've had worse. Have at it," I said in a controlled whisper. "Think about it," I said. "For one lousy lay, you're going to die."

He shoved himself off me, the belt unraveling from his hand. "Cunt," he said. He spit on my face and stumbled for his clothes.

I crawled for my torn clothes to cover myself.

"Stupid fucking bitch," he said. "You're not going to say anything. The doorman saw me come up with you and everything was hunky-dory." He knew no one would believe me. He swooped up his blazer and left without looking at me.

I doubled-bolted the door and collapsed against it in a shaking heap.

I compelled myself to the shower and scoured until my fingers were prunes.

After, I cleared away any evidence of the night, put my work clothes in the garbage with the cigarette butts and empty wine bottle and took the bag to the incinerator. I wouldn't be returning to the job.

Chapter 52

Plaza Athenee oozed the same prudent distinctiveness as the townhouses that shared its Sixty-Fourth Street block. It was the ideal place to re-initiate myself to the life I'd so pompously dismissed as beneath me only months before.

I'd been matter-of-fact when I called Blair in Miami for a number. She introduced me to a madam who lived in Gramercy Park; they'd worked together in their heyday, now they referred each other girls. Courtesan alumni. God help me.

This one was pulled tight and buffed like marble. She called me to her boudoir, a canopied, heavily-draped sanctuary where she lounged and studied me like a prospective owner might the lines of a racehorse. "Turn around," she said, her tone perfunctory.

I did because I didn't care.

"I'll be sending you to the most conservative and elite men," she said.

Yeah, I thought. Aren't they all?

"You'll come here before every date so I can check what you're wearing," she said.

"No problem," I said, but I had no intention of cabbing it to her place every time I got a call.

The Athenee's lobby was festooned with shiny black shoes, gold watches and cufflinks. The lovely world of money greeted me with the smile I'd become used to. Doors were opened, second glances discreet. Prince somebody, the madam had said. I was to meet a Marla here.

Simple to dress in Valentino, easy to flaunt my beauty, effortless to slip back into the warmth of being in demand.

A butler answered the bell and led me to the living room of the suite; everything unpretentiously lavish. The Prince in his sheets was visible from the other room. His attendant in navy Italian released the cork from the champagne but poured only for me.

Marla, my partner, arrived, sublime in taupe Chanel and sling-backs, her casual charm enhanced by Marilyn-blonde curls. At dinner, we pretended to be friends, and after a couple of quick hand jobs, the usual routine with Arab royalty, we left together.

"I took one of the Lalique ashtrays from the bathroom," Marla said once we were on the street, tilting her purse so I could take a look. "It always makes me feel better," she said. The chuckle in her voice made me laugh, too.

We stepped into a Korean market, bought smokes. "Two-seventy-eight?" she said to the little man behind the register. "Tax? The next thing I know you'll be taxing the air," she said out loud to the store.

Brash with style. I liked it. "By the way, it's Robin, not Mandy," I said, extending my hand over a bucket of cut flowers.

"Claire," she said. "You want to get a drink?"

We crossed Central Park in a taxi. The September night blew a good feeling through the windows, dissipating the rancid vinyl odor.

"Mortgage and a new Andrew Marc jacket," Claire said. She stuffed the folded cash deep inside the zippered compartment of her bag, the crystal on her lap. "Who says crime doesn't pay?"

I felt like we already knew each other. There was no *why are you doing this* to wade through.

"Things have really gone my way since I bought that brownstone," she said. "It's been a good year. I'm socking away plenty in mutual funds."

"I spent all I had on my down-payment," I said, trying to sound like I was on her level, knowing I wasn't.

"Don't worry about it. There's more where that came from," she said, her voice a combination of sarcasm and authority.

I knew my shame hadn't served me and my guilt absolved nothing. Resistance hadn't kept me from being an actual hooker. If I embraced it like Claire, I'd get out of it sooner.

I took the stick of Dentyne she offered, savored the familiar cinnamon taste.

"When I'm done getting a degree, I plan to make millions investing my blood, sweat and tears," Claire said while she blotted her nose with powder.

"Where are you going?' I said, casually, like all escorts were merely errant coeds.

"Hunter College," she said. "I can walk there from my place."

I'd never heard of it but what the hell did I know. "I want to go back to school, too," I said.

"Why not? It's never too late," she said with delight. "We're beautiful girls, no one can blame us for cashing in while we're young."

A violinist played in harmony with the car horns, his case open for donations on the corner of Central Park West.

"You'll like Columbus," she said. "The last time I was there, Tom Selleck bought me a drink."

A couple of dancers, skirts over tights and their hair pinned in buns, crossed the street, their carefree strides almost a skip. I was saddened by their lighthearted beauty.

We stopped in front of the restaurant and I paid the fare. When Claire said she'd get it the next time, it felt good, like we'd already decided there'd be one.

Chapter 53

Stan Rhodes *looked* like someone I should be interested in, so when I got on the plane for an English country weekend he'd invited me to, I convinced myself that he'd be a viable boyfriend. I also took pleasure in knowing that since David had introduced us, our dating would get back to him.

The sex, however, was disappointing. Stan was ham-handed like he was storming the gate of a medieval castle. I suppose I'd have been floored if he drew a weeping orgasm out of me, I'd have to marry him then. And the wine hadn't helped; it made me sleepy instead of horny.

I'd wanted to like him because he was rich and handsome. I'd planned to overlook his hair plugs and his boorish self-involvement for his hefty stock portfolio. The moonlit chandelier sent shadows across the heavily molded ceiling and I thought how outmoded the room felt, like we were being projected in black and white.

Stan collapsed on me. I might disappear and he wouldn't notice. I wiggled from under him. I knew where I was going without the light but turned it on anyway because he bugged me. I felt him drip down my leg and I thought how unjust it was that not only did I have to wash while he snored, he was probably lying in a puddle on my side of the bed; another argument for *leave the money on the dresser.*

His flat was cold as I remembered when I'd stayed there before going to France with David. I wrapped myself in an itchy wool blanket and went to the barren kitchen. I wanted something warm and sweet to eat but instead picked at a leftover scone. I didn't understand scones; no amount of sugar or fruit made them taste any better than sawdust.

We were leaving in the morning for the country. The engraved invitation was from Lord Timothy. Funny that Stan didn't invite a date from town, I had to be imported from another country; some local girl probably wouldn't be impressed by suburban royals. I didn't want to be mean, but it was going to be a challenge to tolerate him for the rest of the weekend without pay and then let him go with his dignity intact.

I couldn't remember when I'd been so insufferable or treated somebody with such obvious scorn as I did Stan on the drive to Cheshire. My patience with him dwindled after his second wrong exit. "West," I said, pointing with venom. I loathed nothing more than caution behind the wheel mixed with incompetent navigation.

"*You* try driving on the left side of the road," he said.

I squirmed in the passenger seat and sighed, as if doing so would force him to hand over the keys. But he ignored my petulance and continued to forge ineptly ahead. We sustained our discourse through Stratford-upon-Avon and over the rolling lush Cotswold countryside.

The trip had already taken four hours, and we were still two hours away.

"I think it should be mandatory for anyone who wants to get married to rent a car in England for a weekend," Stan said. "It would immediately answer any question of compatibility."

"So then you'd never get married," I said.

"You can't let up," he said.

We stopped and leaned on the car, pretending to be interested in a flock of sheep while Stan chugged the rest of his ginger ale and I smoked.

"You really should quit that," he said.

His moral superiority grated my last nerve. "Now who can't let up," I said, close to screaming *take me to Heathrow.* I inhaled deeply, enjoying the lightheadedness the nicotine provided. I'd tolerated much worse than Stan, but then, I was getting paid, so the money took the edge off. Unfortunately, I wouldn't get the satisfaction of throwing *that* in his face.

I stepped on the butt and blew the last of my smoke at him.

The wind made whimsical patterns in the tall grass on the hillside. The moment needed to be shared with someone special. I felt guilty. He was dull, but he was a nice guy.

"Hey, I'm sorry I've been a pill, can we start over?" I said, hoping to salvage the weekend.

"No problem, kiddo," he said.

So easy. Smile, shut up, fuck. That's what he wanted, that's all he needed.

We continued up the countryside.

"I talked to David," he said. "It's funny to see him so heartbroken. Since he prides himself on being such a Lothario."

My face flushed. Wasn't David the one who insisted Stan might be a good choice for me? At the same time, I felt validated by his jealousy.

"Uncanny, to see him so in love," Stan said, shaking his head.

Something wasn't right.

"The girl he met in Paris this summer while you were visiting," he said, responding to my confused look. "The married redhead from Toronto."

I lowered my window, suddenly needing air.

"Talk about devious," he said. "Wearing her perfume around the house, pretending he's avant-garde so his wife doesn't notice he smells like another woman."

I was wearing that perfume, as we spoke. Ombre Rose had become my signature since David had introduced me to it. I was horrified. How could I have been so naïve? David didn't want me to be like him, he wanted to commingle his deceit. He was sure to have had a good laugh at my expense. What an idiot I was. My throat ached from stifling the rage. I stared at the passing scenery, unable to absorb it.

Stan was quiet and drove deliberately for the remainder of the trip while I swallowed the poison of my humiliation; he didn't need to know I cared in the least.

Stan and I arrived before sundown and were promptly shown to separate rooms. Maybe it was good taste not to assume one was already sleeping with their weekend companion, or maybe it was the usual hypocrisy –everyone fucking but nobody copping to it. Whatever it was, it saved me from having to share the cramped antediluvian room and gave me some brief privacy.

My suite was all starched linen, doily-covered antiques and burdensome drapery. I was surprised by the gift basket filled with chocolates, French body lotion, and monogrammed slippers. I popped a fat dark truffle into my mouth, climbed onto the high bed and mulled over what Stan told me about David. I hadn't gotten past the first swallow when Stan tapped on my door, peering in before he was invited.

"You wouldn't have any hair gel, would you?" he said.

"Not really," I said, but got to my feet anyway and stormed over to my train case. I produced a tube of VO-5 which I used to smooth my ends. "This should do, but don't use too much because it can get greasy," I said.

I was putting on the finishing touches of mascara when Stan burst in, red-faced. "Look at me!" he said.

He'd used too much; I could see his hair implants neatly divided on the top of his head. "Don't yell at me, I told you, only a tiny bit," I said. "Take another shower."

"I don't have time," he said. "They've already waited cocktails for us."

"Don't worry about it," I said. "No one will notice."

"I will and it'll bug me all night," he said. "Fuck, fuck, fuck." He stooped in front of the ancient bureau mirror, parted and re-parted his hair.

He was worse than a teenage girl. I laughed. I couldn't help it.

Lord Timothy introduced us to an anteroom full of guests. Gibsons were served and I flitted through the hellos, being my most lovely. I grazed on the egg salad filled tarts and lobster pimento cheese spread on celery stalks and animatedly narrated the salient particulars of our misguided ascent through the countryside.

The prattle continued into the dining room where we dispersed and found our place cards. The light from the hefty crystal chandelier was dim above the oblong table and a fire smoked from the open hearth. No one was seated next to their date and I was relieved to find that I'd been positioned at the far end of the table from Stan.

It all felt very Agatha Christie and I half-expected the butler to inform us of a dead body. A more reasonable excuse than my poor judgment, I thought, for the weekend detention.

We were served white wine with some chilled oily fish on limp lettuce. I wondered how much of the food was going to be similarly flavorless. I thought how being paid for the weekend would have made it all go down like honey.

Surrounded by Millicent, Felicity and Patience, all equally gaunt with mousy hair, pale skin and bad teeth, I could be pragmatic about my profession. I understood why it was easy for me to endure such clumsy interactions when it was my job. I could forgive my choices.

Brisket and peas with boiled potatoes. Warm wine. I knew I risked a sick hangover from too much booze but I guzzled it anyway and giggled wickedly whenever I caught Stan's seething eye and matted locks.

He told a loud story, the group was engrossed, all gin in one hand and "fags" in the other, laughing wildly. How he stood out with his tanned skin, bright smile and strapping height. He couldn't fathom why I wasn't smitten with him.

The carved paneling went up to a crown-molded ceiling; the imposing credenzas, the polished silver, all setting for the stodgy exclusivity that I refused to want. I felt its established superiority, security. Stan and I, the boisterous Americans, were merely the entertainment. I could see it in their inane fascination that screamed, *how amusing*. Like a Labrador puppy.

We filed into the conservatory, cigars were passed and lit. The room divided into pairs —a touch of hand with this one, a stroke on the back of the neck with that one, a peck between drags. I wondered, were these obsequious couples really in love? Would I ever feel that again? I had set up a system to protect me from this stifling sense of doubt. I shook off the thought, accepted another glass of wine.

Stan stood courteously when I took the seat near him, though I could see he'd have been quite pleased to let me alone. I felt bad for teasing him; he pulled it off, acted like nothing had happened to spoil his night and I figured one more day wouldn't kill me. I'd play nice, we'd stay friends and I'd return to the safety of Manhattan.

Chapter 54

I'd chosen a thigh-length cobalt blue sweater, black leggings and ballet flats for the interview at the Culinary Institute. It seemed right for the cool autumn day, and I thought, looked collegiate enough. The bright sky defined the steamy exhaust emanating from the back door of the clanking diner kitchen at the corner of Sixth and Fifty-Eighth.

People moved down the avenue on their way to jobs. Careers.

I walked toward the park to catch the subway. One of my regulars, Georges, a French chef, had given me the phone number to the Institute and like a dare, I'd called. Now I braved humbling myself before the admissions process more to defy my fear than with purpose. Sure, I liked to cook. Georges taught me to use Muscadet in the beurre blanc, the difference between morel and champignon mushrooms. I was absorbed by the fun of it, but passion? It didn't matter, it was *something*. I hadn't the courage to mention my reconnaissance to Daddy after Melanie's congealed response.

"A two-year program to cook for people?" she'd said on the phone.

"Chefs are not cooks and it's only the beginning, there are apprenticeships in Paris, Italy," I said, trying to give the notion more shine, despite knowing that Melanie would regard anything I did as average, if that.

At eleven, Columbus Circle wasn't busy; everyone inside, working. The downtown R train to Twenty-Third Street; orange seats grimy in the fluorescence of the near empty car. I sat opposite from a model-type, long boots, cheekbones, hair stringy, unbrushed, staring at nothing; heading to a shoot, no doubt, even her boredom carried function.

My stomach was nerves. Why, though, escaped me. Talking to strangers was easy; putting it on, my nature. But I felt obvious, like I had a stamp on my head that read failure.

Chapter 55

My reflection was warped in the polished matte-brass elevator door as I waited. The image resembled how I'd been feeling inside, like overstretched taffy.

The doorman tipped his hat and opened the heavy glass door. The October sun shined full of hope in a cloudless sky, making me squint the moment I emerged from under my awning. I needed the Ray-Bans. The aroma of caramelized peanuts mixed with car exhaust, the noise of taxi horns and construction workers howling "hey, baby" infused the chill in the air which allowed me to don my shawl-collared camel hair wrap. I hated to squander such superb apparel on David but at least I'd make a decent entrance at Bice.

David must have been looking forward to seeing me, though I'd barely spoken with him since I'd visited London. He didn't have a clue that Stan had told me everything and I planned to cut him loose but hadn't quite figured out the particulars. All I knew was that he wasn't to be trusted and my pulse quickened and throat closed in anticipation of seeing him.

I booked across Fifth Avenue through the oncoming pedestrians, bike messengers and anonymous hands extending flyers.

Why had I even expected David to be different? A married man. I'd wanted love without the responsibility.

But from the start, it was only fucked up people doing fucked up things.

I carved a line down Fifth and gracefully stepped over the outstretched legs of a homeless man reclining joyfully against a garbage can out front of Tiffany's; he'd brazenly made peace with his situation and I envied him.

The challenge was to keep myself from strangling David long enough to get something from him other than hurt feelings. He deserved to be treated like a common customer, but I didn't know if I had the strength to be as ruthless as I had been with other men. I'd never so much as asked for cab fare from him. Maybe that was the whole problem.

By the time I turned on Fifty-Fourth, my face was flush and I was perspiring. I took my off my jacket and slung it over my arm, tugged down my red sweater dress and quickly gave the bra a push in the window of a French laundry. I dodged the linen and garbage steam stench that rose from the sidewalk grate and headed for the restaurant.

David's betrayal felt as bad as anything I'd experienced. At the very least, I wanted some monetary satisfaction. But I didn't know if I had the courage to stick my hand out to him, because it hadn't been our arrangement. I'd been somebody different with him, but I reminded myself that there was dignity in the transaction. Needs fulfilled, no emotional casualties.

Bice was packed and David was seated at the best table, peering over his new readers. Were they Gucci, Courreges,

Armani? He'd toss them aside, pretend total captivation at my presence.

He stood, I gave him the cheek, dumped the coat and my Charles Jourdan hobo between us. I let the maitre'd slide in my chair, immediately opened the menu and took a breath to calm my nerves.

"I'm starved," I said.

"The city agrees with you," he said, trying to make eye contact.

"I'm in the mood for the farfalle," I said, glancing at him for a millisecond. Then I shut the menu with a snap and turned to the waiter. "Diet Coke, please. And a straw."

"So, tell me how things are," he said. How long was he going to ignore my distance?

"I'm applying at the Culinary Center for the spring," I said. I hadn't heard anything since my interview there, but he didn't need to know that.

"Since when have you been interested in cooking?" he said with a hint of snobbery.

"There's a lot you don't know about me," I said. "And it's to be a chef, not a cook."

He seemed amused, which deepened my loathing. The sommelier opened a bottle of Pinot Grigio and poured. David nodded his approval.

I covered my glass. "No thanks," I said.

"I thought you'd come back to the hotel with me," he said.

His disappointment emboldened me. "I have a life," I said. "I can't drop everything because you come into town."

"And I wouldn't want you to," he said.

As long as I'm doing what you want me to do, I thought.

"Aziz and Charlie are in for a match tonight, you'll meet us afterward?"

That was his reason for being in town, not me. He lied about the woman in France; I lied to myself about everything else. I'd tossed the Ombre Rose into the incinerator when I returned from London.

"I can't. I'm leaving for Florida tomorrow," I said.

He babbled about his recent travels, a thing he bid on at Sotheby's. I picked at the focaccia, but I wanted to grab the collar of his Paul Stewart button-down and pound him with a right-hook.

The waiter replaced my salad plate with a bowl of creamy bowties. "You know, you remind me of someone," I said, looking at him, stabbing the pasta.

"Don't say it," he said.

"My father" "Your father," we said simultaneously.

"It's not that much of a stretch," I said, pausing to sip my drink. "He may even be younger than you."

He laughed at that.

Over coffee I said, "I could use some help for a new suitcase." Delivered like an indictment for all he hadn't done for me.

"How much do you need?" he said, his face stuck between confusion and annoyance. He pulled out a clip full of cash, peeled off some hundreds.

"More than that," I said with gained confidence, my tone unapologetic. After he'd counted eleven bills, I took my hand away and stuffed the money in my wallet. "I'd really have loved to see Charlie and Aziz," I said.

I was brutal, and he let me do it. Disgusting. Was that what he always wanted, to be treated like dirt? One thing was certain; it wasn't close to how much I wanted him to suffer. He thought my being a whore gave him the moral high ground, but did it really? Maybe being a whore was the *only* moral high ground.

I took my coat and slung the bag over my shoulder and left without looking back.

Chapter 56

The week of Thanksgiving, Melanie called in tears. "He's having an affair," she said, overwrought through swollen sinuses.

So Melanie's Prince Charming was like every other man, though I took no delight in the confirmation of my suspicions. Propped against my pillows, I settled in and lit a smoke for the saga. "How did you catch him?" I said, assuming the absence of his sincere confession.

"He'd been working late since the election," she said, blowing her nose. "I called over there, his partner said he was in Chicago. I pretended my dates were confused, laughed it off, then searched his desk." She stopped, wrangled herself. Blew again. Sniffed. Her voice grew haughty. "All I found were two numbers listed under Northwestern. No name. I *knew.* I dialed and a girl answered. I asked to speak to Chad," Melanie pitched her voice, "He won't be here until eight."

"Fucker," I said, surprised by how personally I took it.

"I called back. He was there," she said, anemically. "A paralegal at the Chicago firm. *A paralegal.*"

"He told you?" I untwisted myself from the phone cord, got up, paced. I wanted him dead for injuring her.

"He didn't deny it," she said. "I told him to get his crap out of my house." She paused, cleared her throat, regained her composure. "So you better make other plans for the weekend because I'm not cooking."

"I'll come anyway, we'll eat out," I said, fearful from hearing her broken, knowing she shouldn't be alone.

"Let me see how the rest of the week shapes up," she said, controlled. "I'll let you know when I've made some decisions."

Even at Melanie's most vulnerable, she could wound me.

Chapter 57

For the first time in years, I looked forward to seeing Melanie. When she heard Chris was staying at the Plaza, she took a Metroliner up for the weekend. She needed the diversion, and I knew, if nothing else, that's what I could deliver.

"Do my hair and make-up for me," Melanie said, letting me perform the one task at which I was superior.

We dressed for dinner at a punk rock sushi bar on the Upper Westside and did lines off a plate. I took her departure from her straight arrow image as a sign of confidence. She sat in the vanity chair and smoked while I sprayed glitter and tied a high teased ponytail on top of her head. After some black liner, short spandex and patent leather, she said, "I could never get away with this in D.C."

"Fun, right?" I said. It was all I wanted, to know I had a hand in my sister smiling.

Chris called from the limo. "Get your skinny asses down here, we're late," he said.

When I hung up, the framed picture of me and Donna in Mickey Mouse sweatshirts, seventeen, in front of the giant Epcot sphere stared up from the table. Jeff had taken the picture; we'd driven all night on whim to Orlando. Was that the last time I was content? Maybe it was as far back as Laine. I pushed the sadness away.

For the moment, Melanie was here, she seemed to love me and it was all that mattered.

We stuffed satin clutches with lipstick, money and drugs, scrambled for keys and cigarettes, then stopped for the doorman to take our picture on the way out.

Chapter 58

The feeling was always the same the second I'd made the decision to cop. It was as if I'd already snorted my first line. My heart quickened, my palms began to sweat, my stomach cramped and I'd run to the bathroom. I'd make sure I was dressed and made-up before making the call. I kept my manicure impeccable; the corners of my eyes clean from black liner, my lipstick perfect.

My dealer lived only a couple blocks away. A glossy high-rise. I could've walked from my place.

I hailed a cab. "Fifty-seventh and Park," I said. The driver didn't flinch. I wore my mink, a black catsuit, boots. I powdered my nose using the glow of Christmas Manhattan outside the taxi's window.

I'd spend the evening on Josh's leather sectional, with fancy people I just met. Maybe there'd be someone I'd seen before, drinking champagne, communing over our shared habit.

Josh was the maitre'd from Regine's. Claire made the introductions when we'd gone there for dinner. We didn't eat much after our first drink. We didn't eat at all. There were always plenty of non-dining diners at the white-linen tables. So many trips to the bathroom, it seemed like rush hour. Gold-boxed cigarettes burned in crystal ashtrays. Josh smelling of Dior, wearing a gardenia tucked in the hole on his lapel, his dark hair slicked back. He told me to call anytime. I did. At least twice a week.

My visits to Regine's had become more frequent. My trips to the bar, waiting for the matchbook with the magazine paper that was filled with a gram or eight ball, depending on what my night had in store. There was the dependable silent exchange, the handshake with the folded bills, a comped glass of wine. It was a cabal; you knew instinctively who was in and who was out.

Josh's lobby Christmas tree glistened through the window with silver bows and oversized orbs, a single color, the mark of elegant holiday decoration. I tipped the driver, put my gloves on, rode up to the fifteenth floor.

Ronie was easy enough to hang with, she was stunning; shoulder-length blonde hair, with small breasts on a long, lean body, like a dancer. I invited her over after we'd met on a date at the Waldorf. We'd spent some hours doing our own drugs and chain smoking in my living room.

Unrestrained candor was typical of early morning coke chat, but I was shocked by her openness. She'd run away from an alcoholic mother and a stepfather who climbed into her bed every night. She related this as if she were recounting a trip to the grocery store, then gave a detailed account of turning tricks at thirteen on Hollywood Boulevard. How the Johns would drive up and ask for whatever, how she charged different prices, from twenty to a hundred, for each act, most times in the back of a car.

"This is all a major step up for me," she said, gesturing

her hand about her in deference to my apartment. "I don't have a pimp anymore." There was triumph in her tone.

"Wow," I said, because I felt the need to say something and the only reference I had for her previous lifestyle was *Baretta*. "I could never give my hard-earned cash to someone else."

"He protected me when I needed it," she said, as if I was naive, then split a line, did half and handed me the mirror.

I was shaken by what she told me. I'd never met anyone who'd actually been on the street. Had a pimp. Had it been providence that I'd met Jeff when I did? If I didn't, would I have ended up like her? Never. And my father hadn't been fucking me. But here we were, in the same place.

We washed off our make-up. Her face was still dewy, even in the inevitable harshness of the all-nighter. "Thanks for letting me stay," she said.

She didn't know she was helping me; I hated being alone when I was high like this. I placed two valium on the counter and lent her a t-shirt. We migrated to my bed, sat crossed-legged and smoked.

"I hate coming down," I said, curling my knees, covering my legs with my shirt.

"It's not so bad, we have each other," she said without hesitation, blowing smoke up to my ceiling, not the least self-conscious. Intimacy was effortless at three a.m.

"I won't work for a week," I said, "probably spend the whole wad we made tonight because I always feel so guilty when it's over."

"Guilt's stupid," she said. "You either do it or you don't, and you're doing it. You don't have to answer to anyone."

Only to myself and I could only be invisible in small doses. Ronie may have lost her conscience but I hadn't. Meanwhile, I wasn't the only one jonesing for another line, feeling like shit, was I?

She put out her smoke and started rapping, the Sugerhill Gang, moving her hands to her beat, *I'm tons of fun and I dress to a T, you see I got more clothes than Muhammad Ali.*

It was an uncomfortably random outburst but I listened while she kept relentlessly at it since it seemed important to her.

I gotta Lincoln Continental and a sharp new Cadillac. So childlike, happy, bopping in her seat. "I'm going to record my own rap album one day," she said.

"Really?" I said, with nothing to add because it was a weird aspiration. But at least she had one; I couldn't say that for myself.

By morning, two candles remained lit and the Cult droned in the background. Cigarettes ceased to distract us from the ache of withdrawal and the valium did little to bring on sleep. Ronie snuggled close in the tangle of pillows and pressed her lips to mine. Her vulnerability enveloped me and I gave in to the kiss, but I withheld my pleasure because I sensed this wasn't a whim for her and didn't want to take advantage of it.

Those flings in Florida, that time with Leanne in Panama, I indulged the passing urge. But I'd become increasingly self-conscious and too selfish to expose that side of me. What if Ronie wanted more? And, she might talk. I didn't gel with the dyke label; the other girls might not want to work with me. It was crazy to care; we were all so fake none of us knew the truth about ourselves or anybody else.

I pulled back, despite my hunger for the embrace and the desire to be loved.

"What's wrong," she said, her eyes liquid in the dwindling light.

She was broken but I had my own damage. I didn't want her in my life and I didn't want her to need me in hers. I turned over, blew out the candles. "I'm not into girls," I said.

Chapter 59

In a half-hour I'd walk to see Georges. Monday was our regular night, the slow night at his restaurant. Dark had fallen at four-thirty and New York's Christmas blinked silently from the street below. Snow was imminent beyond the double-paned glass and radiator clatter of the steam-forced heat.

I called Leanne, Chris hadn't returned any of my recent messages and she was the quickest way to get the headlines. We'd all been busy with the holidays and it'd been hard to stay in touch.

One of the things I loved about Leanne, she answered her phone. I never did, or my pager for that matter; my machine blinked a red twenty at me from the kitchen counter. I feared the ring; it was an intrusion into my imperfect state. I enjoyed the control of call-screening.

We sailed through our customary jabber about the balmy Florida winter, money, clients.

"Come see this guy with me, I'm taking Claudette tonight," Leanne said as her hairspray bottle pumped ceaselessly in the background. "Easy, a lot of talking." Then she said, "You've gotta be shocked about Chris."

I felt a film of sweat beneath my turtleneck. "What about Chris," I said.

"It hasn't been that long since we've talked," Leanne said, her Pomeranian barking, as a table full of breakables were obliterated.

It'd take patience and time I didn't have to get the story. "What. Focus. Tell me everything," I said, smoking, swiping bagel crumbs into the sink.

AIDS, she told me. Like that. Simple. About my best friend. As if my feelings meant nothing. I wondered about her casual delivery. But then I asked for it, didn't I?

"He was sick for a couple weeks and he never would have known if he hadn't ended up in the hospital with pneumonia. They tested him," she said.

"I knew something was wrong when he didn't call me back," I said, though what I really meant was that I felt left out. Chris didn't think I was important enough to tell.

I stared at the dried grease on my stovetop but saw instead Chris's family and friends communing in his empty home, me in tears behind a black veil, and then I'm emaciated with an IV sticking out of my arm, my sister and father shaking their heads as they leave the cemetery.

I didn't mind seeing Georges Fournier twice a week or that his poor English forced us to pantomime conversation. He was the chef and owner of Maurice. Short and sturdy, with thick dark hair and a strong nose, black lashes curly around gold eyes. He prepared elaborate meals with the effortlessness that I made a pot of coffee, paid me in cash without requesting a regular's discount and didn't require me to wear make-up. Two hours with him was like visiting a buddy who got to see me naked.

"My friend has AIDS," I said, sitting on the kitchen stepstool so I could watch him chop onion.

"Yes, this is a problem," he said, wiping his hands on the dishtowel he'd tucked into his belt, pouring me a glass from an open bottle of Burgundy. "A waiter of mine, too."

My stomach was sour; I tore at the baguette he'd set out, slathered it with warm brie. I could've been eating dirt for the way it tasted. I washed the lump down with wine.

"I worry about myself," I said, wishing I'd mentioned the humidity instead. We were only pretend confidantes; I was paid to listen.

"He is gay, no?" he said, sautéing the onion in butter, its sweet aroma barely tempting me. "The fags do not pay women for sex." He raised his eyebrow, smiled at his lame stab at humor.

When I didn't laugh, he said, "You cannot get it by drinking or touching." He removed a pan from the broiler. "It's the blood, yes?"

His recitation of the commonly-known facts failed to cheer me. Straight men never thought they were at risk. "We lived together in Florida and it's not just a gay disease," I said, miffed, the conversation had gone too far. I stood, combed my hair with my fingers into a ponytail high on my head, let the tresses fall down my back.

Georges put the spatula down; put his lips on my neck. "Come," he said. "I will feed you."

I moved bites of Dover sole around my plate, chewed a baby carrot, toyed with the roasted potatoes. "Delicious." I said.

Chris and I had shared everything but the bed, though that wasn't what bothered me. I'd played Russian roulette. Asking a client to use a rubber was considered street and putting one on was like admitting you were a prostitute. High-end girls didn't use them. We'd all been careless. Testing positive would be an apt punishment for my sins.

After Georges put the dishes on the counter, we moved to his bedroom. He folded his slacks on the crease, hung them on a wooden valet; climbed onto the high bed in tighty-whities. His gold cross still hung around his neck.

It was always the same. The strong scent of cologne mixed with his wooly chest. The taste of wine and spices beneath toothpaste. His quick release at the sight of me on top of him. A rinse in the shower while he cleaned the kitchen.

I was still damp while I dressed. I glossed my lips in the mirror over the mantle, glanced at the gilded clock. Still under an hour but he always paid for two. I'd leave anyway. I rolled my head but it didn't ease my stiff neck. I thought how that boy I'd worked with at the Yacht Club in Florida had died, and that DJ we knew from the Alley, like they'd been in a movie I'd seen once, not real, and now Chris would die, too. I could be the next one, with all I'd done. I'd get tested in the morning.

Chapter 60

The familiarity of Ft. Lauderdale International had a calming effect as I steered the rental car onto US-1. Just being in Florida felt like I had some control.

Leanne said she'd be home, she wanted me to stay there, but I went straight to Chris's. He still hadn't returned my calls and I'd heard from different people that he wasn't seeing anyone. I even phoned his father and he said that Chris was declining fast and that his mother wasn't up for talking. She'd taken to bed herself and I couldn't blame her, but still, I felt I deserved more without having to ask for it. Call me if anything changes, I'd said.

I felt nervy, entitled to use the key but I knocked and rang. It was an eternity before I heard movement. A woman I didn't know answered.

"Can I help you?" she said. She was pale, skinny, older, with her blonde hair in a clip.

"I'm here to see Chris," I said.

"He's not seeing anyone," she said.

"Just tell him it's Robin," I said. I shifted, put my sunglasses on my head. I wanted eye-contact.

"I'm on strict instructions," she said, leaning against the doorjamb, arms crossed.

"Are you his nurse?" I said.

"I'm his friend," she said with an amused smile. "And I'm taking care of him."

I was outraged. "I'm his friend, too, and I've never heard of you," I said. "Look, I've come all the way from New York and I'm not leaving until I see him."

"I've given him all his messages, Robin, but as I've said, he's not seeing anyone." She said my name like I'd been discussed and eliminated.

What had I done to make Chris not want to see me? I was deflated, rejected and helpless against the woman's detachment. I'd go to Leanne's, call Sophia and Vincent – they'd tell me what was going on. There's no way they'd stay away at a time like this.

"Do his parent's know that you're keeping people from him?" I said. "They've all been told," she said.

But I hadn't. Birds sang in the hibiscus but there was silence beyond the threshold. The sunny day did little to brighten the inertness that emanated from the once lively home.

"Will you at least give him a note?" I said.

I dug in my bag, wrote on the jacket of my plane ticket: *C – Was here but your "friend" didn't let me in. I'm worried about you. Page me. I'm in town for the weekend. I'll come anytime. I love you. –R*

There was nothing else to do.

Chapter 61

I scoured off my make-up and tiptoed around my apartment like a thief, afraid my neighbors below, above, next door would hear me, judge me. I wasn't disturbing anyone but myself, it was only my paranoia. Like being scrutinized by the strangers I co-existed within our capsule of anonymity mattered more than my mangled soul.

I was a cold slab in my sheets, my pillow awkward, my sweatshirt confining. I closed my eyes in failed attempt to settle myself. My heart stormed with exhaustion.

If I was less reckless, if I could be truthful when no one was listening, that this time was *never* going to be the last all-nighter, I'd have the temerity to have a Valium, the Halcyon or the Xanax –the scrips I should've had handy to quell the crash. This I knew in the void of my pre-dawn torment. I cursed myself, when begging God to let-me-sleep-it-off-and-I-will-I-swear-never-take-another-hit, that I couldn't just be what Niles said I was, what Ronie never denied. A coke fiend.

"God, why don't I have a tranquilizer," I said to no one, rummaging through the jungle of my bedside drawer. I sat, lit a cigarette in the dark as consolation. It only worked to torch what was left of my fictional decency.

Why I invoked God in these black moments –the He I did not believe in, the He that left me to flounder faithless, the He that didn't know I existed –I'd never know. My communion with the Supreme whatever didn't dent my self-deception. Wasn't it the Devil who I was really in business with anyway?

I stubbed out the butt after two drags because my lungs couldn't manage another hit, returned to my coffin and wished for death. Not really. That was plain fucked up. That was certifiable crazy time. Not me. I was just having a shitty day. Tomorrow, no the next day, after I recovered with split pea soup and mashed potatoes with gravy sent up from the Greek diner, and all day re-runs of Andy Griffith, I'd change my life. Maybe I'd call Georges. Pick up some money, let him cook for me. Be healthy. I'd only drink Chardonnay, plead my circumstance, cry even.

Chapter 62

Daddy and I rarely spent more than a meal together and his staying the night was unprecedented. It was dark by the time he arrived.

"I found a space way over on West 56th," he said, his smile full of warmth, gripping my shoulders as he kissed my cheek.

"Great," I said, "You'll be good until eight." My anxiety had mushroomed and his long-anticipated presence caused my heart to settle like the remains of a boiled-over pot.

"Nice place," he said, dropping his bag in the foyer.

The maid had just left and I'd bought cut flowers, put out the mixed nuts I knew he liked. "Are you hungry?" I said, hanging his coat in the closet.

With the exception of a Korean market run, I'd been hibernating in the sanctuary of my apartment since my last night out. It had taken the two days until Daddy's arrival to recover and I'd been an emotional wreck. I'd prepared myself as meticulously as I had the room. My demeanor was bright, every hair smoothed.

I was relieved when he wanted to order Chinese.

"It's antiquated and the entire thing needs to be upgraded," he said about the new job somewhere in Connecticut.

I sat across from him at the dining table I'd set with paper napkins and black-rimmed Mikasa plates, wanting nothing but to stare at the creases around his eyes. His hair had been buzzed by a barber, giving him a boyish appearance despite the gray and I examined his face for threads of my identity, a strand that would remind me of what existed inside me.

I resolved to listen complacently. That I was interested in his every word was not an act; each scrap was treasured. I was suspended in present time. Nothing before or after.

I talked about the February cold, the difficulties of navigating dirty ice piles at every corner, the cost of cable, impersonal things that prevented me from crumpling into a bawling heap.

I cleared the plates, closed the boxes of leftover Mu Shu and fried rice.

Daddy rubbed his eyes, stretched out on the sofa and used the remote. The Sixers were playing; the rhythm of the announcer calling the shots, panacea for an exhausting day.

I still had hometown pride, cheered unerringly for anything Philly. It had been ingrained like DNA and, as a kid, I'd prided myself on knowing the teams and being able to talk about the plays with Daddy, but instead of joining him, I busied myself in the kitchen. I washed, dried, put things away. Neat. Clean. Please and thank you. A model daughter. Keep the anxiety at a low simmer.

When there was nothing left to avoid him with, I sat in the chair opposite the couch. "Alright," Daddy shouted at the screen, clapping as Dr. J dunked the ball. He patted me on the knee, gave it a squeeze.

Then, without warning, I wanted to talk with him, like when I was sixteen and I'd confessed that I'd lost my virginity. It'd been like hurling *the worst has already happened* at him. But there had been no big lecture or reproach, no life without parole. All he said was, "I don't want any illegitimate grandchildren running around." I thought then I'd gotten away with it, that maybe we'd profoundly understood each other, but now, as if I was surveying my history like a map, I saw that I'd needed more from him.

Charles Barkley swooshed it in from the foul line and the players dispersed across the court.

"How are things?" he said, eyes half on the tube.

I fixed on my father, the lighthouse that had guided me to safety and, as if a breeze blew my sense out the door, an avalanche of honesty tumbled from me. "Things haven't been as good as I let on," I said, focusing on the freckles of his tanned hands. "I think I may have a drug problem."

The game ended and Marv Alpert recounted the scores while I chronicled pot smoking in high school to the illicit substances that now permeated my life. I spoke quietly through a throat sore with the containment of tears. I blamed circumstance, availability, cocaine on the cover of Time magazine. I tried to see beyond his granite reaction, wondering if he'd ever even heard of such things.

"I'm in therapy," I said, instantly regretting this admission rather than the probable diagnosis.

Was his frozen expression a scrim over churning thoughts? Then his face changed. Was that compassion? "I've known people who've wrestled with alcohol," he said. "Get the help you need."

"I will," I said and cleaned my face with my hands, wiping the sticky sheen on my leggings.

That Daddy didn't judge me meant an understanding that I'd rarely felt from him. Maybe I deserved something better than what I'd created, maybe he'd be on the other end of the gauntlet that lay ahead of me.

The news came on. Oliver North, stiff in his decorated uniform, took the Fifth. We watched silently, tuned in to the private parades inside our heads.

I went to the couch, put my arms around his neck, collapsed into him and wept. He didn't console me with *there there*, he only lay prone, motionless. It didn't matter; to be with him would have to be enough. But he could no more manage me next to him, a full-grown howling disaster, than he could assuage the rejection I felt from his distance, so he remained uncomfortably still until I stood to get ready for bed, promising to set the alarm.

I hadn't slept without dreaming in ages and I was surprised that I awoke rested, before the alarm. The dawn seeped through the cracks of the Venetian blinds, spilling a matte wash of gray over my bedroom.

Daddy had slept on the sofa and I wanted to make coffee before waking him. It had been years since I had breakfast with my father and I knew the value of the occasion. I pulled on sweats and tiptoed to the kitchen, I heard movement in the hall and adjusted my eyes to the dim. There was Daddy, coat on, his hand on the doorknob. The sight of him sneaking out made me dizzy.

"Daddy, where are you going?" I said, steadying myself with the wall, unable to mask the injury in my voice.

"I wanted to get an early start," he said, barely concealing his guilt.

"Without saying goodbye?" I said.

Numbness spread through me. I'd gone to bed deluded that my father loved me, even understood me and that I'd been pardoned. But it wasn't true. He'd desert me before I could need more.

"I thought we'd eat together," I said, clinging to the original plan.

"I'm not hungry," he said, impatient, readjusting his stance. "Better to beat the traffic."

"But you've got to have coffee," I said, looking at the parquet, tearing the cuticle on my thumb, hating myself for begging. "I can have it ready in a flash."

When I looked up, he seemed frightened, and I felt sad for him. His daughter adrift, in pain; he wanted distance to think. I'd been self-indulgent with my confession, when I should've protected him.

I hugged him, but it was more like clutching. "I'll be OK, Daddy," I said, but the false optimism tripped in my throat and dissolved. I wrapped his scarf tight, tucked it into the yoke of his navy overcoat. "Stay warm," I said."

I watched him walk down the corridor, hoping he noticed the bright floral arrangement on the landing —a splash of sun for the bitter day that lay waiting. When the elevator arrived, I kissed my fingers and waved. "I love you," I said, and listened for the whoosh of the closing doors before retreating into the emptiness.

Chapter 63

I paced and smoked and mixed my coffee almost white so I could guzzle it, and then I called Melanie's office, dialing the number with the same familiarity that I signed my name.

"Chris died this morning," I said, the words a whisper, panic pressing my chest; my voice echoed in my head as if wrapped in tin.

Melanie sighed with the impatience of someone deflecting a nattering child. "I see cases of people losing loved ones every day," she said.

"I know, but not *your* loved ones," I said, tapping ashes in the kitchen sink. Stress surged into my cramped neck and shoulders, my pulse thumped in my fingertips. "You were friends with him, too."

"Yeah, but I don't have the luxury of being melodramatic," she said.

It was hard to get air into my lungs. I opened a window to a symphony of horns and the damp chill of air mixed with bus fumes wafted over the forced heat of the radiator.

"The funeral is on Thursday," I said, still hoping she'd want to go with me.

"You knew there wasn't a cure," she said.

Her indifference flattened me. "Knowing that doesn't make it easy," I said, sitting the dining table chair scraping against the hardwood as I dragged it out.

Chris had honored her not only as my sister but as a friend. And though I knew he did it for me, Melanie didn't. The attention he paid, the money and time he'd unselfishly spent in Florida and New York to make her visits memorable meant nothing to her. She refused to mourn and could care even less about my loss.

I arranged wads of soggy tissues as if I were lining up balls of cookie dough on a baking sheet. When Melanie failed to offer any further wisdom I said, "We were best friends. I loved him."

"You haven't even seen him since he got sick," she said, papers rustling in concert with her irritation. She was heartless to say it, knowing it wasn't my choice. I'd told her about the disappointing trip. When I didn't answer she said, "You're living in New York now. You've never been short on friends."

Chris loved my peculiarities, overlooked my destructive habits and understood my cynicism. He accepted me despite my embarrassing choices. I *had* been short on real friends and Melanie didn't think I knew the difference. "I just thought you'd like to know," I said, exhausted.

Chapter 64

The bells tolled in deep tenor and wreathes of sympathy covered the steps leading to the pulpit. I sat with Leanne, engulfed by the sickening scent of flowers.

I'd changed in the airport bathroom while Leanne waited curbside and we'd gone directly to the church. Niles was a couple pews away with his new girlfriend. I thought I'd say something nice to him after the service. Be gracious like Jackie O. I'd gone for that look with my choice of sunglasses, black pencil skirt and hair up in a hat. It was how I imagined I was supposed to look in grief, as if by playing the part I actually felt something, but I was disconnected from the pain, and seeing Chris's urn didn't change that.

I was grateful they'd burned his remains, I didn't want to see Chris's emaciated painted corpse at the wake. I didn't need to observe his abandoned flesh. I only wanted the memories of his love and the good times, of us together in Key West after our all-town bar crawl, in front of Screaming Mimi's Resale on Columbus Avenue, at the Panamanian airport. That person wasn't the stranger who'd turned me away.

The congregation was appropriately sullen through to the Absolution. The last time I'd been to mass, I'd gone with Donna and her mom during my junior high religion -sampling era. I'd knelt, fraudulently eaten the wafers and sipped the blood of Christ. Some of the prayers were similar to the Episcopalian ones I'd grown up with but with Catholicism there was more pageantry and candles.

The black-robed priest circled the remains, sprinkling holy water. Incense for the finale. "May the martyrs receive you at your coming, and lead you into the holy city," he said. There were tears and sobs.

Leanne and I followed the procession to Chris's parent's home. I thought: where was the urn? But I didn't dare say it. What about the house on Las Olas, I asked his sister. They hadn't dealt with the cleaning out of it all but they planned to donate and sell everything.

I wanted the Lalique Singing Robin figurine that Chris used to mimic my voice. His attention meant love. I thought he knew me best. Because I'd been honest with him about how Melanie and Daddy and Donna had hurt me and how nuts Leanne could make me and how I'd never really liked Niles. And he'd been there when I needed him. But not at the end, when it mattered. And Chris hadn't thought to leave the Singing Robin for me and I wondered about the things we made up in our heads. Would a piece of crystal in my hands have changed the fact that he's dead? Would I believe he loved me? And could I have been the one to sit by his side in the end, nurse him, feed him, change his sheets? Surely, I didn't have that in me. I didn't deserve the Singing Robin anymore than to be sitting on his mother's gold-striped sofa recounting funny stories, or washing her dishes, or taking out the garbage.

Leanne and I hugged bravely at the airport and agreed that it was the worst thing that ever happened. And maybe it was and maybe it was a lie, because Chris's death should mean something. But I had yet to understand what.

April 1987

Chapter 65

Donna's street seemed a mile long when I was growing up, but now it felt like half a block. Her mother's tiny house was shabbier than I remembered.

The cement driveway was split by weeds but the azaleas bloomed vigorously in the sun despite their neglect. I walked to the door on the trampled dirt path through the crabgrass. Things the way they always were, though I'd never noticed. There were a lot of things I'd overlooked then.

I ignored feelings of suffocation and tried to breathe in the familiar sweet Pennsylvania spring. I was there for Donna. Despite the resentments, regardless of the distance, I was the dutiful friend.

Donna answered the door, brown eyes sunken into sallow skin, gray sweatpants and a threadbare Aerosmith t-shirt. She'd swallowed a bottle of Motrin. Mrs. Milpas said on the phone that she found her lying in a pool of vomit, dressed in a yellow pencil skirt and white linen blouse. Nice choice of clothes. Lame choice of drugs.

I'd left from Penn Station on the next train.

Donna and I held each other and cried. "Don't ever do that again," I said.

She cleared the clothes from the rocker for me but I kicked off my pumps and sat next her on the unmade bed. It was hard to believe I'd spent so many nights among her clutter, but her house felt more like home than Carpenter Lane ever had.

The Smiths on the turntable. For once in my life, let me get what I want, Morrisey sang.

"You look great," she said, handing me the Kleenex, using some herself.

"Yves Saint Laurent will do that for you," I said, blowing my nose, wiping the streak of tears from my well-made-up face. Wadded tissues everywhere. "It's been a real sobfest, huh?"

Donna knotted her unkempt hair into a pink scrunchy. The last time I'd seen her was in New York when she was jonesing for another base hit. I wasn't very sympathetic then.

"What the hell were you doing?" I said. I took it personally, her wanting to die.

"Haven't you ever felt like the sadness just wouldn't go away?" she said.

"Yeah, every day," I said, tucking her stray bangs behind her ear so I could see her face.

"No. I mean, hopeless," she said.

"Not enough to kill myself," I said, feeling the distance between our present lives.

"Rolfe's got a new muse," she said, taking two Parliaments out of the box.

"He's surrounded by poontang, it's his job," I said. It irritated me, her obsession with the ex-boyfriend whose carnality resembled a chimpanzee's, who was so hyper-critical of her weight that she was driven to bulimia. "You left him, remember?"

"But I didn't think he'd fall in love so fast," she said, shaking the Bic to get it to light.

"Who says it's love? You can have anyone you want anyway," I said, lighting my smoke from hers. "What happened to the racecar guy?"

"That was like eight months ago, and he shaved his pubes," she said.

I'd missed entire chapters of her life. "Well, it's no reason to end it all. I mean really, man. Motrin?" The tin she'd been using for an astray was overflowing; it looked like she'd burned through a carton. I emptied it, brushed ashes and cat hair from my skirt.

"It wasn't planned," she said.

"You could have called me."

"You'd just tell me to buck up," she said. "You're doing it now."

"I should let you wallow?" I said and realized how much I sounded like Melanie.

"No. Yes. Shit. That's why I don't tell you everything," she said.

Being rational with Donna always worked until it didn't. There'd be lengthy phone conversations with tears. She made resolutions and agreements, and then she did whatever she was going to do anyway; the same course she'd been on.

"You think you're helping but you're not," she said. Donna never had trouble sniping at me. "Not everyone is as strong as you," she said.

But I wasn't strong, I just didn't complain, and I wasn't going to get into it with her under the circumstances. I picked up the guitar that stood against the wall, started strumming Give Peace a Chance. All we are saying, I sang. And after a couple bars, Donna chimed in.

She put my cigarette to my lips. I leaned over the Yamaha, took the last drag.

"What can I do for you," I said, squinting through the smoke.

"Nothing," she said. "Feed the cat."

I chose to believe her because I wasn't in the position to proffer any wisdom.

"What did you bring me to take the edge off?" she said, going for my purse.

"Xanax and Valium." I said, and dug out the enameled pillbox Niles had given me. I didn't mention the gram I had stashed in my wallet.

"I'll take the Valium," she said and swallowed it with water cupped in her hand from the bathroom sink.

I fed Amadeus a can of Fancy Feast, straightened the dresser, folded some laundry and threw out the trash while Donna showered with the door open so we could talk. I told her about the funeral, Georges' giving me the referral to culinary school, and my upcoming weekend in St. Maarten with a Swiss banker, careful to downplay any minimal enthusiasm, so as not to make her envious.

"At least you have some options," she said, wrapping herself in a flannel robe.

"You do, too," I said. "Look, the only reason I haven't slashed my wrists is because there'd be no one to find me. Consider yourself lucky you're loved by so many."

Donna rolled her eyes. "Well, I love you," she said.

"Yes, you do," I said, knowing she was probably the only one who did.

I picked up my purse to go.

"You sure you're not up for lunch? It'll do you good," I said, believing that a meal at a trendy spot was the salve for all that ailed anyone. "Come on, my treat. I'll wait while you get ready."

"Naw, I'm going to go back to bed," she said.

I stopped in the hall, looked at Mrs. Milpas' shrine to her daughter. Years of her school photos, with braids and braces, a freckled nose that accented her innocence. Donna in high school, her chin jutting defiantly. The girl I knew she'd been. I straightened a picture and ignored the jolt of despair I felt when seeing testaments of family love. There were no framed pictures of me or Melanie in Daddy's house.

As if she read my mind, Donna said, "Are you going to see your dad?"

"He doesn't know I'm in town," I said.

Donna raised an eyebrow. "He could be dead tomorrow, then how would you feel?" she said.

I'd only been to his new place once, for an hour or so when Cheryl wasn't there. I was afraid how I'd be received. I hadn't even heard from him since he'd bolted from my apartment that morning after the drug confession.

"Maybe I'll swing by," I said.

Donna walked me out; the sun on my face felt reassuring.

"Call me if, well, you know," I said, before closing my car door.

I watched the rearview of my rented Taurus as she waved goodbye from the stoop then disappeared behind the shadow of her screen door.

Chapter 66

I drove up Conshohocken to Gladwyne where Daddy and Cheryl had migrated. The tracts of land were more expansive, the hills greener, the columns taller, whiter than on Carpenter Lane. Philadelphia Country Club was central to the community and I knew if Daddy wasn't home, he was on the back nine. This place made me cringe, I'd never felt like anything but an outsider here.

The gravel crunched under my tires like a siren in the cathedral of nature. A deer froze, half-hidden in shrubs aside the circular driveway to Daddy's door.

I knocked and waited instead of pushing the bell, not wanting to blister the serenity, not wanting the door to be opened. I watched a couple of blue jays on the bushes near the landing, waited an interminable thirty seconds. When no one answered, I retraced my route down Lafayette to the club.

I parked in a guest spot; my heels echoed from the lot to the heavy door of the pro shop. "I'm looking for Will Daniels," I said to the girl behind the counter, wondering if the visor she wore was part of her uniform or if it hid a bad hair day.

Her startled smile failed to cover her confusion. I'd seen that look a million times from preppies like her; they were so thrown when I came into the room, like they'd never seen a woman before. "Jack?" she called.

The graying pro joined us from the back office. His face and arms were tan from the early spring, though his body was probably pasty-white under the pink golf shirt. His demeanor shifted from preoccupied to attentive the moment he laid eyes me. "How can I help you?" he said.

"Maybe you could tell me when Will Daniels will be finished," I said. "I'm his daughter." He didn't say anything, so I added, "I'm in town for the day, so I thought I'd surprise him." My tone was gracious, but I was irritated that I had to explain my presence.

"I've known Will for years, he never mentioned any kids," the pro said. He smiled, leaned against the counter, checked me out.

"Well, he's got them," I said sweetly. What the hell did this jerk know, he was the hired help. "Would you mind checking to see what hole he's on?"

"I saw him on the 16th, so he should be in soon," the pro said. He was handsome, straight teeth, blue eyes. He probably plowed the member's wives after their lessons.

"I'll wait," I said and feigned interest in a rack of pullovers, feeling his eyes on me.

I was unusually self-conscious. I knew I looked fabulous but what did this tennis rat and golf jock know about style? I must have been as exotic as a henna-painted belly dancer to him, and though I'd survived these types in the past by feeling superior, it wasn't working. I was on Daddy's turf and he preferred me to be invisible. If he didn't come in fifteen minutes, I'd drive to 30th Street, catch the Metroliner, be back in time to meet Claire for dinner.

I perused the wall of clubs. Woods, irons, a wedge. I toyed with the tags on the powder blue ladies bag. Jeff and

Susan played in Myrtle Beach. Susan even tried to get me into her regular foursome. I'd seen her cheat and never said a word because I didn't give a shit about any of it.

Daddy had never mentioned me and Melanie to any of these creeps, but he was never like most parents. That he'd change one day kept me hooked, but I knew it wasn't an innocent oversight, the club's pro never having heard of his children. Though I was sure it was Cheryl, not Daddy, who insisted we didn't exist. Could I fault him for wanting peace? I certainly didn't wish him unhappiness.

Minutes later, though it might have been a century, Daddy walked in, hat on, pencil and scorecard in hand, a look of astonishment on his face when he saw me. "What are you doing here?" he said.

He stiffened when we gave each other a careful kiss hello and I felt the sweat of the afternoon on his shoulder, smelled his familiar scent. I didn't perceive anger beneath his shocked pleasantry, which was all I could ask for with my father.

"You met my daughter, Robin," he said to the pro, covering, like I hadn't embarrassed him.

We went to a diner in West Conshohocken near the tracks. The red vinyl of the booth creaked when we sat. Daddy tossed his hat on the seat, roughed a hand through his hair to relieve the pressure of our sudden meeting.

It was these rare moments when I was in my father's company, that I felt each of his movements, that I was one with him. I reached across the table, touched his hand. "It's good to see you," I said.

"Me, too," he said.

This was the truth, even though we never saw each other, even though we didn't phone and the conversations were stunted when we did. He loved me and words, though I craved them, weren't needed. This is what Donna found hard to understand; she'd only seen his cruelty, my loneliness, the desertion.

I flipped through the tabletop jukebox. Buddy Holly, the Platters. Daddy dropped a quarter in and I pressed E4 for I'm All Shook Up.

He smiled. "Remember?"

"Our dance parties," I said, and sang the chorus.

Daddy ordered a root beer float and I got a Diet Coke before the waitress had a chance to put the sticky plastic menus on the table. "You sure you're not hungry?" he said.

"I ate. Thanks," I said, knowing I'd only move the food around my plate; the gravity of our reunions always killed my hunger.

Daddy stretched an arm over the back of the booth. We talked about his golf game and the new course in Georgia he'd done the drawings for. The weather. I told him how I was doing much better –I'd registered with a temp agency and maybe going to the Culinary School, though I hadn't really followed through yet.

The waitress returned with the drinks, Daddy's in a fountain glass topped with a cherry.

"You take care of that problem of yours?" he said, licking the whipped cream from bendy-straw before putting it on the table.

"Yes," I said. I'd done a couple therapy sessions with a woman who had an office in one of those huge pre-war Riverside apartments. She'd wanted me to come twice a week and attend a group but all she talked about was my mother's death. I hadn't even gotten to the drugs and my profession, so I stopped going because it wasn't helping. And I certainly hadn't stopped partying.

"Good," he said.

There wasn't anything else for us to talk about because he didn't know me. I'd leave without telling him about Chris or the therapist or that the agency I was registered with had nothing to do with typing. I smiled at my father, thought about what the golf pro had said, *he never mentioned any kids.*

"You sure you don't want something to go?" Daddy said before he paid.

I declined. He wanted me to eat but not take up his time doing it. We'd parked tandem at the curb.

"How's the Taurus?" he said.

"Not bad for a rental," I said.

He pressed a roll of cash into my hand, folded my fingers around it, then gave me a squeeze that said, you be OK because I need you to be. "Talk soon," he said, then kissed my forehead and his touch remained like a ghost on my skin.

Chapter 67

I felt strong. Two days without drugs, my morning work-out behind me. Fresh fruit and bottles of mineral water would only fortify my commitment to self-improvement. The sun warmed my hair and the fragrance of blooming Dogwoods dissipated the bus exhaust as I walked up Broadway with new confidence.

The produce at Fairway was still dripping from the morning rinse and buckets of daffodils added evidence of seasonal change. I prodded the navel oranges; it was still too early in the year for anything else.

"Excuse me." The man's voice behind me was deep and breathless and startled me.

"Yes?" I said, devoid of invitation. Like every city girl, I'd learned to shield myself from strangers without overtly insulting them.

"I passed you at 70th and had to turn around," he said.

I gave him the once-over. About my age, neon orange t-shirt, sleeves rolled and skinny Levi's, his posture was unthreatening; there was sincerity in his dark eyes. Not hitting me up for a hand-out. I smiled and continued squeezing and weighing.

"Justin," he said, extending his hand, then retrieving it upon realizing that mine were full. He scratched the back of his neck, kept his gaze on me. "Would you like to have coffee with me?"

"I don't even know you," I said and moved to the cart brimming with assorted grapes.

"One hour won't kill you," he said, his expression playful, assurance in his tone.

I had to look up to see his face. Tall, lean. I liked it. Probably didn't have a cent to his name. He wasn't a serial killer but he was trouble. "Why coffee," I said. "Seems awfully cheap."

"You're right, it's much more gentlemanly to ask you out for a drink, get you drunk," he said, making fun.

"I'm sorry, I'm too busy," I said. He was distracting me. I snatched up a bunch of the green seedless and struggled with the plastic bag. He took it from my hand, held it open for me while I put the grapes in. I retrieved it and headed for the register. He followed.

"What about later this week?" he said, leaning his elbow on the counter so he could get a better view of me while I paid. "You could give me your number."

"Look, Justin," I said, walking back down Broadway, gracefully dodging oncoming pedestrians while he continued behind me. "You seem nice, but I don't meet people on the street and give them my number. Besides, I don't have a pen."

I stopped at the light. He raced in front if me. Faced me. "I'll remember it," he said.

He was cute. "I'll tell you once, it's up to you to remember it," I said and told him.

Chapter 68

The breeze dispersed cherry blossoms through Riverside Park, provoked my sense of well-being, and I felt impractical as Justin and I trampled the remains of an abundant spring. Like I'd learned nothing.

We flirted and I observed myself gush and cling to each of his words like gentle gospel, all the while Daddy's voice in my head drowned the birdsong. *You can fall in love with a millionaire as easily as a gas station attendant.*

Was Justin the gas station attendant? No. He was a bike messenger with an Upper Westside studio apartment, applying to grad school, who looked at me like I was his beginning. I'd hung out with plenty of millionaires, hardly worthy associations, any of them. Mostly philanderers, frequently dishonest, even a few gun-toting drug dealers. Daddy's was a distorted lesson, a puzzle with a missing piece in the shape of a heart.

We sat on a bench and watched a tug lumber its barge up the Hudson in the afternoon sun. "You seem unhappy," Justin said.

The blanket of my dream was yanked away, leaving me exposed, even embarrassed. I was content to be with him all afternoon. And that was surely the hitch, my watch was down. Here in the daylight, the one thing I was good at, constructing a credible veneer, was deficient.

"Uh huh. Single, beautiful, gorgeous Manhattan

apartment, money in the bank," I said. "It's horrible being me."

"I didn't mean that. I meant you're smart, funny," he said, sunlight reflecting the fuzz along his jaw as he turned to look at me. "You underestimate yourself, you could be doing so much more."

He didn't know a thing about me but it's what I wanted someone to see in me all along. If he was feeding me a line, at least it felt good. "I've applied to go to Culinary School," I said, wanting his approval.

"That's cool," he said, reaching over to brush a petal off my shoulder, letting his hand linger. "When do you start?"

"The fall, I think," I said, but I didn't know because I hadn't finished the process of all the paperwork and referrals. Maybe because Melanie laughed at the idea –but more so because they probably wouldn't want me anyway.

"You don't know?" he said.

The sincerity, his innocent curiosity got to me and I became flustered. I was too exhausted to lie anymore. Breathless, as if a wave had knocked me down, I started to cry. He put his arms around me and I fell into him and for the first time in forever I was safe. Safe to tell him everything. And I did. And he listened.

About running away from home when I was sixteen and my desolation when Daddy didn't come for me and Jeff and my relentless guilt and how Melanie hated me but I needed her and my persistent loneliness for Mommy and how Chris was dead and how dating rich men by the hour was the way I afforded the high-end life that shielded me from it all.

Chapter 69

Justin and I spent two uninterrupted nights in my apartment, sent out for food, cigarettes. On Sunday we pried ourselves from my warm bed. My white tee and navy silk mini felt light against my electrified skin. We kissed uncontrollably at my door. "My hair," I said, but it was useless to think I wouldn't look like I'd been fucking for days.

We took the One train to Canal. The sun was high and so was I, on waves of bliss, on flashes of disappearing into him. I could do it for a week, then I'd let it go. This sort of thing didn't last, did it? He'd never stay, nor would I.

The street was crowded. We bought incense and a Panda covered in unidentifiable fur from a Chinese vendor with a goatee who made change from his pink vinyl fanny pack.

We walked to Broome, Justin's big hand soft, cradling mine as we crossed brick streets. We fed each other bites of pancake and Spanish omelet at the Moondance, his arm around me in the booth, toying with my hair, me turning my sticky crumb lips to his. Did we look like we were in love? I'd seen people like us and always thought: God, get a room. I wanted not to care. I didn't. I used the butter, poured more maple syrup, calories were non-existent.

I was the way men wanted me to pretend to be for an hour but that girl was far from here. Justin was the experiment; could I love someone? Was it his weakness to want me? This felt consuming. Frightening.

We wove up West Broadway through the SoHo funk, music spilling out of glass storefronts. "Why don't I live down here," I said, knowing it was too south of acceptable for my image; I had to be "uptown" for whom, I didn't know.

"Not shiny enough," he said, playing at disdain for my high maintenance.

I kissed him because how could he hate that part about me? He wasn't with the cashier with the pink hair at the secondhand music store, he'd chased me.

We stopped for espresso on Prince, sat on the same side of the shaded café table that faced the uneven street, surveyed the procession of black jeans and sunglasses, and mauled each other between sips.

We bought cheese, veggies, brisket and wine at Dean & Delucca's before getting back on the subway. I wanted to feed him, sustain the bubble we'd made for ourselves.

I'd been in the apartment for almost a year and had barely used the cookware. I oiled and washed the Dutch oven, put the roast in and the place smelled like home for the first time.

We'd made the room cozy with candlelight, set out the hot food, and in the perfect moment it occurred to me that we'd done little more beside make love and eat. How could we subsist like this?

After dinner, I cleared the table while Justin washed dishes and I thought: his mother trained him well.

"It's an annual thing," he said about his upcoming trip to his parents' Michigan lake house.

Any sadness I felt for never having had that with my own family was squelched by the panic of separating from him. "Sounds like fun," I said nonchalantly, scraping food into the trash. "How long will you be gone?"

"Ten days," he said. "Mom gets her fix and I catch up with old friends."

He'd probably run into his high school sweetheart, I thought, another reason that I couldn't allow my emotions to get away from me. He was too young. Ten years into his career, I'd be traded in for his secretary.

"That actually works out great, it's during our trip to Zurich," I said, stretching plastic wrap over a serving bowl.

"Why are you going again?" he said, rubbing his cheek with the back of his soapy hand.

He'd want to know everything, all the time, I thought. "A friend of Claire's lives there," I said, wiping suds from his chin with a dish towel. "You know, never been, free place and all."

"I'm jealous," he said, without the slightest hint that the feeling was about me. Then, referring to his fall internship in Peru, he said, "I was hoping to get one more trip out of the city before I leave."

Did he mean a weekend away with me? I'd already conjured absurd images of us in a country cabin with a litter of kids, but I was nuts to think beyond the summer. He was leaving and it would be hopeless –like what happened with Melanie and Chad, their marriage doomed by serial sabbaticals.

"Then you'll have your Masters in Education?" I said, confused by most of it, though like everything else, I'd figure it out eventually. I dried the silverware.

"The endgame is Applied Anthropology," he said, taking off his wet shirt, drying himself with it.

"Like Indiana Jones?" I said. He had the body for safari gear.

"Not exactly," he said, taking the last sip of wine. "More like studying the migratory patterns of indigenous African tribes, or getting them to use condoms."

I couldn't follow a research-obsessed bookworm to the dusty ends of the Serengeti, regardless of how horny he made me. "Six weeks," I said, concerned. "You won't even remember me by the time you're back." But really, I only wanted him *around*, I didn't want *him*.

"It's required," he said, leaning on the counter, the flush in his cheeks made him angelic. "Then I'll have to get a real job."

Melanie's response would be, *What's he going to do, teach,* her tone likening the occupation to that of a janitor. I wrapped my arms around his waist, nuzzled my face in his chest.

"Talk of gainful employment and you're putty," he said, breathing into my hair.

"Always," I said, but it was his scent that deconstructed me.

Chapter 70

As promised, Justin left for Michigan at the end of the summer, turning our assertions of love into something illusory and unstable. To fill the void, I accompanied Claire to Saint-Tropez where we met one of her regulars, a Swiss banker, who'd hired us to entertain his clients. The plans served well enough to distract me from my inevitable feelings of rejection.

A taxi took us to the Byblos, where Claire and I met the three old men. The banker's clients were balding American manufacturers of some kind of steel widgets. And though we were relieved that Claire and I were given our own room to share, the arrangements over who'd pay us remained vague.

"Don't worry," Claire said with convincing authority, fixing a wide-brimmed sunhat to her head. "Whatever happens with these guys, Peter will make good on the tab."

After breakfast, the men took us to Cinquant Cinq, a private shore club. "It's the most elite place here," Peter said through bad European teeth, his colorless eyes squinting under thick wire-rimmed glasses, sagging flesh loose over his stick-thin, gray-haired body. All his beauty accentuated by a tiny blue Speedo; the hallmark of the beach.

Once again, I found myself underwhelmed by what the South of France had to offer: a rocky coastline where leather-tanned inhabitants walked their poofy dogs, with the same bored expression with which they chain-smoked and ate hunks of cheese.

The experience was hardly enhanced by our American escorts, who were dressed in swimming trunks, stridently expounding their enthusiasm for the slender naked breasts that dotted the cramped shoreline, oblivious to my and Claire's polite laughter and embarrassment.

Above the chatter, my thoughts were of Justin. The drug of him. A saturated memory that felt eerie and compulsive. Claire and I would be gone less than a week and I'd have time to shake off Bad Robin before reuniting with him. But before I could concern myself with more than that, he'd leave for Peru, and like now, I'd be the furthest thing from his mind.

Peter left that afternoon for Zurich and Claire and I went to dinner with the Americans to a mountaintop restaurant where, to my disgust, they gutted the fish at tableside. I took consolation in the low-calorie meal but drank myself hungry again. There were no drugs to be had in this purgatory of riches and nothing quelled my longing for Justin.

I already knew I'd never make it through the fall without him because I couldn't endure thoughts of insignificance and self-doubt. It was why I couldn't be in love. The not knowing. What he wanted, what he thought, what he expected. And I was evidence that you never *knew* someone.

Back at the hotel, Claire went with the tall gray-haired

guy to his room and I went with the stout whiner. The whiner was more trouble than I could stand, wanted to touch me all-over, take his time. The usual easy fifteen minutes lasted an eternity and the facility with which I'd done the same thing so many times before failed me.

I met Claire back in our room before heading for the nightclub.

We changed from yacht attire to club dress, but I didn't have it in me to be sexy. I threw on a short black sleeveless shift and sandals while Claire put on a red silk backless number with stilettos.

"Thank God they don't want to go out," I said, downing two extra-strength Excedrin with the remains of a liter of Evian.

"Yeah, it's the perfect time of year to snag a rich boyfriend," Claire said, squinting through her cloud of Coco perfume while she re-pinned her chignon.

Claire blurted these absurdities with humor, but I knew, for her, man hunting was no joke. She refused to give up on her belief that Prince Somebody was merely one disco away. What she hadn't learned was that she could no more tolerate subjugating herself full-time to a trust fund baby than she could to some geezer. If money was her criterion, it would always be easier to take the unfettered cash.

We joined the Americans for breakfast on the umbrella-covered terrace. The sun had already burned off the morning cool and the puddles on the terracotta had evaporated. The Whiner feigned manners by reaching for my chair but he was too lazy to actually stand. Instead he pecked around for a waiter. "We've settled the bill," he said, proud of himself. "Your late check-out is confirmed, but your ride to the airport should arrive before then."

I shot Claire a worried look over the top of my sunglasses. We still hadn't addressed the matter of *our* bill. For the rest of the meal, unable to rally small talk, not maneuvering for repeat business, I kept my shades on and smiled intermittently, with minimal civility.

Saltwater fishiness blended with the floral sweetness that blew through the air while hummingbirds flitted in the bougainvillea; so beautiful, but wasted on me without Justin to share it. I thought how, with growing discomfort, that it would be impossible to put all of this behind me. I'd have to remove my brain. Until I believed in what was happening with Justin, my secrets were all that kept me in control.

After a basket of croissants, the only thing on the breakfast menu other than wine and coffee, we got the signal to go back to the men's suites.

As Claire and I followed them under the pristine gazebos, it became more apparent to me that making money would never be sufficient, it no longer merited the inconvenience.

A packed suitcase was waiting at the door of his room littered with used towels and empty glasses. To close the deal, and because I suspected Claire was doing the same thing across the breezeway, I dealt the guy a quick blowjob while he sat like an expectant child on the unmade bed.

When I fixed to leave, he sheepishly handed me two hundred and fifty dollars, a pittance for what we were owed. "Is this for the car?" I said. "Because this in no way covers my fee."

Claire came back to the room and tossed the same two hundred and fifty dollars on the dresser. "I'll call Peter in his office on Monday," she said, trying to sound casual. "He'll straighten everything out."

It was evident that the old men had agreed on the price. "Peter told them what the deal was," I said, stunned by her lack of outrage. "Plain and simple, they stiffed us."

"What do you expect me to do?" she said. "I can't piss him off." She took out her suitcase, began packing.

"He doesn't give a rat's ass about pissing *you* off," I said. Her concern for Peter was lost on me and I was too angry about not to getting paid. I picked up the phone. "When do the shops open?" I said to the operator.

When I hung up, Claire said, "I'm not spending what little we got, it's mortgage time."

"We have our room keys," I said. "We can still sign on the account." I wasn't leaving without some compensation. I came to St. Tropez with Claire to avoid my predictable loneliness, and the experience had been barely tolerable. Going home without payment meant humiliation and I didn't have room left in me for an ounce more. I grabbed my wallet, shook my key in front of Claire's face. "I intend to go back to New York with my dignity intact."

"What if we get caught?" she said, the worry on her face turned into skepticism as she followed me to the door.

"The hotel doesn't care and it'll be a month before the goons get their credit card bill, so screw them," I said.

The stores at the Byblos were filled with posh resort clothing, designer luggage, French perfume and Cartier. I grabbed Courrèges sunglasses, IZOD shirts, Italian sandals, careful to evenly parse the inventory so as not to appear to be hoarding. An MCM bag, a white parachute duster, friendship bracelets, some Nina Ricci. We only looked as if we'd left a few things at home. I signed the charges without flinching and the near ten thousand dollar tab helped ease the sting of having been conned.

The bounty was packed and our suitcases stowed in the trunk of the waiting Mercedes while Claire and I sat for a three-course champagne and caviar lunch that we added to the tab before heading for the airport.

Claire and I couldn't get to the forgetting fast enough. I tried to remember when I'd last ingested food. Did I eat the sushi before we went to Nell's? Our uptown dealer delivered the eight ball three hours after we landed in New York. We'd been up since, and were now in my apartment. Claire, showered, smoking and pacing, me hugging myself on the couch, more coke on the table. Day two.

August dusk and city lights dawned beyond the hum of the window air-conditioning unit.

My answering was machine full. Justin and Justin and Justin. Who else. Madam what's-her-face from this one, that one. I was done then, wasn't I? I should've gone home before that last call with the movie star client, *the last call,* but Claire and I had to recover the lost week with a lost weekend. A final bet with borrowed chips. It'll be easy together, Claire had said when we hailed the cab in front of the club. But it never was.

We went to the young actor, a beautiful blue-blood whose Mayflower parents let him out of a psycho-sanctuary to pursue his film career. He showed us his movies, did our drugs. Then he brought out his hospital diaries, shared his insane hieroglyphics and took Claire in the bedroom. I hadn't even disrobed, I wanted to leave. When he paid us and asked Claire to come back later, she thought it meant something.

Now she sat on my sofa, chill bumps on her bare thighs, a towel wrapped tight around her, moisturizing herself as if she were going somewhere.

The new French clothes, tags still attached, beckoned from atop my unpacked Vuitton, but the memory of Saint Tropez would soon be stashed alongside that girl-I-might-have-been.

I coughed weakly, reached for the cigarettes. I was depleted, disgusted, disconnected. Now all that remained of my swearing-it-all-off, declarations of renewal, feelings of love even, was the haze of someone else's dream like a low-watt bulb blinking to its end.

"Check your messages," Claire said and did another line.

But that was impossible. Justin was back by now. We'd had plans. *Plans.* More than dinner. Life. I guess. I was too high to produce the lies. "Tomorrow," I said.

Justin tried to reach me repeatedly but I refused to listen to his messages, because I'd have to confront the truth – that reduced to my simplest form, I was a drug addict and a hooker. To admit at the outset, how entirely unworthy I was, would have made it easier to reconcile my fear.

So what about guilt? I searched through my narcosis for a connection between who I wanted to be and who I was, tried to decipher if it was worth the fight. My emotions were willy-nilly and I tied all hope with a ribbon and sent it packing on a raft ablaze.

A hot shower with lavish soap that I could no longer smell only washed away my outer layer of dirt.

When Claire called for a second delivery from the dealer, I was onboard. The come down too unbearable to meet, the pain all too excruciating. Better to die, was the judgment call.

You girls could use a night off, was what dealer man said, but nonetheless, he took the money. Ready for the night ahead, he'd slept, picked up his cleaning and gone to the gym like a normal person.

When I finally saw Justin, it was as he crossed paths with the dealer on his way out my door. My first thought, *how did he get past the doorman?* was replaced by the knowledge that I made this moment happen.

"Why haven't you returned my calls?" he said, staring, confused by the picture and too frozen to push beyond it, his outdoor freshness incongruent with our squalor.

"I can't. Not now," I said, looking as hideous as I was crazed. And in the moment before he stormed away, I registered his disbelief and realized how inevitable it was that I'd witness the agony I'd perpetrated, the dismay in his eyes.

"He'll get over it, they always do," Claire said, opening the baggy, spilling more white on the table. "No point thinking about it now."

Nothing was clear other than that she knew zilch about love and that Justin's exit was quite possibly the end of the only decent thing in my life

"OK," I said, jaw clenched, my fingernails digging into the enameled paint of the closed metal door behind me. But I knew I'd marinate in the ugliness of what had happened until I passed out.

Chapter 71

The heat had begun to recede from Manhattan and the anticipation of a crisp autumn renewed my hope of transformation as I walked along Central Park West toward Seventy-Sixth Street.

It had been five days since Justin had bolted from my apartment. After a day of recovery, I left many unanswered messages. Despite my desperation, I'd reconsidered going to his messenger hub for fear of making things worse with an embarrassing confrontation.

Though I felt bruised, I carried myself over the busy sidewalk, wondering how many times I'd felt this way. The disgrace and remorse of having disappointed someone, unworthy of forgiveness but needing to be forgiven. It was all too familiar but it had been a long while since I'd felt such responsibility for my actions.

I had reached the empty nothing that was me and there was no chance of losing more, so I accepted the glances of oncoming pedestrians as I continued up the Westside, without shame, as if I belonged.

Maybe all I expected was for Justin to tell me to go away, that he hated me, that he never wanted to see me again. Then I could forget him and heal. He would leave for Peru in five days and the weeks he was gone would be enough time for him to stop thinking about me. But would it? We'd said we loved each other. I hadn't believed I actually did until now. Surely, it was too late.

Doormen in their cumbersome uniforms stood like soldiers in front of the famous parkside tenements. With renewed fascination, I remembered what was special about New York, and I knew I wasn't going to run this time. I was home. The only question was would I share it with Justin.

But what had he really seen? He didn't know that Claire and I had been with clients. All he saw was two strung-out girls and an unknown guy leaving. I'd tell him that my drug use was more than I'd revealed and let him know that I was getting help.

At Seventy Sixth, my stomach turned. I'd be OK until I made it to my daily meeting. Ninety meetings, ninety days, they said.

Over coffee and cigarettes the afternoon after our binge, Claire revealed the neatly folded pamphlet from Cocaine Anonymous that her brother had given her. I'd read it in disbelief. There was a name for what we were doing and help for it, like Daddy had said about his friend, but I didn't understand it then.

Claire and I sat at the dining table and answered yes to every question listed on the form. That night, we went together to the Presbyterian Church on Madison to a full basement of Upper East Side addicts spilling their guts. It was the first time I'd felt optimistic that there was another way to live.

Sober, a word that I had trouble grasping, but it felt good. Four days and counting. I was getting clear.

Justin's brownstone came into view, faded compared to some of the fancier owner-occupied ones on the block. The trees reflected the low afternoon sun and jostled in the light wind that blew the scent of seasonal change my way.

I sat for some time on his stoop, watched a girl, red hair in a ponytail and white sunglasses, walk her Doberman and pick up the poop with a plastic Gristede's bag. A limousine pulled over, waited two doors down. Its black windows sparkled in contrast to the dusty street-parked cars.

Then Justin was suddenly in front of me. Never more real, the flush in his cheeks, a random curl jutting from under his helmet. I reached to push the hair out of his eye but he recoiled deliberately, dismounted his bike. He wanted me to feel his contempt, and I resisted the urge to throw myself at him.

Though I prepared a speech, all that came out was, "Did you get my messages?" It was stupid. Of course he did.

He refused to meet my eyes.

"I'm sorry," I said. He was removed, cold, but through his detachment, I could see how I'd hurt him.

"Who was that guy?" he said.

"No one. Claire's friend," I said with conviction. But I wanted this part over with, to move beyond the whisper of forgiveness, for him to tell me that he still loved me.

"What, then?" he said, impatient and stoic in the same breath.

He wanted an explanation and I knew he'd bolt if I didn't give it to him. "I have a drug problem. Cocaine. It's why I didn't answer your messages, why I couldn't see you," I said.

"Not possible. We spent too much time together," he said, a curtain of confusion across his face. "I've partied with you!"

"I was hiding it. Lying. The behavior, it's called binging," I said, continuing because he hadn't run. "I went to some Cocaine Anonymous meetings and haven't used for the last couple of days," I said, feeling the strange ghetto sound of the word "used" in my mouth, wanting to retract it. "The place was full of people just like me."

I tried to read beyond his shock. His t-shirt was sweaty, the film of the city had settled on him and we were close enough that I could smell his earthy skin. I almost touched him.

"School begins for both of us next week," I said, trying to suggest a common challenge that would open a dialogue for what happened next but he didn't reply.

"I know you're leaving, all I'm asking is a chance to pull it together. I'm going to get sober regardless," I said. Sober. The jargon was corny and surreal at the same time.

I took the softening in his gaze as a good sign. "I can do anything if I know there's hope for us," I said, believing the banal sentiment.

"It's too late. You should have trusted me," he said flatly.

"I'm trusting you now," I said, shifting on my feet.

"I don't have time for this," he said, looking away.

He was right, it wasn't only my life at stake. There was something bigger for him than me and I didn't have the right to fuck it up.

"But you love me," I said, though I wasn't convinced my notion was accurate. The chatter of the evening birdsong was hard to ignore in the brief silence that followed.

"I do," he said, as if through me, down the street. "But I love myself more."

There was nothing to counter it, it's why I wanted him.

A truck bounced by and car alarms blared in a chain reaction. I fought to keep Justin's focus, but he hoisted his bike on his shoulder and edged past me, careful to avoid our touching, then climbed the stairs without looking back.

Chapter 72

I tucked an umbrella into my backpack, buoyant despite the forecasted rain. Six a.m. and clear-eyed, I walked north into the dawn.

"Regular light," I said to the coffee vendor on Columbus Circle, paid with change and peeled back the plastic lid for that grounding first sip.

The walk to the Sixty-Third Street Y was part of my commitment to the new me. Five-plus blocks to wake up, to plan, to reflect. I'd chosen the six o'clock meeting because I couldn't rely on getting to one unless I did so first thing. The rest of the day was entrusted to my eight hours at the Culinary Institute. At my apartment, a dinner of yogurt awaited me and sleep was my respite.

The homeless silhouettes asleep in front of the abandoned Civic Center reminded me of where I didn't want to end up, and I felt the gratitude. I wanted to live, maybe in truth, for the first time. Those passing thoughts that Chris got the easy way out had dissipated and I was encouraged.

Thirty days without drugs or alcohol, I would receive a chip to commemorate it. The Y's round-robin, where each person had a chance to talk about their struggle or joy, one at a time, was now the place I checked into daily. My *home* group. I was Robin at the round robin. The God part was still an eye roller to me, alongside the pithy signage and over-sharing-which-sounded-like-whining.

My life was now measured increments. Twelve steps. Ninety meetings in ninety days. Three weeks in school. Twenty-five years old in October. Twenty-seven days since I'd last seen Justin.

I'd called him a couple times and hung up. He'd left for Peru without a word. Then there was the post card from Lima, no note, only signed with a "J." He thought of me. It was enough for now. I loved him and wanted him back but I was happy that he was gone for this part.

My route took me up Central Park West. The lobby of the Paramount building reflected the gritty morning dew on its empty stairs and a lone security guard looked on from his interior perch.

School and meetings. I was friendly with a girl from Paris and a black guy from Atlanta. We smoked together at breaks, made empty plans.

I had the tools, the uniform, the schedule. And it felt worthwhile. I'd kept the Wusthof knife Georges had given me at home. Numéro un outil, he'd said. But as far as I'd seen, most of my classmates came without expensive accoutrements and I didn't want to stand out. Anonymity held its attraction.

I talked with Georges the first week I was at the Institute, told him how my feet hurt and how I'd cut myself learning proper julienne technique. I thanked him for vouching for me. "You took an interest in my future when no one else did," I said.

"You will keep touch, no?" he said.

"Definitely," I said, understanding how our friendship had moved beyond its beginning. Paradoxically, had I never been a call girl –defined by being subjugated to someone else's desires – I'd have never experienced what it was like to receive another's unconditional support. Georges helped me find my calling and for that I'd be eternally thankful.

My nose dripped in the morning chill. I wiped it with the napkin from the vendor, it was a wonder how my sinuses had gotten away intact.

On my birthday, I'd be over two months clean. When I told this to Daddy with pride, his response was vanilla. Sounds good, he said, before jumping from the phone. Sometimes I wished he'd yell at me, then I'd know if he at least cared, but as it stood, his silence only meant rejection.

A doorman stood sentry outside a glass entranceway as a white-haired lady emerged with a poodle. Her Burberry pocket bulged with plastic baggies and the dog's tags jingled. I greeted them with good morning as they pranced by, leaving me with the feeling that I'd rejoined humanity.

The Burberry reminded me of Melanie. Her retort to my circumstance had been that addiction was a convenient excuse for my failings, but for once, I was undeterred by her and almost felt forgiveness. I'd avoid awarding her premature pardons, or expect to receive them from her. In time, I thought, I'd learn to absolve myself.

I waited for a yellow Checker taxi to make the left turn, then crossed Sixty-Third to the Y.

Chris had loved riding in those big, silly things, said they made him feel like he was Doris Day. Sadness fell over me, though the loss of Chris was clearer before he died. Missing him now was like contemplating a dream I'd awakened from, haunting me only until it was replaced by a new one. The memory of our friendship would remain shaded by the emptiness I felt from him not wanting me there at the end.

I'd searched repeatedly for someone to shelter me, and now that the haze was lifting, I realized that the ghost of my mother's lap was the comfort I'd blindly sought. But Chris was dead, Justin was gone and Daddy's arms were never open.

As always, I found my own refuge.

The side door of the Y closed behind me with a thud. Metal chairs dragging across linoleum and voices emanated from the fluorescent basement. The aroma of coffee wafted up and I counted the twenty-two steps down.

Acknowledgements

John Jahrmarkt, without you, there's nothing.

Apryl Huntzinger and Beverly Kennett-Lindberg, who took the writer's journey with me from page one.

Les Plesko, for teaching me to love the written word.

My UCLA peeps for enduring my many drafts and providing brutal feedback. My Adat Ari El gang for comments on the finished product. My comrades at Tertulia.

Kim Castle, your beauty is limitless.

Sasha Ruocco, for feeding my courage.

Carrie Kneitel, for your generous and inspired eye.

Dianne Cohn Case, Thessy Mehrain, Nina Sventitsky, Amy Scribner, Lisa Ann Walter, Nora Lynch, Linda Branca, Cecil Kepner, Christy McBrayer and Kathleen Guthrie Woods who continue this great experiment of the life with me.

Michael Jahrmarkt for seeing me;

My one and only mother, Roberta Jahrmarkt;

Bella, who makes everything worthwhile;

And, last but not least, Linda Nelson, for sharing the ride.

www.ingramcontent.com/pod-product-compliance
Lightning Source LLC
Chambersburg PA
CBHW051437260626
47162CB00001B/140